# DOCTOR KINNEY'S HOUSEKEEPER

D1469167

## SARA M DAHMEN

Doctor Kinney's Housekeeper

Sara Dahmen

Copyright 2014 Sara Dahmen

Printed in the United States of America

First Printing 2014

ISBN 978-0-9982661-0-7 (6x9 paperback)

Coppersmith Publishing LLP
PO Box 149
Port Washington WI 53074
www.coppersmithpublishing.com

Proofreader: Annie Bahringer
Cover Design: Perry Elisabeth Design | perryelisabethdesign.com

*To Katie and Heather*
*always my first editors*
*and for always reading*


*and my husband,*
*who allows me to disappear for weeks*
*in the crazed writing silence that comes out of the blue.*

## SITUATIONS WANTED

THE MILITARY

ALL VOLUNTEERS WHO DES
ire to receive the highest bound-
ies paid cash down in hand should
apply to CAPTAIN & CO., 300
Broadway, room 12.

ALIENS - ENGLISH, SCOTCH,
Irish, German and all foreigners
wishing to volunteer are guaranteed
the highest bounties, cash in hand.
Apply early. CAPTAIN & CO.,
300 Broadway, room 12.

A NUMBER OF WELL RECOM
mended Irish females want situations as cooks, chambermaids,
nurses, girls for general housework
&c., at Mrs. KELLY'S Home &
Orphanage, No. 20 Dartmouth.

A NURSE, THOROUGHLY
trained and competent to take the
entire care of an infant or two small
children wishes a situation; is a
Protestant and a good seamstress.
Superior references. Call at 31
Bridge Street

A WOMAN WISHES TO TAKE
in a gentleman or family's washing
at her own residence. Call at 45
Gray St.

A COOK WANTS A SITUATION
understands English and American
cooking; is an experience baker;
good city reference given. Can
be seen for two days at No. 4 W.
Canton.

WANTED: 20 4-OX TEAMS and
10 Wagons for Freighting from
New York to the Black Hills. For
particulars, address Smith & Parker,
New York.

## SITUATIONS WANTED

A YOUNG ENGLISH GIRL
wishes a situation as nurse and plain
sewer; willing to make herself useful;
good city references. Call at 5 Med-
ford Qt.

A SITUATION WANTED - TO TAKE
care of children to do plain sewing or
light chamberwork. Call for two days
at 11 Yarouth St.

A RESPECTABLE GIRL WISHES A
situation as a plain cook, washer and
ironer; has good city reference. Call at
Waltham St. in the candy store.

A SITUATION WANTED - AS WAIT-
ress; no objection to chamberwork and
waiting. City references. Call at 202
East St. Botolph.

A YOUNG WOMAN WISHES A
situation - to take care of growing children and do sewing or chamberwork
and waiting; wages not so much an
object as a quiet home. Appointments
at Chester Sq.

WANTED: BY HOLLAND GIRL-
chamberwork five days a week. No
English. Room 3, South St

HOUSEWORK, WANTED, A WO
an for general housework in the western territories. Must be sturdy. Send
word Box 30.

WANTED PROTESTANT PLAIN
cook, washer and ironer; inquire
through Lewis Law.

THE ADVERTISER (WHO HAS JUST
lost her baby) and has a full breast of
milk wishes a situation as wet nurse.
Can be seen at 8 Oxford Pl. between
Oxford & Harrison Ave.

## SITUATIONS WANTED

WANTED - COOK, GENTLEWOM
an elderly preferred. Write to Box 48,
care Hampton Law.

IN RETURN FOR PASSAGE TO AU
stralia, refined young lady will render
services as Companion, Secretary or
Nanny. Expert stenographer, Highest
references. Box 16, care Surry & Associates.

HONORABLE AMERICAN, 30,
with some means and hiw own office,
desires acquaintance of sincere, affe-
cate, Protestant girl; object matrimony;
correspondence onfidential. Box 98,
Boston.

HOUSEWORK, WANTED, A WOM
an for housework in the country. Ital-
ian or French. Apply through Box 16,
care Surry & Associates.

HELP WANTED IMMEDIATELY:
Cook laundress and housekeeper for
Great House. Apply in person 170
Pemberton Sq. References required.

HOUSEWORK - MIDDLE-AGED
woman for housework: plain cooking.
Possibly could use woman with small
child. Boston. Apply 67 Chauncy
Ave.

MAID, WHITE, WANTED FOR GEN
eral housework; reference required.
Call at 11 Chatham St.

WANTED - A MIDDLE-AGED OR
elderly woman to assist in general
housework and plain cooking. Inquire
Box 59.

Box 48
Hampton Law
Dear Sir or Madam


I am writing in regards to the advertisement in the Boston Advertiser for a woman and cook.

Until my husband's passing, I managed our household and some plain cooking, as well as general nursing for him.

You may contact me through my late husband's offices. I appreciate your consideration.

Sincerely,


*Mrs. Jone Weber*

c/o Ward & Weber Shipping
Boston

Box 30

Dear Sir or Madam

I am writing in regards to the advertisement in the Boston Advertiser for a housekeeper.

Until my husband's passing, I managed our household and some plain cooking, as well as general nursing for him.

You may contact me through my late husband's offices. I appreciate your consideration.

Sincerely,


*Mrs. Jane Weber*

c/o Ward & Weber Shipping
Boston

*Box 59*

*Dear Sir or Madam*

*I am writing in regards to the advertisement in the Boston Advertiser for a housekeeper and cook.*

*Until my husband's passing, I managed our household and some plain cooking, as well as general nursing for him.*

*You may contact me through my late husband's offices. I appreciate your consideration.*

*Sincerely,*

*Mrs. Jane Weber*

*c/o Ward & Weber Shipping*
*Boston*

Mrs. Jane Weber
c/o Ward & Weber Shipping
Boston


Madam,

I write on behalf of my colleague, Doctor Patrick Kinney, who works in Flats
Junction, Dakota Territory and requires a housekeeper and cook.

Your background in simple nurse duties is helpful as he handles all manner of
illness and issue — both man and beast — and any assistance would be beneficial.

The death of his elderly relation has left him without means to keep up and he has
asked me to solicit someone as soon as possible.

Are you able to travel to the Territories soon? Forgive my forwardness as well,
but will you be able to withstand the harshities?


Sincerely,

Dr. Robert MacHugh.

Dr. Robert MacHugh
Box 30


Dear sir,

Thank you for your prompt response to my inquiry. My husband has only recently passed, and I must set his affairs in order before departing, and would ask some weeks delay; perhaps until April.

I understand that may not be possible for Doctor Kinney, but I must be available to settle the estate if I am to move west.

As for my sturdiness, I assure you I am not lacking.

Please advise.


Sincerely,

*Mrs. Jane Weber*

Mrs. Jane Weber
c/o Ward & Weber Shipping
Boston


Madam,

Thank you for your patience. Contact with the territories is slow.

I have enclosed the correspondence between Doctor Kinney and me pertaining to your employment. You may contact him directly.

My best to you.


Sincerely,

Dr. Robert MacHugh.

*Doctor Kinney*
*c/o Postmaster*
*Flats Junction, Dakota Territory*


*Patrick,*

*Two women have responded to the advertisement I placed at your request.  I have enclosed their letters.  One comes without reference but has claimed a background in home nursing.  If you wish, I can meet with them to gauge each ability to manage out west; I can consider it a favor.*

*I understand you do not wish to delay too long in a decision.  Whichever you prefer, you may write or send a cable.*

*At your service,*

*Robert.*

Doctor Robert MacHugh
Box 30
Boston


Bobby,

I do not care so much for references as much as for ability. I'll take the one with the bit of nursing. It'll be much needed out here. If she is capable, it will be worth waiting the extra weeks.

Please tell her she might plan to board in my aunt's old rooms, which will be part of her wages, and to bring whatever serviceable items she can.


Patrick

Doctor Kinney
c/o Postmaster
Flats Junction, Dakota Territory


Sir,

My thanks are to you for allowing me to finish my late husband's affairs and for the opportunity. A reduced wage of $3 per day is sufficient if board is included.

I plan to take a weekend train, and hope to be in Flats Junction by the end of the first week of April.

My sincerest regards,

*Mrs. Jane Weber*

# Dakota Territory

## 1881

# CHAPTER 1

He was the husband expected, the one who my mother liked and my father approved. Dark haired, well dressed and kindly, I found him dull and yet appropriately attentive. Our courtship was briefer than most - he because he wished a bride and me because I was happy to finally run a household of my own. We were not often without the ears of a chaperone, and the stilted conversation that began our relationship continued throughout the marriage. Once our vows were spoken, he came to my rooms as required, and did not demand much of me even when it became apparent a child would not come easily for us.

I was not happy, but I was happy to be married. It was not a good life to be a spinster, living with family forever, only to end up alone in the lateness of age. It was something I had never wished to happen, so I was glad Henry had taken me for his bride, even though I was perhaps a few years older than most girls when they took their wedding veils.

His kindness came from old chivalry, and while I knew he doted on me, ours was not a passionate love, nor a passionate marriage. He sometimes seemed uninterested, unable to be aroused, and it was only after we'd been married for a year that he unburdened his worries under duress and I understood his apathy.

Henry was ill. He'd been told by numerous doctors of a wasting illness that they could not fix. It seemed to wax and wane without warning, and lived in his blood. Sometimes he would be beset with pain, and would sit in his study at home in utter horridness. I then understood why some days he would be at the table for dinner pale, grey and drawn. For months I had wondered if it was his marriage to me that caused him sadness. Because there was no love between us, I found I could not throw myself into cheering him, and began to think I was an unsound wife. Perhaps, I had reasoned, it was no wonder he did not smile at me, for I did not try to charm him.

Once he had made the comment, quietly, that I must not trouble myself on his account, for I was exactly the wife he had hoped for. Henry was one who would not ever make light of his words. Over time I had grown to think of his color was due to the roughness of his job. I never thought it was the delicateness of his own condition.

As our marriage tripped along slowly, I still enjoyed my life, for I had purpose. We had become closer, friends even, and eventually I became more a nursemaid to him than the one that stopped by at intervals from the hospital. Sometimes Henry's illness would seem to disappear. He'd have good days, and we would rejoice with them. But those days were fewer and fewer.

We had one last day, filled with sun, smiles and even kisses before he took a turn for the worse that never changed. My Henry; husband, lover, and kind friend, eventually succumbed to the disease and I wore the black veil of the widow. The gowns in my closet turned to ash and grey and black.

The color does not suit me. I rather miss being married. I miss having a direction to my days.

I am on a train, heading west. I am not impressed with the landscape - it grows flat, then rolls, and is a bit disconcerting. This is amplified by the fact that I am pregnant, and the motion of the train, at times, can cause my stomach to feel queasy.

There is much irony in this pregnancy. Henry did not know of it. In truth, neither did I, until he was buried. Only weeks later, as I was packing, did I pull out the drawer of rags and realize they had not been used in a while. That somehow, in one of those last, happy moments together, we had finally made a baby. Now, I will raise this child alone.

Henry's estate has left me a few things, enough to get by if I greatly reduced my way of living, but I want to be useful again.

With luck, I am headed to one of the newest areas of the union. There is relief in ridding myself of the rented house and the meager staff we kept on. For the first time in a while, I feel the freedom of the ocean.

I've heard good and bad of the Dakota Territories, but most natural fears are not as pressing as my worry that I will not hold up to the rough and tumble of western life. I will not have running water in the bathroom, nor a library. Most of all, I will not have the ocean.

The train levels onto flat land again - flatter than I have yet to see. I am struck by the landscape, a mixture of lush trees and flat or undulating prairie. There are a few bison in the distance, a shimmering horizon of pink as the sun sets. My pregnancy makes me drowsy and I slip into an interrupted sleep.

# CHAPTER 2

"Ma'am."

I am gently woken by a gruff whisper. I blink in the dusky morning. The kindly face of the conductor peers down at me through the soft gloom. "It's your stop, ma'am."

I am grateful he has remembered to tell me this, I would have slept through, and I tell him so. He nods sympathetically. My ring tells a story of its own. Either I have lost a husband or go to this wasteland to stay with one. Neither is easy, and I think this old gentleman likes to take the lone female passengers under his wing. A kind of fatherly gesture, his gentle tap perhaps makes him feel needed, particularly by the ladies. His life must be a lonely one for all the wonders of travel.

The platform that lets out at Flats Junction is dusty and weathered. The creak of planks, boots, and wheels is still subdued at this early hour. The train creaks and groans behind me as the steam billows under my skirts. I stare across the land. It is a rather large town, with a main street that is intersected by a few other rutted dirt roads. I am surprised to see so many houses. I had thought the territories were so sparsely populated, and while it is unexpected I am pleased with the number of families Flats Junction sustains. Perhaps it will not be so desolate here.

Across the street is the general store, with many goods crammed into barrels along the windows. I see a woman hanging a lantern at the door, as she is just opening for the day. Grabbing my satchel from the empty seat next to mine, I hurriedly cross the crusted street before she can disappear into the darkness inside. As I move, the chill of the spring morning hits my cheeks and hands. Even with the early sun, I can tell winter is not far gone.

"Excuse me," I call, as I breathlessly mount the stairs. My Boston accent betrays me immediately and she turns to me with a frown. Already I have made a bad impression. "I am so sorry, please, if you could tell me which way Doctor Kinney's practice is, I'd be obliged."

"What do you want with the Doctor?" She stands over me, strong hands in fists on her hips. Her eyes narrow and she looks me over, taking in the dark grey frock and plain cuffs of my dress, the new polish on my black shoes. I am not ashamed of my clothes or my body, though her scrutiny makes me pause. She is frowning slightly, but suddenly her face softens.

"You're his new housekeeper?"

I nod.

"His place is two streets over, the house with the blue shutters." She smiles at me with a new warmth in her eyes.

"I am thankful," I say, as I start back down the stairs.

She calls after me, "He won't be awake yet; don't bother heading over there. Last night Alice Brinkley had her babe and he was up all hours. Doesn't pay to make a bear of him by waking him earlier than he ought. Come in for a cup."

I pause, but realize the sense in her generous words. I do not wish to start my employment on a bad footing, so I turn back once again and follow her into the store. It smells of warm grain, rusty metal and molasses. There are shapes looming everywhere inside, most of which are displayed once my new acquaintance finishes lighting a few lamps to ward off the last of the early morning shadows. There are steps behind the counter, and she turns to me, beckoning with her hand, "Pour a cup and sit behind the curtain a spell. I'll join you shortly. Always a bit of a rush right after the train pulls through."

She disappears behind a large pile of seed stacks, and I am left to peer around a faded calico curtain, where a large blue flecked urn is steaming. There are mugs hanging on hooks over the black stove and I pour myself a cup, absently sipping it before I realize what I took for tea is actually strong coffee. It is thick and muddy, and I cough a bit, glad she is not here to see my face after I try her concoction.

These are her private spaces. There is a short plank table with a few stools and a bench gathered around it next to the stove. The crockery and pans are piled up haphazardly on a shelf over the stovepipe. I can see she is just as disorderly here as she is in her store. Rugs are faded with use and fraying, but the bed is neat and made precisely. Curtains are nothing more than long rags hiding the blinding sun as it rises. There are no photographs or portraits on the walls, no artwork hanging or decorative vases on the table. She is spartan, a bit like me. I am eager to learn more of her. Perhaps she can be my first friend here.

I hear men's voices, flowing fast and loud, though I do not trouble myself to eavesdrop. Instead I pace the room. It feels good to move after being so many days on a train. She has a tinkling laughter, a booming sales pitch, and a flirty way to send the customers out the door. I can hear all this in the sounds of her voice, even without truly knowing her words. I wonder if she is like me: widowed and alone. The bed along the wall in the far corner is a single one. If she was once married, she has adjusted well to being alone.

She enters the back room. I am worried I have imposed on her, but she immediately starts to question me, familiarly, as she pours her own cup and guzzles the horrible coffee.

"So you're coming to keep house for the Doc?" she reaffirms. I nod, twisting the handle of the mug in my hands. She sits across the table, perched on the edge of her seat, continuing to scrutinize me, though I am sure I am not much more interesting than any other woman. She is the opposite of me: tall, straight, with high cheeks and a straight nose. Her hair is pinned up, but it's obviously thick; so much so that it must be a struggle for her to contain, with glints of red in the almost black color. I am fascinated with her hands, long fingered, strong nails and scarred. She wears no wedding band. What is her life story?

"I am. He answered my letter in response to his ad?" I hope the question in my voice lends itself to an answer, so I don't have to guess completely at the situation I approach. I know nothing about my new employer, only that he is, by complete lack of option, doctor, midwife, dentist, vet and chemist to this town.

She takes the comment and dutifully responds. "His former housekeeper died a few months past. She was his great aunt. I've been stopping by when I have the time to try and keep his place tidy a bit, but he is used to the charity of others for a hot meal, and he's rarely home." She pauses for a moment and then looks at me squarely. "My name is Katherine. Kate."

26

I nod at her and smile encouragingly. My formal name slips out, though I do not mean it to do so. "I'm Mrs. Henry Weber."

While she nods in return, more questions crowd my mind with her involved response to my initial question, but a rooster crows nearby. It is the third cock to sound since I've sat in her kitchen, and she stirs in her seat. How late in the morning is it, now?

"He'll be getting up now. You best be on your way if he's expecting you."

I stand with her and take my emptied cup to the washbin. "Thank you for your hospitality. I am incredibly grateful."

"You looked like you needed it. Your man must be down on his luck for you to hire yourself out for home work," she states, but I know there is hidden meaning in this, and that I betray a personal confidence by not answering truthfully.

I look down, as it is expected of me to be woeful. I am not completely upset by this turn of life, by the fact that I am free to do as I please in the aftermath of Henry's death. While I feel guilty at times because I think I should mourn him more fully, I cannot deny that I am happy to be free of a loveless marriage. Still, I sigh and say to Kate, "My husband Henry is recently deceased. I need to make my own way now. You said Doctor Kinney is two streets over? The house with the blue shutters?"

As I look up at her for confirmation, I see her face, once again, darkens, but she tries to mask her scowl. I have recently been a guest in her home, and now I see her try to master her fiery emotions. To feel so passionate about things... I wonder how that must be to live life with so much feeling trapped inside.

She gives a tight "yes" to my directions, and I take my satchel and turn my back to her. I decide I will figure out her moods later, as I hope to stay in Flats Junction for a while, allowing my past to filter away.

The roads are bumpy, but also muddy in certain low points. The earth is both dark and brown as well as soft, and I find it easiest to keep my mind on my feet as I pick my way around the wagon ruts and horse prints. I try not to think of the cobbled streets I left, and the swept front porches and painted wood of the homes. It is simpler here, I say to myself. And simple is good. When the Doctor's home looms in front of me, it is cast in morning glow, and the shutters are brilliant blue though I can see the chips and scratches in the paint with the starkness of sunlight on them. I take the few stairs to the doorway, which is open and a makeshift screen stands between me and the dark dimness of the interior.

Doctor Kinney is rustling in his back rooms as I arrive. The windows at the front of his house are open, and there is a muttering and a short curse as I knock on the screen door.

A pause, then a clambering from the rear of the house brings a shadow into my sight. He is not as tall as I expected, and not nearly as old as I assumed. Though there are lines along his mouth and wrinkles in the slants of his eyes, but they are more from fatigue than age. I guess him to be five years my senior, perhaps ten if I am careful in my opinion. He pauses, and we stare at each other from both sides of the screen.

I find my voice. "I'm Mrs. Weber. Here to keep house for you, Doctor?"

There is a long moment as if he is measuring me, considering. I don't mind the wait, and do not fidget. He finally opens the door and stands aside to let me in. "Come in - my study."

His voice has an Irish lilt, and I bite back an impulse to comment immediately. My roots are in Massachusetts, and many neighborhoods are filled with Irish voices.

His office is tiny, a narrow wooden desk covered in files and papers: boxes stacked on the floor, bits of paper haphazardly sprinkled through his overloaded bookshelves. The chaos reminds me of Kate's general store.

He goes to stand behind the desk and I perch on the only other seat available, a worn straight chair with a spindle back. It is not very comfortable. His blue eyes peer at me in the lamplight; only a small window brings in the morning sun. I see his hair is auburn, too, though it is more red than Kate's.

"Mrs. Weber," he says my name slowly. "I'm glad you're here."

"Yes," I say guardedly. "Thank you for responding to my letter. I am grateful for the work." It is all I can say. I am more than grateful, but I cannot dissemble so cleanly. This work will give me a purpose and save me from the quiet fading of widowhood.

He sits down so we are more eye level. He sighs and looks away from my face. There is a pause before he dives into the subject with a straightforward manner. "I'm sorry for your loss. Ye must miss Mr. Weber very much."

I give a small nod, not trusting myself to answer. I am often afraid the truth will come out, and it would be unbecoming. Though I should be glad that I had had a husband at all.

"We need to go over the particulars of your duties. But first, there is the matter of your room and board."

"Oh?" I panic inwardly. Our correspondence, though brief, had been particular about the bigger points of the arrangement, and he should know I do not have enough to pay for a room at an inn. We had confirmed that I would stay in his previous housekeeper's quarters.

"Yes," he pauses again, then meets my eyes. "Ye are younger than I supposed, and it would not do to have you stay in my auntie's old rooms upstairs as I'd planned."

His words deflate me. He's right. But I still cannot afford the inn, and I voice as much, though I say so with some apology. He waves it away with a large bunched hand.

"I'm not goin' to have you stay at the inn, Mrs. Weber. But the only other place I can think of is boardin' ye with old Widow Hawks."

"That sounds fine," I say soothingly. I am embarrassed to have caused issue already.

"Widow Hawks is Sioux." The statement is said almost defiantly.

There is a part of me that hesitates. I am worried that she is by definition an outcast. That by staying with her, I will be shunned immediately among the townsfolk. But I look at the Doctor and realize he wishes this. I must trust someone, and why not my new employer? If he does not doubt the widow, I have no reason to do so either.

"If she is a fair landlady, I have no objections," I manage to say evenly, and he relaxes slightly, then leans into the worn wood of his chair and stares at me. I take the time to look at his stocky shoulders, the round muscles of his arms, the holes in his shirt and the patches in his leather vest, which is shiny from wear. He has curls in his reddish hair, and he is newly shaved.

He nods slowly, as if he is still mulling what we have already decided. "Yes. She's like family to me, and I know you'll be treated well. It is best." His eyes watch me. I do not know if he is just observing or if he is creating opinions already. Finally, he sighs. "I'm sorry again for your recent loss, Mrs. Weber. I know ye are in mournin', but the work here is hard. You'll be advised to cast off the blacks and greys soon and wear more suitable clothing."

His pragmatic attitude soothes me. I do not like being fussed over, and mourning Henry has been chaffing enough as it is.

"My period of mourning will be over in a fortnight. I have enough saved to make what is need. I would think Kate can steer me in the right direction on cloth."

The Doctor's head comes up a bit at the mention of the grocer. "You've met Kate already?" His voice is softer.

"Yes. She was kind enough to offer me coffee when I arrived on the train. We spoke briefly."

He smiles for the first time since we've met, and I like the way the lines bunch on his face and how his blue eyes squeeze to half moons. I think he will be a kind employer.

We fall into discussion about my duties: cook, clean, organize, mend, care for the garden and home, and generally do wifely duties without being his wife. This is good. I feel I have a purpose again, and thankfully it does not come with the strings attached that my marriage had. I have vowed to never tie myself to another union that is so detached, and am glad I can hide myself in this new role for decades should I wish.

As we reach the part of the discussion pertaining to the use of patient files, there is a knock on the door. It is a young cowboy, covered in dust and clapping a hat to his thigh as he pushes through and turns directly into the office. There is little privacy here, I note.

"Doc! Hank's horse ain't getting from the far side of the pasture this morn. We've tried everything short of force. He thinks something's wrong with him." As an afterthought the boy looks at me. "How do, ma'am."

The Doctor sighs and stands. I notice he does not bother to clear any of his clothing. His slightly disheveled state must be a standard. He glances at me.

"I'll be back for midday dinner, I'd think, Mrs. Weber. If ye could manage to fix up a bite, we'll head to Widow Hawks' place later to get you settled."

As they amble out, I see the Doctor grab a well worn stetson from a hook behind the door, and the screen slams behind them, echoing across the street. I'm left in semi-silence. I hear a few morning larks yet outside, and a drip of a faucet somewhere deeper in the house. Around me, dust settles across the beams of watery sunlight, trailing slowly down to one of the piles and piles of patient folders on the floor and desk. Thoughtfully I turn off the gaslight in his study, and step out of the small room to set my wrinkled satchel on the scuffed plank floor.

Following the narrow hall, I glance briefly in each door. Next to his study is the surgery. The instruments are a dull silver that gleams in the half light. The walls are whitewashed, and a few nails hold thinly framed certifications. There is a large black cabinet with wide beveled glass doors. Through the glass I see bandages piled neatly, beakers arranged according to size, and other utensils I don't understand. His surgery is the opposite of his study; neat, tidy, and precise. The dripping comes from a pump nozzle over a basin. He must bring in water directly from the rain barrel outside.

There is a staircase to my right. I assume the bedrooms are up there. At the end of the hallway the kitchen yawns open before me. The room is wide and the stove is large, double the size of Kate's, and the pans and pots that are not soiled are still hanging on hooks Perhaps his great aunt had kept a good fire going, maybe keeping the meals hot and ready. Shelves line another wall, where a few plates and knives sit in a line. The rest are all dirty in a nearby wash or still sitting holding half eaten food on the wide slabbed table in the center of the room. There are a few chairs around it and one long bench that can sit 4 guests. There is even natural light slanting in from the northern windows. I will be spending much of my time here and I find myself well pleased.

I do not know how long it will take Doctor Kinney to do his veterinary services, so I decide to mix up a batter of flapjacks, so long as the ingredients are in the pantry. Surprisingly, the place is rather stocked, as if he hasn't much touched them or didn't know what to do with the dry goods. I was not so well off when married to Henry to have a cook, though I did have a maid to help with the cleaning. The chemistry of the kitchen comes natural to me. It is one of my few heaven-given talents. I shift around the kitchen, cleaning bowls and spoons as I need them, and stoking the stove and griddle pan so as to be hot when he came in. The cast iron is black and smooth with age and use. His auntie must have cooked often.

Flapjacks are not really lunch, but they are all I can think to do without knowing his schedule. Perhaps in the future, I will learn his methods so as to properly guess the lengths of his work.

While I wait, I decide to start working at the mess of the kitchen. I am only halfway through the suds of the dishes when I hear him racketing into the house, slamming the screen. I think, strangely, of the babe in my womb, and how I might ask the good Doctor to not slam the door when it is sleeping.

He pauses; I guess at the door of his study, but then I hear water and realize he is at the tap in the surgery, probably cleaning up. I am grateful he at least thinks to wash his hands. It is not so uncivilized here, then.

He walks into the kitchen with a sturdy stride, and I give him a small smile and motion wordlessly to the place I have set at the now cleared table. I pour him a cup of my own coffee brew. I make it differently than Kate, though I am, myself, used to tea. My coffee is strong, but not thick, without the grains floating deep inside, and tastes rather good. Henry used to compliment me on it often. I wait for the Doctor's reaction, or a word of approval from behind, as I have my back to him while I tend the flapjacks. He is fidgeting behind me, and when I finally turn with a plate of golden jacks, he arranges his face to blank, but I am too quick and see the look of annoyance that was first setting there. I am immediately worried. I need this work for my own sanity and do not have the possibility of returning, but worst of all, I had thought to do a good job from the start, though I see now he is frustrated instead of pleased.

He tucks into the flapjacks so fast I move to make more immediately. This time when I turn around, he is just finishing the food so he is not watching me and I am saved from the disapproval on his face. I make more, hoping I have enough batter to fill his stomach. This batch he seems to eat slower, for when they are finished I put them on a plate near his elbow so he can take them when he is ready.

I make the rest, and put it on the slab, and he eats nimbly, quickly. I twist the coffee in my own hands nervously, staring at my hands so as not to watch him. My hands are not lady's hands, there are burn scars from my oven back in Boston, blunt fingernails and a few small callouses. My veins are blue and visible. They are not long-fingered hands, nor very powerful, but they are capable and strong.

Finally, I sense him move and I look up to see him leaning back in the chair, looking content. He sips his coffee, piercing me with his stare over the rim.

"Were they good?" I ask the trite question to fill the silence.

A smile flits its way across the craggy features. "Delicious, Mrs. Weber."

"Thank heaven," I cannot help but murmur. "Then you won't fire me right off?"

He sets the mug down hard on the table; it had been halfway to his mouth again. "Why ever would ye think that?"

"You were so displeased with me, I thought, when you first came in?" My voice is quiet and low, but he hears me and gives his unruly head a small shake.

"Don't take it so personal, Mrs. Weber. I beg ye. I was starvin' hungry from the late night birth, and annoyed with Hank, who has no business bein' a cowboy and keeps draggin' me out to handle his horse... which has nothing wrong with it."

"Oh."

There is another pause. He sips his coffee again, then mentions off-handedly. "But if ye wanted the full of it, I was a wee bit amazed you had the food all ready. Did me a bit of a shock."

"Ah. I was wondering!" I cannot help but lean forward toward him, earnest to placate.

He makes a dismissive noise. "The flapjacks I'll take over what my old auntie would have done. Had a cold sandwich on the sideboard for me to pick at whenever I showed back up. I couldn't complain. I don't have the leisure or time to manage the house or yard or make food for myself. Hot food beats cold any day."

I press my lips together, then offer tentatively, "Is there a way, perhaps, to guess at when you might be home so I can manage hot food more often than cold? I can see... I mean, if your schedule is never ending, then it could be difficult sometimes, but perhaps you could always send word along?"

He gives me a shrewd look, and I wonder if this conversation had not already happened between him and his aunt. Perhaps I am completely naive.

"That is not a bad idea, Mrs. Weber. We can try it out and see how it goes?" He does not condescend to me, so I take a bit of heart. Maybe I will be able to appease him or find a rhythm to his daily work after all.

I am relieved to find him as fair minded as I'd hoped, though a Doctor ought to be more pragmatic, I suppose. He leaves me then, and I hear him rustling in the surgery before he sticks his head around the door, giving me a bit of a lopsided grin.

"I need to do my rounds, but before I do so, shall I walk ye over to Widow Hawks?"

I glance around the kitchen. Now there are the dirty dishes from breakfast as well as the earlier mess, and give him a smile back.

"Perhaps I had better stay here. Clean up a bit. And if you'd be so kind to let Widow Hawks know to expect us after dinner? Would you be back then?"

He gives a shrug as he tugs a medical bag from the room. "If I'm not, I'll try to send word."

The screen slams. I stare around myself, and then do not pause to think further and instead concentrate entirely on my chores.

The kitchen takes up the remainder of my day. I find the well out back, and haul water to clean the floor twice and the benches and tables thrice. I black the stove and hang up the pots and pans in an order to my liking. The shelves are restocked with the cutlery, and the pantry is reorganized. Almost immediately, I find I like having a home to tend to again, that this is a good purpose. I muse that perhaps by tending to the Doctor, I will be helping those who are ill and sick as well. It is something to live for.

The sun is setting. I stand at the stove, placidly spinning a thin soup. It is just spring, so there is not much in the garden for eating. I note I will have to find seeds from Kate to plant and I hope I am not too late to get started for the year. There were navy beans, some cured ham and a few old beets and I am glad there are spices enough to make the soup edible.

37

Just as I wonder if he will send word that he is to be late I hear him springing back into the house. He is loud, even for a man, and I wonder that his patients are not immediately overwhelmed with the racket he makes coming into a place.

"Smells good, Mrs. Weber!" He is in the room, and I glance up at him, glad he is joining me for another meal. I have so many questions, though I am not sure he will have the interest or the time to answer them.

"Set yourself down. I have a tea ready."

He nods absently at me as he leaves the room again, and I hear the water tap run. Once he is back in the room, I hand him a proper big mug of tea, which he sips while staring out the window, where the shadows are slowly growing long.

"I sent word to Widow Hawks. She'll expect us at dusk," he says, without looking at me.

"I thank you for your thoughtfulness. It sounds like it was a busy day. Would you care to tell me over supper?" I turn to the table to ladle the soup. He catches me mid-movement and swiftly takes the hot iron pot out of my hands and deftly places it on the table. I am unsure about his helpfulness. Is this his nature, or is he simply being kind this first day? Henry never helped in the home.

"Ye wouldn't know anyone I speak of," he says, sitting down on the bench as I bring over the spoons. He is not looking at me now, but his eyes are traveling over the surfaces of the home, and along the walls where the newly washed dishes are standing up straight and proud. He glances at me as I sit across from him and ladle out the soup. "Besides, I don't want to bore you."

I smile at him tentatively. "I should learn, somehow, to know my neighbors."

His face breaks into the same lined smile, briefly in return, and he gestures for me to fill my plate and join him. I sit across from him and we share the salt and pepper before he dives into the day's rounds.

"First, of course, there was the check on the Brinkley newborn and Alice. It's her first, so I knew she'd be nervous to start. Her milk hasn't quite come in yet, so I had her set to suckle the boy they call Pete. The longer he goes, the quicker her milk."

I set my spoon down to listen closely to this. It is new for me to hear these earthy matters, and as I will be a mother now, these stories have a bittersweetness that I yearn to hear, and yet struggle to accept as my story. The Doctor continues, stabbing at his stew with vigor as he goes on. "Her husband, Mitch, is set to stay with her as it's spring planting, and the family'll be too busy to care for her much."

This need for help is something I understand, and I am quick to jump in and break my own empty stare at my plate. "I could make overlarge portions these days and take the leftovers over."

This makes him look up at me squarely. "They won't take to charity. None do here, really."

"Who does?" I counter rhetorically. "They'd be doing us a favor, taking off leftovers that would soon go to spoil with only two to eat them."

He laughs heartily at this reasoning, leaning back from the table. I am pleased with his laughter. It is free and fills the space briefly, seeming to fit his size perfectly. It is almost captivating.

"Very good, Mrs. Weber. Very good."

His hands are immediately busy again with the stew as he outlines his other calls; an elderly crone with arthritis, a few broken bones on the cowboys, a case of infected saddle sores and one sickly early spring foal in a rancher's stables.

We finish the stew over the story of the foal. I think perhaps I should have made a dessert, but there was not much time and I hadn't thought so far ahead. He settles this worry for me by standing and looking outside.

"We'd best get over to Widow Hawks' soon enough."

I stand too, and stack the cutlery, chiding as I move. "I'll not go until the dishes are done. You've gone too long without a clean place and I can't finish my first day with a dirty kitchen."

Moving to the washbin, I begin to suds up the bowls and forks, moving quickly as I can as I see the sun is starting to set. I do not know if nights are safe outside.

There is movement next to me; the Doctor has taken a rag and is drying dishes as I finish them. This makes me pause. Surely the ease with which he deftly dries and replaces on the shelves comes with practice. Did he help his old aunt with home chores? I find myself voicing this wonderment without thinking, and he nods.

"Yes. When I'm at home, I like to be involved with the upkeep. It's a nice change from the daily work."

"May I ask... were you close with your aunt?"

He shrugs, but I find myself doubting his lack of feeling. "She was family. Who doesn't care for their family?"

"You must miss her."

The Doctor is quiet. He places another dish on top of the first, the tin clinking. "She was all I had left."

I think perhaps I should say he has time to marry and have a family of his own, but these words choke me. I should not be so quick to prescribe marriage as an answer. I thought it was, and I was proven wrong.

"I am so sorry, Doctor. Truly, I am. I did not know her, but she must have been something to handle the work here."

He looks down at me. The Irish eyes are not twinkling now, but I sense he is glad to discuss this quietly, even though I am a stranger. He says, "She was. Thank you."

We stand there for another moment looking at each other, until our hands reclaim the washing until I finally reach the last pot. The copper is gleaming a bit in the lamplight, and I hang the towels to dry. Dusk has settled, and we are clearing to leave for Widow Hawks' home when a horse comes skittering out of the gloaming from the main street, stopping in front of the Doctor's home. The rider doesn't even bother to dismount.

"Doc Kinney! Tate's leg is swellin' up something fierce, just like you said it might -"

He doesn't finish before the Doctor is swinging out of the house and heading for the hitching post out front where his horse waits, patiently munching on its own dinner.

"Infection. Got to watch for gangrene. I've got to go, Mrs. Weber. Head straight over to Widow Hawks; down the main street, last house on your left. Be back tomorrow. Seven sharp."

They race away before the screen door has time to slam.

Because it is growing dark so quickly and I have no wish to walk alone any more than I have to, I head out immediately with my satchel.

Thankfully, the main street is peppered with homes, saloons, the general store and a few other buildings that have their gaslights still blazing strong. The sun has only just set, so the light is gray and low but not completely dark. I see how the spaces between the wooden structures could become black holes in the night and am glad I am walking while there is still a touch of light in the sky.

The main street is long and wide, but as I clear the most populated part, it becomes apparent even in the gloaming, that the Widow Hawks' home is not hard to miss.

Set quite a few paces away from the second to last home, her place is a longer, rambling house. As I get closer, I see a few hides airing out, and there is a fire pit in the front yard. Strange native artwork is roughly painted on the door, and a warm light glows from the two windows.

I knock, but barely finish when the door swings open wide. In my mind's eye, I had expected her to be a stooped, tiny little widow. Instead, she is straight and towering, a tall black shadow against the fire in the hearth behind her. A whiff of air from inside smells of burning sage and hot meat. I sense her eyes on me before she silently moves aside with a dancer's step. It is my invitation to enter, and I do so tentatively. I have not ever met an Indian.

The fire is crackling, and the one long room is dark in the corners so that I cannot see much around me. She is moving next to me, near silent in her mix of hides and skirts, and fluidly squats near the fire where pieces of straw are half braided. Her hair is bound in one long plait, but even in the firelight I can see it is mostly a steel grey.

I stand, uncertain, for a long moment before I realize she is not going to offer my ideas of expected social norms for visitors. Setting down my satchel, I go to kneel on the floor next to her. She does not look up, but her hands are busy, quick and nimbly braiding and weaving. I think to help her, but I doubt my prowess in making the pieces tight and proper enough for her purpose.

As the silence stretches, I wonder how I will live like this now. How will I work twelve or fourteen hours for the Doctor, never knowing his true schedule or his needs, to mind his whole household, only to come stay every night and wake every morning with this strange specter of a woman who does not speak to me? Nor do I know how I am to repay her for this kindness. I am a stranger. An easterner. A white woman.

Though it is early, my pregnancy weighs on me quickly in the evenings. There must be a shift in my breath or my knees to rouse her, because she suddenly stands and walks to a dark wall. Not knowing what else to do, I stand and watch her. In the shadows, she gestures, so I approach to find a small cot simply prepared and covered in a hide of an animal I do not recognize in the night. This is to be my bed. She walks away before I can even murmur a thanks.

It is a far cry from anything I had prepared to handle. But it is not worth a fuss. Nothing will change my circumstances now.

She is quickly back at the fire, and I assume that she will not take kindly to my requests for privacy in this wide open room. It is her home, after all. I must abide her rules, whatever they may be. Turning my back to her, I unbutton my dress, already stained with black along one sleeve, and strip to my undergarments. A simple nightgown, an unadorned nightcap, and I am ready for sleep, save for washing up. Widow Hawks does not move, and I am too embarrassed to disturb her. At this point, I am not entirely sure she speaks any English. I open the bedding up and turn toward the wall. I think I will spend all night wondering about my new job, the Doctor, and the Indian woman with whom I live, but instead I fall into a deep sleep, immediately.

# CHAPTER 3

I wake with her as she rises early. I can barely see the sunrise through the cracks in the hides and faded calico over the windows. She is stirring the fire embers, and generally making a racket, which I did not expect from her. My body protests the earliness of the hour, but I get up and pull the cap from my head.

As I must wash up today, I tentatively step toward her and she swings to look at me. She is not quite as tall as I remember from last night, but she is still many inches above me; her face is inscrutable.

I gesture with my words. "Do you have a cup and water I might use please?"

She looks at me a long moment, then walks out of the house. I wait, hopeful she understood me. There is a sloshing and the door bangs open to show her wrestling a good size wash bin into the room. It is full of spring rainwater, and my eyes widen.

"Widow Hawks,I thank you. But this is too much trouble. I will gladly wash outside tomorrow."

Her back bends smoothly to put the bin by the fire. She does not acknowledge me, but turns back to the embers to continue rousing them. I watch her, spellbound and uncertain for a minute. It is then that I notice she has no clocks.

This thought rouses me and I bend to wash up quickly in the chilly water. Pulling on the same dress as yesterday, though it is travel worn, I lace up my shoes, noting they will need to be replaced with the sturdy kind I saw Kate wearing. Widow Hawks wears soft leather shoes, native made and decorated with faded paints. Are they comfortable? There are no sturdy soles like the boots I saw Kate wear, but she has a steady gait. Half her clothing is almost exactly what I have been told the Indians wear – primal, savage clothing – but they do not seem out of place, nor threatening now that I see it all together.

Plaiting my hair up neatly and coiling it with pins, I am ready without much fuss. I allow myself a little private smile to think of the ladies at home and their finery and needs. I am thankful I did not need a maid to dress me out east, or I would be lost today.

The widow is still working the fire when I go to the door. There is a part of my nature that is tactile, but I sense, as I had when I was married to Henry, that touch was not welcome. To be a person who craves the touch of another in love or simple friendship has caused me often to pause, to think, to consider before I reach out. My hand on another's is so often disapproved of in society, even between family members. Here, too, I am uncertain enough that I innately pull in myself from placing a hand on the older woman's shoulder. Instead, I try to use my voice to portray my thanks.

"The Doctor said you would be a fair landlady, Widow Hawks. I see you are. And I thank you for allowing me a bed. I know I am a disruption. Please let me know how I might... offer my thanks to you."

She does not turn or move during my speech, so I press on, anxious to make at least one decent impression. "I am... I'm a widow too, like you. I--." My words choke me, because I know nothing of her marriage, and I cannot make more out of mine than what it was.

It seems she will not speak, so I leave the house and walk briskly in the dusky morning toward the Doctor's house. I take my time to look about as I walk today. The land is flat and easy to read. There are hills in the near distance, covered in tall trees, though most of the landscape is flat prairie. The road and the railroad cut a scar across the pale soil. The main street is wide, and there are the few streets that curve out from it, the Doctor's house being one of them. These streets are all dead ends; there are perhaps fifty homes in all throughout the town, some scattering haphazardly out of the edges of the streets. The packed dirt under my feet gives no loud sound, and by the time I reach the Doctor's home, I have not seen more than two people who give me curious glances, but do not speak to me, and the silence is soft.

His house is quiet, so I let myself in and take care for the screen door to close with barely a squeak. I see a soft glow in the kitchen and realize he is already awake. Perhaps it is after seven. Entering, I see he has a lantern on the table to help him with breakfast preparation, though he is nowhere to be seen. Now, as I am in the house, though, I hear him puttering upstairs.

Putting on the kettle for the coffee, I move to the pantry and think a good hot breakfast of eggs and bread would do him well. As I finish up the coffee and heat the pans, he enters and breathes out loudly so I need to turn to acknowledge him.

"Good morning, Doctor Kinney."

He nods in response, but nothing else, so I pour him a cup of coffee and turn back to the eggs, mentioning off-hand, "Widow Hawks has no clock, so I hope I am on time."

He comes to stand next to me, watching me beat the eggs. I watch him take the bread and begin to slice thick slabs. Finally he says, "You are on time. Ye are early in fact, Mrs. Weber." His voice is contrite, and I stop the beating of the eggs and the kitchen is suddenly silent.

I look into his eyes. He is not smiling at all, and fear wells in me. Have I displeased him already, again? His lips press together and finally says, "I am sorry ye had to go alone last night. It is embarrassin' to me. To ask Widow Hawks to take a boarder is easy. She is a good woman and we'd do anything for each other. But to ask you to go alone, without introduction... It was inexcusable."

I look down at the eggs sloshing in the bowl cradled in my arm. It would not do to be truthful with him now, to tell him that I was nervous in the dusky night walk through town, nor that Widow Hawks does not speak to me. Not that I am sure I could be so honest with my employer anyway, regardless of how kind he is.

"You would feel better if I forgave you, then?" Instead, I am merry to appease him.

"Please, yes."

"Then you are forgiven. Though I don't think it's necessary," I rejoin, and looked down to continue the eggs. He stands next to me for another moment, as if words are trembling on his lips, but he says no more. I should have expected him to be a gentleman, but his worries are still touching, nonetheless. I have other anxieties, such as the babe I carry. At this thought, I am stabbed with guilt. Perhaps I should be honest and tell him about this coming issue, but my words are stuck. This baby seems so much an illusion. Perhaps it is why I have not mentioned my condition outright to him. Why does my confession stick in my throat? It does not seem real that I carry Henry's baby.

We eat companionably. I appreciate the meal. I suddenly realize that I am hungrier than ever and quietly hope he leaves some eggs in the pan so that I could have a little extra. Unfortunately, he leaves me nothing, but at least he praises my cooking. As he finishes his coffee, he leans back.

"How did you find Widow Hawks?"

Swallowing my own mouthful, I answer carefully, unable to meet his eyes. "She was accommodating. Thank you for arranging a bed."

He stares at me, as if measuring a response, and gives a slight nod while he sets down the empty mug. "I'll work in the study a wee bit until I start rounds. Thank you for the breakfast, Mrs. Weber."

Once he leaves the kitchen, I stare about. I am still hungry, but I think I will just make a bit more during dinner and supper to allow me seconds and still have leftovers for the Brinkley family.

The day is overcast, so I decide to manage the garden, as I worry the spring will get on faster than I realize, and it is nice to not have the sun beat down on my hair and back as I turn over the soil.

As I pull the hoe through the earth, I mull over the schedule of the days and try to find a rhythm. I will make breakfast and we will eat. Then he will do paperwork and I will do chores. He will visit morning patients, arrive back for a lunch, and then head back to rounds until dinner. We will have dinner and I will clean and head back to my silent rooming partner on the far end of town. It is full and busy, and it will not be an idle existence. More than anything, I'm grateful that I have a house to keep and someone to feed.

The sun breaks through the clouds and hits my hair and the back of my neck, heat soaking into the dark fabric of my mourning clothes. I do not realize how hot I am until I stand up and immediately feel dizzy, falling to my knees to keep from fainting.

"Mrs. Weber!" There is a call from the house, and I see the Doctor has stuck his head out of the window. I did not realize that he could watch me from his office. "Are you alright?"

I nod, feeling my heart pump hot blood through my head. His head disappears back inside. He was right. I need more suitable clothing for this type of work.

The garden needs seeds. I finally finish prepping the dusty ground, and wonder what I should plant. I do not have much of a green thumb and I have no understanding of what grows well in the soil out here. A few wealthy acquaintances back east kept greenhouses, though I did not have that luxury and have little experience planting and maintaining. But I want fresh vegetables for cooking, so I take my apron, wipe my face, and head back into the cool shade of the hallway. The Doctor is taking his hat from the peg by the door, but stops and looks at me in concern.

"I have two patients to visit this mornin'. Don't trouble much for luncheon."

I wave away his worry. "It's no matter."

He shakes his head, plops the hat back on the nail, and marches into the kitchen, calling to me over his shoulder. "You should feel free to wash up in the surgery, Mrs. Weber."

I pause at the door of the lab, with its pale whitewashed walls and shiny glass and silver instruments on the tables and cases, carefully labeled and organized. The tap has a soft condensation on it from the morning's warmth. I pour some water out on my hands and clean the dirt from under my nails.

Turning, I see him standing in the doorway watching me, blandly, a tumbler of cold milk from the ice box in his hand. "You're a bit pale. Early sunstroke, I shouldn't wonder," he explains, then hands me the milk before heading back to the door.

"Thank you," I call, belatedly, as he walks out. I am not sure he hears me. I have forgotten to ask him how long he will be. Guessing that two patients might take an hour or so, I calculate that I have time to dust the house before I make the midday meal.

I do not touch the lab. I do not know how to start sterilizing his equipment properly, so I dust around the piles of paperwork and mounds of books in his office, the shelves on the kitchen, noting the curtains will need a spring wash. Hesitating a moment, I wonder if I should intrude on the living level upstairs, but decide that as housekeeper, I cannot shirk half the house. I walk up the narrow stairs. A few of them protest with pops and squeaks as I ascend.

There are two bedrooms and a community washroom. One room is spare and spartan, the faded flowered coverlet the only evidence that the space once was his great aunt's bedroom. A cross over the bed speaks to the Irish Catholicism, and there is not much to dust other than the bed rails and tops of the bedside table and bureau. The closet is utterly bare. Her bed reminds me of my easy fatigue, but I push the thought away and turn to the washroom. A tin bathtub on planked flooring is shielded from eyes below by a dark calico curtain. There is a string with a matching curtain along the wall, allowing for privacy so a person could bathe while another primped at the wash station. The water in the pitcher is low, but I see he has washed out the bin. The floor needs a scrub and the bathtub, too, but I am pleased that the Doctor is not sloppy.

Bracing myself, I look in his private room. This, to me, is the Doctor's ultimate sanctuary and it feels deceptive to walk into his bedroom without asking for permission. His bed is made, though there are wrinkles in the thin blanket. I am surprised to see his closet is only half full, but the clothes are spilling about haphazardly instead of hung on the hooks. There are a few books on the table by the curtain-less window. Two lamps. One on the floor next to more books must provide him evening light and the other next to the bed. I am struck by the fact that he has artwork on the wall. One picture is a small, simple framed portrait of an older woman. I wonder if this is his recently deceased aunt. Another is a wedding picture. A photograph. I think there is resemblance in the man's face to the Doctor, but their clothing is a bit old fashioned, and I wonder if they are his parents or his grandparents. I like the woman's eyes.

I dust around his things, then head back downstairs into the kitchen. Lunch is a light soup, and as I am stirring as he slams the screen door and walks in.

"How were your rounds, Doctor?"

"Good. The calf is doin' fine and Tate's leg is handlin' my treatment," he says, before disappearing around the corner. I hear the familiar gush of water, and then he is back and eyeing me as I set the table.

"How are you feelin'?"

I think of the babe in my womb, and catch my breath, only managing, "Very fine. It was just a little dizzy spell."

He considers, then goes to the icebox and pours out a bit more milk and wordlessly hands it to me. I am embarrassed that I am already such a bother on my second day of employment.

I say this while we eat, and he shows a half smile. "You're not used to the weather here. It can be sweltering, but then the winters are sometimes surprisingly early and snowy. Until you're seasoned, I don't mind helpin' to keep ye alive." His voice is lighthearted and I stop worrying for the moment. There is too much to learn and figure. If I will stop and really think of all the dangers, the changes, the amount of heavy work I am to do, I will panic. Best bit by bit.

Perhaps I should tell him about the babe. I wish to dissemble to someone, but to tell a man – this stranger – within a day or two of our acquaintance goes against my nature. My quiet life suited my preference for privacy, which Henry fit quite well. This entire situation is beyond comprehending. Not only is my widowhood and surprising pregnancy after so years of barrenness something new, but to be expected to dissemble the secrets of my life without history or relationship is beyond my ability. I must adjust. I must learn.

After some silence, I venture, "Where might I find seeds for the garden?"

"Kate," he answers between bites. "And you ought to get your cloth from her, too. Make yourself a serviceable dress or two and a good bonnet."

I nod, then glance about the kitchen. "Where do we get milk and cheese?"

"Brinkley's. We trade services and goods. It's how they're paying for my help with the new baby, but otherwise, they're the family that supplies most of us 'round here with dairy."

"That reminds me, I've made enough dinner/super for us and them. Might I take some over today for their supper tonight?" I ask. He gives me a true smile with his eyes crinkled, half moons. I smile back in spite of myself.

"Alice'll be grateful. I'm headin' to them next; why don't you come along and meet them. Ye can head to the general from there."

I agree, and we companionably clean the dishes together, when I ask him what plants he would suggest I try in the garden. His aunt had done squashes, cucumbers, dill, herbs, carrots, beans, and potatoes. I wonder about tomatoes and he says I should try it.

We walk out together. He courteously opens the screen door for me and I recall the gentlemanly way Henry had treated me. It is the first time I have thought fondly of my husband in a while and I am surprised to think of him with such nostalgia. He was not a passionate man, nor a very expressive one, but he had been polite, careful, and respectful of me. He had been very grateful to have found a bride he could talk to and could easily take to social gatherings. Unlike Doctor Kinney, Henry was not one to remain a bachelor. Society would not have supported him quite so readily back east.

"How long were you married, Mrs. Weber?" the Doctor asks, sociably, and I try not to start, as if he is reading my mind. Apparently, the months of niceties do not pass here before people move into personal questions. But I should not be surprised by this, especially given the prying way Kate asked questions of me yesterday.

Was it only yesterday I arrived? How strange. I am perhaps more overwhelmed than I realize.

I notice I have not yet answered the Doctor's question. He is trying to be friendly. "Four years. I was older when I married. Well, older than most girls out east, that is," I amend, offering up more information than I intended in my fluster.

"No children?" He asks an obvious question, but I answer without thought, forgetting for a moment that I am pregnant, and by the time I speak, the moment for dissembling is gone.

"No. It was... difficult... for Hen... for us." I pause, then decided to give him a broader picture of my marriage. "Mr. Weber had health issues."

I think he is going to ask more questions of me, but we are drawing up on the farm, and the Doctor turns and hails some of the men in the fields. I think I should remember to ask him about himself, and of the photographs in his bedroom since he is going to be so friendly with me. Besides, it will be good to understand my employer so as to properly manage his home.

The Brinkley's are not far from the town center. Their farm is the first on the main road north, visible even from the town square. It is pretty, neat, and obviously successful. I count four homes on the property as we make our way there. Each one has a woman's touch of a window box, curtains, and painted doors. I can smell the cows, the sheep, and the salty dryness of land and earth tilled properly. These are the scents I attribute to peacefulness, a familiarity that feels welcoming. I see a few garden plots already sprouting tiny green leaves. My garden will be late.

As we level up with one of the homes, I hear the tiny, distinctive sound of a newborn's dry fussy crying. The Doctor gives a brief knock and then, carrying the pot of cooled soup, walks in casually without waiting for anyone to answer the door. I follow him, carrying a basket of condiments to go with the soup.

Inside, I find a home that was once tidy, but now has the disarray of distracted disregard for orderliness. Doctor Kinney is already in the bedroom I hear his accent softened with a croon as he addresses the mother and baby. I see he has put the pot of soup on the stove in his passing.

A young man comes in from the side door with a pail of milk and an empty washtub under an arm. He stops short at the sight of me. I smile encouragingly.

"Hello, Mr. Brinkley. I'm Doctor Kinney's housekeeper, Mrs. Weber. You can call me Jane," I offer, remembering the casual way people address one another in this town. I move to the stove and pull a pot from the sideboard. It needs washing before I can put the soup in for them to reheat later. "We've brought you some dinner."

He is still staring at me, then remembers himself and sets down the washbin. "You're here with the Doc?"

"Yes. He's already in with your wife and the boy."

Mitch sets the milk on the table and brushes past me to the bedroom. He seems an eager father, as if he is willing to learn about his son. I admire this, as well as chuckle at his poor attempts to keep house

56

while Alice recovers. I'm surprised there are not many women from the farm helping her.

I fill the washtub and clean out the pot and a few dishes so the table can be set. Then I pour the soup from Doctor Kinney's crockery into Alice's and set it on the stove. As my hands move around the heavy plates and clay mugs, my wedding band clinks loudly against the rims. It reminds me of life back east. The amount of housework I am doing now is not so much new to me, but rather the roughness of it all, the lack of fine things and city amenities that make it less easy.

"Mrs. Weber?" the Doctor's voice spins me around I see a small bundle cradled in his arms. He looks strikingly tender and I find myself catch at the vision. It is not often I would think to see a man holding a newborn and the sight of it is fetching.

"Is everything alright?" I ask.

"Can ye manage wee Pete while I examine Alice?"

I look past the Doctor into the bedroom, where the husband is sitting next to his wife on the narrow bed. He does not seem interested in coming out and holding his son. I wipe my hands on the apron and go to get him.

The Doctor's hands seem overlarge as he gives over the child and the pass of precious cargo becomes a sweetly delicate moment as we both stare at the sleeping babe, carefully maneuvering his little limbs. The little boy is light, air-like, and smells like warm skin and powdered bedding. Do all babes smell good? I do not know, I have held so few. I hold him a bit awkwardly at first, but Doctor Kinney puts a light hand on my waist, then adjusts the crick of my elbow.

"He won't break so easily, Mrs. Weber. Relax here. Good." With a casual tap, he releases my hip and walks back into the bedroom and shuts the door. I'm overwhelmed by the baby I hold, and am overtly aware of his pale skin, the blue spidery veins on his temple, and the shell of his ear. He is roundly robust even in infancy, and his plump little lips still have a drop of milk on them. I am suddenly filled with apprehension for my own little baby. Will it be a boy like this, perfect and little? How shall I care for him? How shall I love him and provide for him? The enormity of the undertaking I have in my future suddenly scares me. I am afraid to do this alone, afraid of the uncertainty, afraid of the birth, afraid of what Henry has left me. This is not the life I expected and I am almost angry at my late husband.

Henry was not the husband I had dreamed about in my youth, but he was steady and grave. To lose him so early in marriage, before we could build much tenderness or history, leaves me still feeling detached to his memory. I enjoyed being married, but the marriage itself was filled with guarded lovemaking, quiet conversation, and dispassionate expressions. I feel as though I had not fulfilled the potential within me to be a wife, and now I will not fulfill my potential as a mother. I doubt there will be such things as nursemaids out here, besides, I will not be able to afford it. And I have no family in all of the territories to help me.

I bend over the little baby and will myself not to cry. Without realizing it, I am swaying lightly and hold the little face near mine, almost so I can press my forehead to his tiny one. He is not mine, though, so I refrain from actually touching him.

"Mrs. Weber." The Doctor is back. I lift my face, glad there are no tears. He has a half smile on his face, but it is almost sad, and he takes the baby without another word. I go back to the stove and then finish up the rest of the dirty dishes so that the kitchen area, at least, is picked up.

"Ready?" He returns again. I glance at the bedroom. I have not met Alice, but I figure there will be time for that later. I nod and follow him out.

We walk in silence for a minute, or so, before I venture, "There is not much help for Alice?"

He understands my question and gives a rueful chuckle. "Not this moment. Mitch's family isn't happy with him for taking time off from spring plantin' and farmin' to spend time with his wife and babe. The men figure if he's so sure to help with the baby, the womenfolk can keep working in the fields instead of taking over Alice's household. They'll get over it soon, and Alice'll win them over, too. But in the meantime, thank ye for helping."

I nod, pleased he notices my work. "He's unique in being so involved in...women's issues."

"Aye." Doctor Kinney thinks for a moment, then says with bluntness. "I wish more men would be interested. It would help some of the women 'round here who do not have family to help them."

"I can see your point," I say. He touches on a subject I was musing earlier. He gives me an amused sideways smile.

"You don't agree?"

I think. I am rather traditional and, to me, it does not seem a man's place to be with his wife during childbirth, or even after. But then I wonder about myself. What would I wish, if Henry were alive? I would be too embarrassed to have him near while I screamed in labor, or hear the diagnosis after I gave birth. But suppose my marriage consisted of a man whom I loved, instead of simply held in affection? Suppose our child had been conceived in passion, not the careful, chilly sex I've known. Then I might wish for more sharing in everything, from childbirth to childcare and beyond.

"I think perhaps some marriages do not make it easy for such openness," I say.

The Doctor does not rejoin my comment at first. He nods once or twice. Then he says, unexpectedly, "Do you not have family, Mrs. Weber? Parents?"

I smile with reflection. "Yes. I have a mother and father. They are alive and live in Rockport."

"No siblings?"

"Yes. I have a sister who is much older than me."

"Did ye not wish to be with them after your husband's untimely death? Forgive me, Mrs. Weber, but family is important out here. When one does not have any, we tend to create our own to survive. But you left yours. Were ye not able to return?"

I hug the empty soup pot to my chest, wincing slightly against the tenderness of my bosom. I do not know why I did not ask to return to my family. Surely, my mother would have let me have my old room. I'd been married quite a few years, but they had kept my childhood house. My sister would not have welcomed me into her busy life, though had I begged, she would have eventually, unhappily, relented.

"I could have, I suppose," I venture. "But I married late and had enjoyed making my own household. To return would be too... easy."

"And ye are not partial to easiness?" There is surprise in his voice.

"Maybe not. Life has not been difficult for me, nor has it been easy," I explain obscurely. "But that is most lives, is it not, Doctor?"

He shakes his head at my trite comment. "Yes. But when given an easy way out, many would take it. Instead, you embark on a journey, alone, to a place where you know no one. I must say, it's a bit gutsy. Here we be."

We've quickly arrived at Kate's mercantile. I am still mulling on his characterization of my spirit. Do I have a bit of spitfire in me? I think he is mistaken. It was a simple choice for me. To return home, as if I'd never left, would be taking a step backward, ignoring what I'd learned as a wife and lover, and forever succumbing to life as a widow. There would be no purpose. This adventure is still out of my element, but I am enjoying the challenge of it, though it can be still counted in days, hours, minutes.

"Be sure to pick up proper shoes. Kate knows my billing." And he is off, his easy athletic gait propelling him down the street.

The store is warm and I wonder how hot it gets in the heat of summer. Perhaps she could open up the glass windows. They are dusty and smudged, but perhaps that is an eastern expectation. There are no other customers at this moment, and I can clearly hear her coming from the back of the store. She comes out with a dusty burlap bag slung over one of her strong shoulders. I wonder how she keeps up the store without any men to help her.

"Jane Weber." Her voice is more melodious than I remember from yesterday, but she does not seem as welcoming today. "What can I get the Doctor?"

I hesitate. "It's not for him. For me. I... I need proper work things, he says."

"Does he now?" There is a forced lightness in her voice. "Well, he's right. Those shoes won't last the summer." She stands before me, drops the heavy bag of dried beans to the floor, and stares at my light weight city footwear.

"I would be obliged if you could help me, Kate." I find that I am pleading. Please let her be a friend to me here, I think, suddenly. How else will I have friends? I'm sure the other women here in Flats Junction are all married and with children. She and I must be alike, to be alone and need to survive. "I know nothing of what to do here."

She finally meets my face and gives me a hard stare. I think of how beautiful she is. Why is she unmarried? And why is she so skeptical of me? I wish I am a brave person to ask her these questions that would give me an insight to her.

"The shoes are over here." Spinning on her heel, she goes to a table where serviceable shoes are piled together. They are all black or dark brown. There are no laces on most of the boots, though a few have metal toe tips. I pick out a few pairs that seem to be my size and try them on while Kate heads to the counter. She calls to me over her shoulder,

"You won't be doing much riding out, so you'll need mainly clothes for tending house, I should think. Just one split skirt, an overskirt, and a housedress or two should do you."

I am immediately embarrassed about this expense, but do not know if I should express this to Kate. Then again, she is privy to the Doctor's accounts.

One pair of boots fits well, and I wear them over to the counter to get a feel for them on my feet. They are immediately more comfortable than my city shoes. I find Kate on a ladder, pulling down materials.

"Kate..." I start softly, then dive in while she continues to move in silence. "Kate, I am unsure how to pay for this. The Doctor is paying me in room and board, not money, really. Unless we should change our agreement. I don't have much to my name and I'm afraid to spend it all on goods for myself."

She pauses for a moment, then comes down to the floor with a stack of cloth. The look on her face is softer. I do not understand the mercurialness of her moods at all. They are disconcerting, and yet, becoming of her, so that I wish to figure out the enigma of her personality. There is a charm about her that I am drawn toward.

"Jane. It's alright. If I know the Doctor, he will consider this part of your 'board,' but I can make a note in the accounting so that should you ever wish to pay him back, you would know how much."

"Very well," I amend. "But do not let me choose things that are too expensive anyway."

"Well, you've done fine on the boots already," she says, peering down at my feet.

I smile tentatively at her, and then browse at what she has laid out. A good brown work calico makes sense to match with the leather split skirt she recommends. But I find I am dissatisfied with the options for a housedress. Kate has brought out mostly dowdy, plain colors. I am not vain, nor am I prone to dress prettily for a purpose, but I do have an idea what looks pleasing on me and what I would be comfortable in.

"Do you... I wonder if you might have something in more color?"

"It will fade faster," she remarks a bit sharply. I bite my tongue against a quick reply against her, unconsciously staring at her orange blouse and blue skirt. It looks lovely on her and it doesn't seem to have faded much, unless it is very new, which I doubt.

"Perhaps... perhaps something in blue or pink... or even yellow?"

She climbs back up and I detect a huffiness. Is she so easily offended that I did not take to her suggestions?

"You won't need much frill," she reasons from her perch. "No men to dress for here, like there were out east."

I nod sagely, playing along with her irritation. "You're quite right. Besides, my late husband did not take much for bows and things, so I've forgotten how to really adorn myself."

She seems to relent a bit after that, and comes down with some prettier fabrics. I choose a yellow calico, and then I cannot help myself as I ask her to pull down a lavender with no pattern at all. I simply like the color, and I know my dark brown hair and lighter skin looks well in purples.

"I'm just going to be happy to wear color again, you see," I try to explain to her. "The colors of mourning are not suitable here, nor do they look well on anyone."

Kate gives a half shrug of indifference and goes to cut the bolts for me. I ask her to cut enough to make a bonnet of one or two of the fabrics. I hope my sewing skills are up for this challenge. I've learned, as any woman does, the physics of making clothing, but I am more used to making samplers and cross stitches than actual garments.

I wander to the seeds and pick through the small packets rattling with dryness. I dearly hope I am not too late to make a go of a garden. While picking out the packets I had discussed with the Doctor, I spy a case of metal goods. I go over to look at them while Kate finishes my parcels.

My fingers lightly graze the glass top of the case. It is filled with the finer things that I would expect to see more back home. Gold and silver glint in the sun streaking in from the large front windows, curling under the glass and glowing on dust that seems suspended in the air of the case. Like me. Suspended in this new reality where I do not know half of what to make of things. Frozen in a body newly taken over by a foreign condition, unable to dissemble to anyone.

She walks silently, even on the rough plank floor, and she scares me when she speaks lowly into my ear, "They are men's watches."

"I know," I stare at them through the dusty case, where they are laid out in no particular order. "My Henry had one just like that." I point, then turn away . She follows me without a word.

She adds up the goods carefully in a large, thick leatherbound book. The accounts fill over half of the yellowy pages.

"How are you getting by with the Doctor, then?"

"Well, it's only been two days. Barely. It's all a bit overwhelming. And I have so much to figure out. I'll learn, though. I suppose."

"Yes," she gives a little snort. "Every woman's dream, to keep house for a man."

"I don't mind having a purpose, whatever it is." I say, and I realize my tone is a bit like a retort. Apparently her surliness can rub off on me.

She relents a bit. "I don't mean it particularly to you, Jane." She uses my front name comfortably, as if we have been close friends for years. "I mean that... that it's something I wouldn't want to do." She is dissembling now. I wait for her to finish her thought. "I've too much I want to prove. To this town and to myself."

"You're a braver woman than me," I give her. Kate actually smiles at this and I, again, think she is unusually beautiful. It is a good compliment to give her, it seems, for she becomes cheerful.

"Well, then, good luck with your planting. I'm sure I'll have to stop by when I can to see how you're getting on."

And with that, I leave the general store, uncertain if she is a friend or not.

# CHAPTER 4

I sit next to the fire, near Widow Hawks, wrestling with the sewing in my lap. I know this is a peaceful process for some women, but I am too rusty to be able to sew aimlessly and just let my mind wander. I would like to be so complacent about the stitches, for I have much to rethink about the past several days. I cannot believe I have been in Flats Junction for just two weeks. It is all a blur that still feels like eons have passed. I am constantly trying to consider my next step on how to properly keep house for the Doctor, how to keep my garden watered, and how to manage his office, which is my next task.

So far, I have made a bonnet and the bodice of a yellow dress. I hope it fits. I worry at how I will take it out when my body starts to swell with pregnancy. It is early yet, I know, and there will be many months before I really must take care. But I still worry.

Widow Hawks seems content to continue to share silence. She sits amicably next to me and handles her own weaving and arts. I do not know yet if she understands English completely. I have noticed articles in her home that do not seem to fit. There is a silver hairbrush, half hidden by wools, and a small locket that hangs from her neck on a real gold chain. But I do not ask questions and try to respect her quiet. We do not share any meals, nor any conversation. Only a space to sleep and a fire for an hour or so in the evenings.

My mind turns again to my task at hand. I am also worried about my lack of sewing skill. My time of mourning has drawn to a close, but I still have nothing to change into, so I continue to wear the smudged and well worn grey and black frocks I own. The Doctor has not said anything. Perhaps he has forgotten when I was to stop mourning anyway.

The night quickly turns old for me, so I turn to sleep.

# CHAPTER 5

In the early morning, I wake to vivid nausea. It is a constant churn. Waves of it are overpowering until I am able to stumble outside and relieve my stomach of supper. I kneel in the dirt outside Widow Hawks' home, heedless of the dirt and dust on my nightgown, thankful I did not retch in her home, and hopeful I did not wake her. Strangely, the nausea does not immediately subside, so I wait, a hand to my head, shaking and lightly sweating.

She is silent as a cat, so I start when her hand first comes around to my forehead. Waiting a beat, she then lifts me up and brings me back inside to the embers of last night's fire. A fur is thrown around my shoulders and then she bends to wake the flames so any chill I feel is quickly gone with the heat and the coziness of the soft fur.

There is silence, except for the crackle of new wood thrown on the flames. Widow Hawks comes next to me, kneeling smoothly. I still marvel at her easy gaits and bends even for her age.

"Does he know?"

Her voice is low, a melodiousness that is at once familiar and yet strange to hear. There is an accent to her words, I hear it immediately, but her English is pure. I try not to smile with happiness that she has finally accepted me enough to speak to, that I am worth her time. Perhaps she would misinterpret my grin. And I am too tired and worn to smile anyway.

"Henry? No. He didn't know. He died even before I knew myself."

"I do not speak of your husband. I mean the Doctor."

I pause, suddenly realizing that she has appropriately guessed my situation. How could she do it? How could she know so quickly? Weakly, I shake my head negative. She is quiet again for a minute, then says, gently,

"You ought to tell him, so he knows to give you rest."

"No, please," I plead. "I cannot be a bother to him any more. He is taking care of me so that I can take care of him, his kitchen and house. He has to think I am worth keeping on as a housemaid instead of one that is only an expensive trouble."

"He won't send for another."

"But how will he not? I must work as long as I can, so perhaps he will be kind enough to keep me on, or send me back east with a good reference. When this child is born, it will be difficult for me to work properly. He will have to put up with a babe in his house all day. I cannot imaging he will be happy with it, bachelor that he is."

"I will speak to him," she says, as if that will handle it all.

"Please, don't." I beg again.

"Yes," she nods sagely, musing, as if I have not asked against the idea. "And he will be happy to take care of you and the child."

"I don't wish to ask him to do that."

"You won't have to. He will. He is a good man. Now back to bed for you. I will wake you in time."

I try to protest further, but I know my arguments are weak. She does not seem to hear my protestations anyway. He must be told eventually and there is some sort of strange relief in not having to admit to this, myself.

She knows I will be utterly exhausted when I wake and I allow her to tuck me back into bed, where I sleep, dreamlessly at first. But then I am filled with the strange, earthy dreams of pregnancy, lifelike and lustful. One dream is Henry, holding our child, and I am confused, for I know he is dead. Another dream is of Kate, beautiful and glowing in the sunset. And the last is of the Doctor himself, looking down at me.

Widow Hawks wakes me at the last dream, so I am left this morning with this strange thought on my mind. I am almost afraid to walk to the Doctor's house and see him, but when I find him, he is his usual jovial self. It is only the last vestiges of my dream that make the day feel odd from the start.

As I set him breakfast, I broach the subject of his office.

"As I have most of the house straightened, I was hoping I might help you in your study."

"How so?" He peers at me over the rim of the coffee.

DOCTOR KINNEY'S HOUSEKEEPER

"Well... I'm wondering if I might act as secretary a bit? Put things to rights, the papers in order by last name or family, and have everything a bit more accurate to find. That way, perhaps, when you are out, I could access things. Only in an emergency, mind you... to help?"

He gives a little chuckle. "Ye needn't ask so carefully Mrs. Weber. It's a grand idea. Come on, then, I'll help with the wash up so we can march in together."

In taking the dry cloth from the peg near me, his arm brushes mine, and I keep my eyes on the suds and my hands so that I do not have to look at him. I hope I am not blushing as much as I feel. He and I have a casual manner and I hope tomorrow the remainder of my muddled dream will leave so I am not feeling strangely around my employer.

"What nation is Widow Hawks?" I ask, by way of conversation.

He carefully lines up the clean forks with the others. "She will say she is *Sihasapa*, Sioux. Folks 'round here call her Lakota too, or Blackfoot which is more precise."

"I don't see any other natives around town. I wonder why she stays," I muse, thinking perhaps now I might eventually be able to ask her that question myself. Now my nights need not be silent as she has decided to speak with me.

"Eventually, I expect you'll meet others. She has a very interestin' story. If you get her in the right mood, you might hear it one day," he says plainly but with finality, and then finishes the last pieces of cutlery. I pour out the water and follow him into the office.

I cannot imagine how he does any work in here. It is so cluttered that I am at a loss where to start, so I sit on the floor and pull a pile of books toward me.

"Perhaps if we clear off the bookshelf at once and build it back up from scratch before moving to patient files?"

He is standing in the middle of the chaos with his hands on his hips, looking a bit forlorn now that the task is in front of him. He gives a rueful little laugh as he surveys the mess.

"You know, Mrs. Weber, I sit in here every day and generally do not worry about the way it looks, but I suppose it doesn't do for patients to see this disarray, and it would make it difficult to have an assistant help out if nothin' can be found."

"Exactly," I say, and start to sort out the books in front of me by author's last name. He pulls down the rest of the books and makes a pile next to me on the floor.

"Might you want to get the rest from upstairs in your bedroom?" I ask casually, and he stops moving suddenly.

"You've been up there, aye?"

Again I try not to blush, but this time it is from embarrassment. "To dust, really. Clean the floors and scrub up the washroom."

"Oh, aye," he sighs. "I noticed it was all cleaned up and forgot to thank you. Of course, yes. I'll go get them."

I hear his steps above me. A short time later, he clambers loudly, thumping each foot heavily on the stairs with the pile of books in his hands, which he sets down before crouching on the floor next to me.

We work in companionable silence again for a few minutes before my curiosity gets the better of me, and I cautiously ask.

"I couldn't help but notice the portraits in your room when I dust. Are they of your family?"

He continues to be quiet, and I immediately regret my familiarity. Perhaps the easy and abrupt way people ask questions out here is starting to affect my own judgment of conversation and character. In trying to adjust and fit in, I am unwittingly becoming a nosy housekeeper.

But then he suddenly starts talking, slowly, as if whittling the tale of his youth from the depths of memory.

"It was the famine. My family, like so many others in Ireland, were allowed to keep only the potatoes to eat. When the blight came, and everyone began to starve, my parents and my brother and sisters and I were affected, too. I have no direct memory of this. I was the youngest. My auntie, a widow already at the time of the famine and with just enough money for passage to America for herself and one other, came to my parents and asked for one of her nieces or nephews to take along."

"And your parents chose you?"

He nods, then picks up the thread of his story with a quiet voice. "They did choose me, as the baby and newly weaned, they thought I might have the best chance of success and survival, and because my mam thought that I would be the first to die if the famine might become even worse. It was a decision that saved my life."

I want to ask more questions immediately, but wait, pulling more books and putting them on piles. Finally, he sighs deeply, and finishes with obvious resignation, "We often wrote to the village back in Ireland, tryin' to find out what happened to the family. As I grew older, I learned to make different kinds of inquiries. A few years ago, we finally discovered they'd gotten lost in the workhouses and the mass graves likely, in the end."

Now perhaps I understand his determination to be a doctor in the far reaches of America where there is little help, his desire to save people, and his worry about people like Alice Brinkley having enough to eat. He wishes to give back, perhaps, what had been given to him. And now I knew that he really was alone, the death of his aunt depriving him of the last bit of family to his name.

There is silence save but the soft pound of books against books as we finish sorting and start to shuffle things onto the shelf. He has quite a few worn and patched medical books, several fictions, which surprise me as he doesn't seem a reader, and more scientific books than I can count on everything from plants to chemistry to animal studies. Maybe he will let me read some, if I should ever find myself to have time on my hands.

I make us a light lunch, and I realize I am not very hungry yet after the morning's retching. He does not seem to notice my lack of appetite as he eats as heartily as ever.

When he leaves to make his afternoon rounds, I take it upon myself to continue in his study. There are papers in each folder, and soon I realize he does have a method to his disarray. Sometimes it becomes a matter of simply writing a person or family name on a file and putting it into alphabetical order. Most of his scribbling is hard to understand so I could not read about cases if I were to become a busybody. Some names even I have to put aside to ask him later when he is back and we have a moment again in his study.

I take a break from paperwork, and then move to wash the clothes. Today, the spring air seems warm enough that things might dry quickly. I am trying to come up with a way to have a rhythm to my week; certain days for laundry, washing, and scrubbing and cooking, but I have no handle on the weather. I brace myself to enter the Doctor's personal space again. It is time for me to tackle his clothing.

As I bundle up his clothes, which smell of dust, old sweat, medicine and of him, I hear the screen door slam shut. I frown. The Doctor is not due back until supper; perhaps it is not him, but a patient looking for help.

The stairs are steep so I cannot see below me as I walk down, but I nearly run into the Doctor himself as he's standing in the narrow hallway with his hands on his hips. I hope I have not displeased him with continuing in his office. Perhaps there are personal papers there he wishes to keep private. I cannot think why else he is nearly glowering at me.

"Mrs. Weber. Give me those," he growls. The surliness is unlike him. I have not seen him much cross. I think he is ashamed of his dirty clothes, or perhaps does not want a woman washing them, especially since I am not his kin as his aunt was. Still, I am to take care of this house and all within, so I make a move to take the laundry back.

"It's alright, Doctor. I don't mind doing them. It's part of my duties, to keep house, I mean, I thought ..."

He shakes his head and proceeds through the house and he dumps the clothes unceremoniously into the washbin, where I have the hot sudsy water waiting. Staring at the bin, he asks irritably,

"Did ye pull this wash yourself? Filled it too?"

I shrug and give a frown. "Yes. How else--."

"You're to ask me!" He swings around and puts his hands back on his hips, then changes his mind and crosses his arms. Agitated yet, he shakes them out and prowls around me back toward the house.

Suddenly, I realize what has happened. The Doctor has spoken to Widow Hawks. I feel the heat of embarrassment rush my cheeks, and I know I look as flushed as I feel. I've seen myself often enough in the mirrors back east.

I follow him back inside slowly, thankful he at least has the tact not to yell at me out in the yard, where I am certain the neighbors, who I have only met briefly here and there, would hear him. I do not want my pregnancy so public yet. Suppose it is not real. I have not yet felt the quickening, and my entire marriage was without children. For this employer to know, when my husband had not, feels as if I am exposing my private marriage bed to a stranger. I do not want the Doctor to think I am unable to manage so that he will send me back home to be a widowed mother alone, in the quietness of my parents' house. I do not want my identity here to be that of a single mother. And in the back vestiges of my mind, I worry about the ageless tarnish a widow carries. Will anyone truly believe the child is Henry's? No one knows me here. They may think I was not really so married and settled as I say. They may consider that I am escaping a life of shame back east; that the baby is a bastard. There are so many reasons to keep this pregnancy quiet.

He's in his study, but is standing with his back to me, surveying my work. Already there is some order, and it's easier to move about the small space. I can see by the bend of his head that he is still angry, still thinking of what to say to me. I suddenly fear my dismissal. I cannot see how being a mother to a fatherless child, forever at the charity of someone else back east is any purpose, and I know I need this hard working life to keep me interested in living. Please heaven he thinks to keep me on.

"How far along?"

His voice has softened a bit, and I try to relax.

"I...I am not quite sure. I think perhaps six or seven weeks? It is early."

"Does your family know?"

"No. I...Henry didn't even know. I myself didn't realize it until we'd already settled on the date of my arrival here."

"You didn't think to tell me?"

Finally, he turns to look at me. I cannot read his face. It is blank of any emotion I understand. Is he still angry? Frustrated? I am trying to mask my own shaking hands, and my intense fear of his dismissal, my worry that he will disbelieve my honor. He is suddenly completely in charge of my future. Will he condemn me? Send me home?

"It did not seem fitting to bring it up at our first discussion, and life has..." I spread my hands expressively. "It has been busy. It still does not seem possible I could finally...that Henry had..." I cannot bear to finish. To discuss sex, and my husband's difficulty conceiving, if not my own as well, is too much to say. It does not matter that he is a Doctor, and is accustomed to these discussions. He is not my doctor, does not give me exams, and is not my confidant.

"Mrs. Weber." He steps closer and lightly puts a hand on my shoulder. "I am not a bad man, I like to think. I am tolerant. I have always vowed to be so. I am not angry about this coming baby, only that you were too afraid to speak up."

"Please... you will let me keep working?"

"Within reason."

I start to protest, but he shakes his head and puts his second hand on my other shoulder. The weight of his arms are heavy, yoke-like. He is staring at me, serious and determined to have me meet his eyes. "You will let me do the heavy liftin', Mrs. Weber. Ye must. You forget I like to help around the house when I can. And you must just tell me what you need before I leave. I don't mind."

He gives my shoulder bones a quick squeeze before releasing me and then turning back to his office, shaking his head. I am surprised at how light his voice is as he comments, "It is shapin' up quite nicely. Now, back to my rounds. Supper in a few hours, Mrs. Weber?"

"I'll be sure to have enough for the Brinkleys, as well." I respond weakly as he brushes past, as if nothing out of the ordinary has happened, grabs his hat, and swings back onto his horse. From the screen door, I watch him spin the mount around and canter off, his body swaying easily with the jaunt of his horse's haunches.

Once he is out of sight, I sink to the floor and breathe a long sigh of relief. Thank heaven he did not see it fit to send me back on the next train out. A small tremor passes through me as thought, What would I tell my folks? They did not know I was pregnant. Would they think I had somehow turned loose out here? That the child was not Henry's? I shudder to think of such a response from my loved ones and am again utterly thankful of the Doctor's tolerance.

79

# CHAPTER 6

Widow Hawks has sewn my dresses for me. She insists that she can do it deftly, faster. That she cannot bear another night sitting next to me and watching me labor over each stitch. And, of course, she is right. Within three weeks, both house dresses are finished, with neat patterning and easy seams. I have a purple bonnet to match the lavender dress and my brown calico is set with the split skirt so that I might start to ride easily, like the way I see Kate do when she visits one of the neighboring towns over. While I am afraid to do this on horseback with the babe in my womb, I know it is something I must eventually master.

I am beside myself with happiness at the companionship of Widow Hawks. She hums, now, in the morning and night, native songs that resonate throughout the room. I am glad I will have a child who will listen to such lovely, haunting melodies. I tell her this often and it is during those exchanges that she smiles fully and I am always struck by her serene beauty. Her teeth are white against the dark nutmeg of her skin, and the creases of her eyes remind me of the Doctor's when he grins, and of Kate's when she smiles, though that is rarer still. I do not know how she makes a way, how she comes by groceries or dry goods. Like everyone here, she has a garden out back. Sprawling squash vines are reaching out beyond the borders of the garden, while beans curl around poles and potato plants nod slowly. But I do not see how she survives on her own. It is, like many things yet, a mystery.

We do not share meals, nor much other than silence or quiet chatter in the night. I have not accused her of approaching the Doctor about my pregnancy. She has been a constant nursemaid for when I am ill in the mornings. She is my advocate with the Doctor if I am too shy to ask for anything, though that is slowly changing as I find him eager to help however he may and is doctorly about my occasional bouts of nausea. I wonder at this, but then I remember he has no living relations. Perhaps he would eagerly await any babe that would be part of his life, if only to have someone to care for in the way of family. Already I can see how one cleaves to others when alone out here. It is easily done.

Today, I wear the new yellow calico to work. There is no need for me to dress for riding, so I think the serviceable brown will be good for days when much work, especially outside, will be done. The purple will be for especial occasions.

Widow Hawks fits it to me, making a final tug or two.

"How did you learn to sew so prettily?" I wonder. She has made an attractive bodice, and full skirt, with plenty to let out when I grow with child. Her own clothing is usually a mismatched combination of native traditional hides and English skirts, so I do not see how creating a ladies dress is possible for her.

"I learned how for my daughter's sake," she says quietly. It is an answer I do not expect. "And for my husband, for he wished me to wear your English dresses."

"Well, I thank you. I finally feel a woman," I say, and I take her hand and squeeze it. So she has a daughter. I feel relief. I might be able to ask childrearing questions of her. She hangs on to my fingers a moment longer, but says no more and I respect her too much to pry.

I walk to the Doctor's house and past the two usual townsfolk who watch me pass. One is an elderly grandfather who is always out to watch the sunrise on the porch of his daughter's family home. His son-in-law is the town postman. I wave; the friendliness is almost expected of everyone to one another.

The other is a cowboy who is always up brushing his horse, as if the stallion is the most important thing in the world. And I suppose, it is the most important thing, or being, he owns in the world, so I cannot blame him his obsessiveness. Today he stops brushing to give me a second look. Widow Hawks does not own a mirror so I can only hope and guess that the dress looks alright and is not coming apart somewhere or ill fitting.

"Good day, Missus Weber," he says and tips his hat. I nod silently in return, and turn onto the street to Doctor Kinney's house.

As I make the coffee, I think again on Widow Hawks' words. I wonder where her daughter is, or if she too has died as the husband has done. For all my ability to start asking personal questions, I still do not go about asking the important ones, it seems.

"Mornin'." The Doctor is talking as he rounds the corner, but stops up so quickly I turn to make sure he did not trip. Instead, I see him taking me in, a shrewd look in his eye and a little half smile on his face.

"Yes?" I do not understand his look, as other than a yellow dress instead of black, there is nothing much new to smile about. It is simply a change of dress, and I do not like to think of myself quite so vain to care much, though if I'm truthful, it feels utterly lovely to be in a new dress regardless. And I do not think the Doctor is partial to ladies fashions. He is at once back in action.

"It's...the coffee smells delicious."

I lift an eyebrow at his blasé comment, but say nothing. We eat the toast and cheese in relative silence. Today, I am helping in his study again to go over the updates to his files. I look forward to a morning inside and to be seated, as I am quite tired. It is much better than scrubbing the floors, which is my duty tomorrow.

"Mrs. Weber," he says slowly as we finish. I do not look up, until his hand reaches across the slab table and taps the back of my own so I meet his face. "The new dress is very fine on ye."

"Oh!" I exclaim, and try not to laugh. He does indeed have an eye to color, then. It is not what I expected of his character. "I...thank you."

He nods, as if the compliment is sufficient and normal enough to say, and finishes his coffee. We do the dishes together, as we have started to do when he is not called away by patients.

"Widow Hawks mentioned she had a daughter," I stated. I feel more comfortable getting information from him than Widow Hawks, also less intimidated. I glance at him and am surprised again to see his face look tender, soft, and a bit wistful.

"Yes, she does."

"Does? That is to say, is she around here? I hope I have not deprived her of a bed and place at her mother's home."

84

"Oh, no, that you have most certainly not done. Widow Hawks' daughter is quite independent." There is affection in his voice.

Since he does not immediately offer up more, I drop the subject, deciding this is a secret he has promised to keep.

I spend an amicable morning doing paperwork with the Doctor, and then polishing instruments in the afternoon while he does rounds. He mentions over supper that I ought to have my sidesaddle clothing on hand, so that I might dress for patient visits some days.

"I could use a nurse," he muses. "Not for the very difficult cases, but when it would help to have a second pair of hands. You'd be up for it, perhaps?"

"Did your aunt help you too?" I cannot help but ask, curious about the footsteps I am filling.

"Yes, she did, sometimes," he admits. "Though she did not understand much of what was happening by the end. It did help to have a woman's face 'round, even if just for the families."

"Alright then," I agree, though I am uncertain what I have just agreed to do. I have no true nursing training, only how to make an ill patient a bit more comfortable, as I did for Henry.

The reminder of our time together makes me absently spin the wedding band around my finger.

"Now then, we've finished up mite early for the evening. What do you say, Mrs. Weber, to a bit of reading on the porch?" It is a tradition we do now that the light lasts longer and when we can manage it.

"Alright," I say. I set about finishing up the kitchen so it is in order and put away my apron.

We read a bit of *The Conduct of Life*, and I like to hear the Doctor take a turn with Emerson's words, as his Irish lilt is soothing. I try not to drift to sleep. Even a day without hard physical labor leaves me exhausted at times.

"What I cannot understand, Mrs. Weber, is why you waited so long to be married." At first, I do not realize he has stopped reading. "You're quite lovely, you know. And if you don't know, ye should hear the cowboys talk. Did ye pine for your husband before he married you? Wait for him to have enough to pay a dowry for your hand?"

Suddenly, I am now not drowsy at all. The Doctor is asking very detailed questions that perhaps were provoked by our reading material. I am shocked my employer's wishes to know these things about my past. What could come of it?

"Why...I mean... that is to say..." I trail off, then gather my courage to be frank. "I was, soon after I was introduced to society, often asked by young men to dance or to be paid visits. My sister was a celebrated beauty and married young. But I did not really find the men we met to be interesting. They did not have much drive in their life. I knew my duty, to find a proper gentleman and be settled."

"And Mr. Weber was proper?"

I nod briefly. "Yes. And by the time I met him, I'd rather scared off the young handsome bachelors who were interested at all in marrying me. I was known for being a bit...bookish and earnest. Qualities that are not very attractive. Or desirable in a wife. Henry liked that I

86

would listen to his thoughts and sometimes add my own. We had a very... intellectual... match. I was older then and wished to settle down and have a purpose. There was nothing for me, really, other than being a spinster. He wished for a wife to aid him in society for his work and to keep him company. It was a... decent arrangement."

"It sounds proper." The Doctor is watching my face as I talk, leaning forward with the book closed between his fingers. It is a bit refreshing to unwind my marriage, to see it dispassionately and without emotion in the retelling. I did have a good marriage, though it was not exciting, nor romantic. Henry had been true, had not stepped out or held any horrible faults. I cannot blame him, even in death, for a desire that had been missing from the start.

"Speaking of proper..." Our heads snap up at the intrusion. The sun is starting to set and a horse and rider detach from the long dark grey shadows along the homes. "Begging pardon, Doc and Missus."

"What is it, Bern?" The Doctor is on his feet, expecting an emergency, though I do not detect that in the languid manner of the man before us. He slides down, grabbing the reins of his mount and walks up to the porch. He is a bit dashing, with dark hair and eyes that squint at the corners.

"It's getting a bit late, and I was going to offer Mrs. Weber a walk to her quarters."

From the astounded silence in the yard, I cannot tell who is more stunned by his preposition, the Doctor or myself. Is this how it is done? Without proper introductions to this man who goes by Bern?

"Well, I..." I start, then glance at the Doctor. He has a strange half-bemused smile on his face and gives a small nod at me. I am to take my leave with this man I do not know?

"Go ahead, Mrs. Weber. I'll see you in the mornin'. Thanks, Bern."

I press my lips together. This is most unexpected. I know this cowboy only by sight. He is the man who brushes his steed in the mornings as I walk by. Yes, he is polite to me, saying hello, smiling, tipping his hat, but that is all I know of him. He has not shown much interest in me before, but I can only guess that this walk home is a prelude of romance in some time, and I am nervous about this notion. It still seems so early in my arrival. I have been in Flats Junction for mere weeks. What would he think if he knew I was with child?

"Mrs. Weber," he tips his hat to me. We begin the walk down the main street toward Widow Hawks' house. "Bernard Masson, at your service. Folks around here call me Bern. I like that better than Bernie, myself."

I nod, smile, and decide to offer him my own front name, as is commonplace here. "You seem to already know I am Mrs. Weber. Please call me Jane."

We are nearly to Widow Hawks' house, and I am halfway relieved, but also wondering where this conversation is going. Why has this Bern decided to escort me home today?

We continue the last feet of the walk in silence, and he tips his hat to me once again as I reach the door, mounts his horse, and rides off without a word.

"Well, I'll be!" I say under my breath. This interlude has given me new voice today, a new strength. I decide I will ask Widow Hawks about her daughter tonight.

I stop short as I turn back to the house. I see a bundle of animal carcasses next to the doorway, half rotted and black with flies. Thankfully it does not make me vomit, but I am shocked that Widow Hawks has left this out. It is unlike her.

Going in, I see she is methodically making the fire. The smoke of the fire is pungent, filled with sage and other almost acrid fumes. I go to my bed and see my dresses all fitted out and ready. It is a wealthy feeling, but I cannot find full happiness because I am so discomfited by the disgusting objects sitting outside the house. How could she have time to sew but not manage the animals?

The fire is started and Widow Hawks leaves the house. I am too riled to go to bed yet. Usually she leaves to get water or relieve herself, so I grow a bit worried when she does not arrive back inside after a few minutes. I expect her comforting presence in the home in the evenings; we have a mostly silent ritual of drinking tea. Sometimes she will answer my questions about particular townspeople.

I go to find her outside, and I see her digging a hole in the ground. It is not very deep or wide.

"May I help?" I approach her. She wipes a bead of sweat from her brow. Though the sun is nearly set and the light is fading fast, it is still quite warm.

"Get you inside. I'll be in soon." Her voice is hard and firm.

"Please let me help."

She sighs very softly, then juts her chin. "Throw me the bag there, then, but take care not to touch anything but the corners."

I go to the bag nearby, but recoil when I realize it is filled with the animal parts and carcasses from the doorway. Widow Hawks is still digging the hole, humming a chant that is almost like a dirge. Finally holding my breath, I find the courage to pick up the sack and bring it to her. There are strange native symbols written on the cloth.

"What is this?" I wonder. I feel quite out of my element.

She continues her song for another long moment, eyes half closed in the rhythm of the digging, and then hauls herself out of the hole. Picking up the bag reverently, she starts to chant lowly in her native tongue. I watch, fascinated, and a bit fearful, as she escorts the bag into the ground, and sprinkles early herbs over the bodies. Rocking on her heels, she tilts her head to the sky, where the dusky evening is showing the first stars.

Looking past her, I see the last few people in town moving inside their homes for the night. A few townspeople glance down the road to our spot in the yard, then scurry quickly inside. Is there a stigma, then, to Widow Hawks? She seems so assimilated that I did not think so, but then I have not been in public with her.

Finally, the chant is finished, and she begins to scoop the earth back into the shallow hole. I begin to think of it as a grave and say as much as I start to help her, using my hands as a shovel.

"Weasel. Otter. They are sacred animals and should be given high reverence." She says softly, sadly, as if mourning.

I stop moving dirt. "These animals are sacred to your people?"

She nods.

"Then why take their fur and leave their poor bodies to rot?" I try to keep any negative emotion from my voice. I truly do wish to understand her culture a bit, as it is fascinating, but in small doses.

Her head snaps up and for the first time I see what she might be like if angered; she is almost resigned with her emotions. "You must not think I did this! These poor things were left as you saw them on the doorstep. It was meant as an insult."

My heart sinks a bit. So there is indeed prejudice against her in the town. It should not surprise me, but it does, as she seems kind and has not caused trouble since I have been in Flats Junction these past six weeks. I am momentarily worried for my own association with Widow Hawks, but I brush it off. I have learned to trust Doctor Kinney and I know he will not purposefully put me in harms way. He has taken an oath not to hurt others and I believe that he takes it seriously.

We finish the burial in quiet and go back inside. I know tonight I will not ask Widow Hawks any personal questions, and decide to just go to bed, finally feeling the exhaustion.

# CHAPTER 7

I tell Kate about the animals when I am at the general store. It has been a week since the incident, but I find myself thinking about it often. There is a spookiness, an anger to the action, as well as cowardice. It is almost worse because the actions are not discussed around town. Do people know who perpetuates such crimes? Or is it an understanding, unspoken and slightly condoned, that leaves people silent. Perhaps they do not want to know who is so cruel to their neighbor, though it is obviously someone who has some sort of knowledge about native preferences.

Kate frowns darkly when I tell her this, and then she mutters, "It is not the first time, nor the last, that the cowboys will play a mean trick on her. There are some in this town who want Widow Hawks gone."

"But why? She does not cause trouble."

Kate gives a snort. "She doesn't have to. She has done enough to warrant trouble. Were she to live her life in vindication, I still don't think everyone would forgive her."

I pause, wondering if I should ask the question and decide I want to. I want to be a bit nosy and I am in too much awe of Widow Hawks yet to ask her directly. Perhaps my roommate would prefer I talk to her openly, but I feel that Kate is easier to speak to, and I wish to share confidences with her anyway. This seems a good place to start.

"Kate, will you tell me? About Widow Hawks?"

She presses her lips together and looks at the bag of buttons we are sorting. I wonder what it matters that she relays this story. She is always full of town news;. Short of malicious gossip, I find Kate to be a good source of information about anyone the Doctor is treating, or anyone who has an ailment unspoken.

"Come back with me."

I follow, dreading her coffee concoction. She pours the sludge into two mugs for us and I stir mine while she guzzles down the first half. She sits next to me, one eye on the door through the half opened curtain.

"Widow Hawks was the mistress of the town's late banker, Percival Davies."

I am struck silent at this declaration. It is so not what I expect to hear that I absently take a gulp of the coffee and wish immediately I had not. I sputter, but Kate thinks it is because I am so shocked. She nods shortly, peevishly.

"I know. Exactly. There was a tribe of Blackfoot that camped nearby in the hills during some of the summer months and he saw her walking with them. Let's just say, he was...smitten."

"He didn't marry her?"

She gives an angry laugh, as if she is invested in this dead man's story. "He was already married. To a woman who lived back east and refused to join her husband in the rough and tumble of the territories. She was happy with the money he sent back, but preferred her parlor in New York."

I slowly digest this. "She chose him, then? I mean, it was a love match? He couldn't keep her by force, I should think..." I know nothing of the natives, nothing of their way of life, only that it was a few short years ago that a great war had torn the territories apart, and that the natives had seen the loss of it. They were perhaps subdued, but before that I could only expect they would have required some sort of retribution if one of their women had been taken without consent.

Kate tossed her head, and a few black tendrils escaped. "No, she wanted to be with him, too, I guess. They did love one another. So she left her people and stayed with him in town. He was the banker, powerful and arrogant in his own way. And regardless of the tongues wagging and the anger of most of the men, he kept with her. They had two children. Eventually his wife died and he was able to legally marry Widow Hawks. They were only wed for a few years before old age took him. That was ten years ago now."

The story sputters to this halt. I bite my lip and try to picture the older woman I know as sure-footed, strongly silent, steely and stately. She was once a lovestruck girl, brave enough to leave her native people and resist the scorn of the townsfolk to stay with the man she loved. What kind of love is that, that is so resilient and true that it spans nations and manners of living? I cannot imagine it. It is not surprising to me now that she has such fluent English, that many of her habits are familiar to me and not savage. She was gentrified by her lover-husband, and now straddles both worlds. Strangely, this rises my opinion of her.

"And the town? They grew used to her?"

"Oh some, like Doc Kinney. He was an outsider, too, when he and his aunt arrived. Driven from Boston by those who hated the Irish. He wanted to practice medicine, you know, regardless of his youth at the time. And old Davies took him under his wing, knowing the town needed a good doctor. The Doc respects Widow Hawks from that time staying with them, and for what Percival did. And because he understands what it is to be an outcast."

I am astounded at Kate's astute read of the situation, and marvel at her practical approach to it all. But of course it all makes sense, when she explains the past so pragmatically.

"Thank you for telling me this story," I murmur, as it is the only thing I can think to say. "It seems an important one, giving that I live with Widow Hawks and work for the Doctor." I think Kate is becoming a friend indeed, though I cannot truly tell how much information she has given me today that will help me shape a picture of both of these characters with whom I interact daily.

"Well then," she shrugs, and stands, finishing her coffee. I guiltily stare into my cup. I have not touched mine since the first gulp. "Let's finish up your shopping and get you back so your beau can walk you home." She gives a wink. Ever since the first night Bern Masson walked me back from the Doctor's, he has been by me ever since. Sometimes on his horse, and sometimes walking, he strolls from door to door with me. It is a small town and such a thing is noticed. Though I rarely have time for more than a quick exchange with the townsfolk, I know they all see him walk with me every evening. Kate is astute to this, as well, and has started to tease me about having a sweetheart. She does not seem to recognize that I am not blushing about this, for I am not certain how I feel about a suitor at my age and situation. But since Bern has dotted on me, Kate has as well, as if now that I am being courted, I am more fun to have round.

"That will be all, then, on the Doc's account?" she asks, writing in her ledger carefully. "The buttons, the pickled fish, and paper?"

I nod. She finishes wrapping the parcels and ties a string so they are easily carried. As we turn to the door, the Doctor, himself, walks in.

"Mrs. Weber! Kate, hello. How are you?" he asks jovially. He has had a lighter load of patients now with the warm weather of these past few days, and it puts him in good spirits to putter around the house.

"Just finishing up," I comment, and take my packages, but he scoops them up and away from me before fixing his blue gaze on Kate.

"Will ye be helpin' with the usual festivities for the Independence Day celebrations?" He looks at her directly and she gives him one of her full rare smiles.

"Of course. I have not had a chance yet to fully ask Mrs. Weber for help, but, with her assistance, I'm sure it will be the best to date."

He glances at me briefly. "I'm sure then, too. The men have been buzzin' about nothing else, though it's more than a week away. Let me or Mrs. Weber know what you need, then, will ye?"

"Yes, Pat. I will."

As we walk out, I try to keep my eyes low so Kate does not give me her sarcastic arched brow at my shock. Kate called Doctor Kinney by his front name and it is a surprise to me that after working for him a few months, until this moment, that no one I have met calls him so familiarly. She must do it to continue to shock me, I reason, especially based on the conversation we'd just had.

"Did ye have a nice visit?" He asks conversationally. I glance up at him and nod. "I'm glad you're gettin' on with Kate. She could use a good woman friend."

"She's been very kind to me, as most here are."

"And you're feelin' alright these days?"

I give him a smile as he stares down at me. "I am, thank you, Doctor. Most of the evils are passing now."

"Good. You'll let me know when you start to get too tired, though, won't ye?" His voice betrays his worry, as if my earlier omission leaves him uncertain of me and I regret my silence again. I should have known he would not reject me based on something such as a child. I am learning that he takes ideas of family quite seriously, whether it's blood or not. I am starting to think he sees me as a sisterly figure, and I do not mind that. It is comforting.

"I will. I promise," I swear earnestly, and he seems to believe me for now.

Dinner is cold sandwiches and a fresh salad of new lettuce. My garden is becoming a success by the end of June. We eat in the backyard, overlooking the land to the north without obstruction. The shadows are long, but the light lasts even longer now, and it is a bit cooler outside than in. I lift my face to the light; it is a soft pale gold, reflecting off the dusty prairie grasses. There is the low scissoring of insects and the I look out at the green in the distance. One can smell the earth here, and hear the brushing of leaves. I think about Widow Hawks, coming out from those trees and meeting Percival Davies. What was their first meeting like? Had they fallen in love instantly?

"Mrs. Weber," the Doctor breaks into my reverie. "Have ye..." He stops short, gives a small sound, then reframes his voice oddly. "Do you... did you know that the color of your eyes is very unusual?"

I give him a little frown. What an odd thing to say. I recall my eyes as being generally brown, same as my hair, though a lighter shade. I say as much to him, but he gives a shake of his red head, still looking at my face in the sun. "They're brown, aye, but then they give way to green and blue and grey. I could not name a color to them."

"Well, and your eyes are blue," I say stoutly. "In case you were wondering."

He starts to laugh at this, loud enough that I wonder if the neighbors will come to see what was the jest, but he quiets down and resumes eating. I look at him, thinking about how he must have known Widow Hawks and Mr. Davies before and after their marriage, and how he says he will do anything for her. I admire his loyalty and his acceptance of them. I wonder if his aunt was the same. I suppose I will never know unless I ask. He must owe the widow and the former banker a great deal for the stake they gave him in Flats Junction.

"What were you going to say, then?" I ask, redirecting his thoughts. He glances up and seems to think, then shakes his head.

"I forget. Not important. In any way, will ye be helpin' with the Independence Day plans?"

"Kate has not mentioned anything to me yet. She organizes it all, then?"

"Aye. Some years there are fireworks if a peddler comes through in time. But mostly it's the cowboys racin' and displayin' their husbandry skills with the cows, all the womenfolk make a good spread of vittles, and there is generally a bit of a fair with the games and all. We are not part of the union yet, out here, but we like to act as if our joinin' were 'round the corner."

I think of the more grand and stately affairs of the eastern cities, with people attending the big fairs and holidays in their Sunday finery, cannons blasting, bands playing and the sweet cold tang of lemonade and candy. And at the end of the hot day, a walk along the seashore. This will be very different, but I look forward to showing the town my cooking skills, which have been progressing well as I become more attuned to the kitchen.

"Is there a dish you'd like me to make, then?"

"Can you do a pie?" He asks.

I laugh. "With what fruit?"

"Ach, there's a point. Well, then, do the cold chicken ye made the other week. That was delicious. Pick up a chicken at the Brinkley's next time you're out for milk and eggs. And whatever else Kate needs for the celebration."

"Alright, then." I give him a little smile and begin to clear our plates and wipe the table.

As I finish, there is a knock on the door. The Doctor turns from his drying to the front of the house. "Right out!" he shouts through the hallway. Turning to me, he has a smile on his face, half teasing. "Your beau is here, m'lady."

I swat at him with my apron, which he catches and tugs, pulling me along. My face is close to his and the smirk leaves his mouth. Suddenly, he is serious, intense, and asks lowly, "You are sure ye wish to walk with him?"

"What else should I do?" I ask quietly I release the apron so it hangs limply from his hand, and walk out of the kitchen. This exchange unnerves me, but I brush it aside and give Bern a small smile as he waits for me off the porch. He does not have his horse today.

"Everything okay?" he questions easily. I look at him, surprised he is sensitive enough to notice the slight change in my manner, and realize I cannot speak my mind, that I do not know him enough to be honest. Perhaps there is something about him the Doctor knows and wishes to warn me. Perhaps it is best to find out more about this so-called beau, and not hear the news second hand, the way I have learned about others today.

"Yes. Everything is fine. Thank you." I say. I find myself to be chattier than usual. On the way home, he tells me about his family, his parents in Minnesota yet, and his brothers who both work a few villages back down the rail line. He speaks of them fondly, and of his riding and love of husbandry. I know nothing about the quality, value or work of livestock, so I am interested. He is open, talkative, more so than ever, that we stand outside Widow Hawks' door for a spell before his stories end. Then he tips his stetson and leaves.

Widow Hawks is waiting for me when I walk in. She is standing, watching the door open. She looks a bit anxious.

"Is he going to court you in earnest?"

"I don't know. Does it matter?"

She gives a small shrug and motions aimlessly with her hand. "Not now, no."

I see my opening and pounce. I go to sit next to her as she kneels down and picks up her stitching. She is making a bunting for the baby. We figure I will be due in the winter.

"Well, it's not always so passionate, is it?" I reason. "It wasn't so with Henry, why should it be any different now with Bern, if he is interested in me? You were married. Were you happy?" I mean more than happiness, but I do not know how to put the words so that she does not know I am partial to her history.

Her hands still, and she bends her head. I see the silver hairs that sprinkle in her dark braids. Finally she looks up at me. The long lines that frame her mouth are obvious in the light, but her black eyes are soft with faded remembering. "I was very happy. Happier than I could have imagined. It was not always easy, and there were difficult weeks and months, but we had one another always. Not doubting his love was beautiful in itself."

So there was passion between her and Percival Davies. I wish I had met him. I wish I had seen them together, so I could read what a good marriage, a good partnership, looked like. I could have perhaps modeled my own fate along those lines, and would know if a future with Bern had much to recommend it, or if I am trapping myself again, slowly, into another loveless union.

"He sounds very kind," I say instead, and she smiles into the distance.

"He was incredibly so. Kindness with a backbone of strength. I rarely see such a combination. Patrick has it, though not nearly so tough as my husband. Perhaps, though, that is why we took Pat in when he and his aunt came to town. Until they built up the house. Because we saw a bit of ourselves in him."

It takes me a minute to remember the Doctor's front name. We are quiet together. I hear the crackle of the fire eating the new logs, and inhale the sage leftover in the air. My comfort with Widow Hawks comes so much from our companionable silences. So many times I was quiet in my life and my marriage, and while I accepted it, it always felt forced. The silence here is comfortable. Even tonight, when I am wondering about the damaged animals and my mind is whirling with the implications, I don't feel the need to speak. Widow Hawks will talk to me when or if she thinks it necessary, and I try very hard not to worry about my own safety.

She gives the softest of sighs, and moves to begin her evening rituals. I move to my bed, stripping down. I put my hands on my belly; nothing is quite showing yet, though perhaps my waist is slightly thicker.

I do not turn when I ask, "Why do you suppose that cowboy, Bern, walks me home?"

"Because you are a beautiful, available widow woman. And you're not afraid of hard work." Her answer is bald and spartan and unexpected. I do not think of myself as beautiful.

"When shall I tell him about the baby?"

103

"When you are showing, I should think," comes her response.

I do not like to think of that conversation; it bodes uncomfortable and I worry about what the handsome cowboy will think of me. It almost bothers me to think that he will stop courting me, and I am surprised to realize that I enjoy his attentions. It has been many years since I've held a man in thrall of me. It is heady, and it is a bit intoxicating to think I could make him do many a thing to win my full favor.

Though I don't know him well enough yet to feel fully in control of the situation. If-when-he discovers I am pregnant, will he leave me alone? Will he believe me when I say it is the child of my dead husband? A widow is often thought of as a bit of a temptress, a woman who knows the pleasures of the bedroom and is not willing to forgo them and will do anything to entice a man to the sheets. I am not such a woman, but no one here knows me truly enough to not formulate some opinion along those lines. Could I work here with such unwarranted stigma on my head? Would the Doctor want such a woman working for him, who is so shunned by his society?

I'm petrified of my pregnancy and all of its shortcomings. I am a single, widowed mother. I know no one well, and I am a bit too stubborn to run home to my family for shelter. I do so want to make a go of a life of my own. I don't want to lose this, and lose the chance of a fuller, purposeful life. This child will make me risk it all, from the loss of a handsome man's attentions to, perhaps, my employment. I wish I could have come here without such a heavy burden in my belly.

# CHAPTER 8

Independence Day celebrations come up quickly. I am excited as it means a break from the usual workload, and I am especially intrigued about what the Doctor will say about my cooking. His challenge for a pie had me cull the earliest of the tomatoes, all green and unripe, and soften them, cook them, and spice them. I taste it as I go along and I think I might pass the pies off for apple, which are nearly impossible to come by out here.

Bern has asked me to watch him at the races. The cowboys have several specialties they like to show off for the townsfolk's entertainment, and I have said I will try to do so amid the food preparations. Kate has me in charge of the ladies' contributions, while she is busy decorating the general store, post office, bank and other public buildings with new bunting she's found, and organizing the town games. Since telling me in detail about his protective and loving parents, and his competitive, but earnest brothers, Bern speaks more freely each evening, though he rarely asks about me. I do not mind, as I do not have any colorful stories to share, and his lack of probing reminds me of the gentlemen back home, who did not pry with personal questions so quickly.

I finish the pies in the morning and put them off to cool while I go about my scrubbing. The kitchen and surgery wipe up easily, but the hallway, stairs, and especially the washroom, take a good long time, as the wood seems to soak up soap and dirt more readily. It is almost as if it can absorb anything and exist the same. One could call the wood stoic, solid, and give it human characteristics that one would wish for oneself. I mull often along these lines as I scrub.

As I take the dirty bucket of water down the stairs, the Doctor comes in from his afternoon rounds and catches me at it. He frowns a little, and brushes travel dust absently from his shiny vest. Then he sighs and hikes up the stairs, his mouth twisted in a weary grimace.

"Mrs. Weber, really!" He admonishes, meeting me halfway up. "Stop liftin' things!"

"How am I to get any work done, then?" I ask him, a bit irritably as I relinquish the bucket. He pauses on the step, wavering, before finally reaching out across the small space between us and touching my waist, his thumb wrapping around to my belly.

"Use smaller buckets. Anythin' like that," he says, a bit deflated. "Confound it, Mrs. Weber. I don't want ye or the wee babe hurt." With a soft squeeze he releases me.

I am heartened at his worry, but what woman does not like a little pamper now and then? I meekly follow him down the stairs.

We eat a good soup for supper. I have enough early vegetables in the garden to make a heartier broth than usual. The food heats quickly in the copper pot, and I am glad of it, as I'm quite hungry.

The Doctor spies the pies that are cooling and exclaims in delight. "Where did ye find fruit?"

106

I laugh. "It's green tomatoes. Please, heaven they are good. I've made three."

He peers at them, then gives me a halfway hopeful, and devilish, grin. "I could try one to make sure for you."

"Doctor Kinney!" I smile. I cannot help it. "Wait for tomorrow."

"Barely," he chuckles. In a bout of lightness, he grabs me and does a quick two step about the kitchen. I cannot decide what has made him so silly, the July heat or the coming celebrations. His arm comes all around my waist, his large hand grabbing mine tightly as he spins us around the table. I laugh again at him, at his sudden freeness. He gazes down at me, a gentle look on his face, and he stops us in front of the stove. At first he does not release me, but holds me, lightly, searching my eyes. I do not understand his intensity, but I am surprised to find I enjoyed our little jig, and the masculinity of his embrace.

"You'll dance with Bern, I suppose," he finally says, loosening his arms. "There was your practice, then."

"If he asks me," I shrug indifferently, and turn to the stove.

"I'm sure he will," he mutters, before setting out the plates. I stir the soup, noticing the tin along the edges is wearing thin along the copper. I will make a stop at the foundry soon enough. The soup has a meaty flavor thanks to the handful of beets and turnips. I think of my day. Soon after lunch, he will be off to afternoon rounds while I circle the neighborhood to check in on some of the women to make sure all is set for tomorrow's festivities. We eat in easy companionship, discussing his cases and my duties. He gives me tips on some of the women.

"Don't approach Sadie Faucett head on, you know. She knows what she is supposed to make this year. And when Kate gave the casseroles to Henrietta, she bent Sadie's nose, or so I was told when I was there checkin' on their youngest's broken arm. Go about that one gently and use lots of praise, or you'll have burnt puddings for the town."

I file away the information.

"And please wear a bonnet. And take water when you visit." He finishes up the meal with reminders. "No faintin' in the heat."

"Yes, Doctor," I say, and move to take the dirty dishes on the table to sit in the washbin with the knives. He gets his bag and hat today. So busy is he again that he does not have as much time to spend with me in the kitchen. I miss our banters when I wash and he dries the crockery, but I say nothing, as I know his work is far more important than my company.

He pauses in the doorway. "Mrs. Weber."

I glance back at him.

He gives me a little smile. "Save me a dance, will ye?"

"Of course." I am pleased he asks me. It is nice to know he wishes to spend some time with me socially.

I make my own rounds in the afternoon. It is hot out. I feel the sweat trickle down my back and under my collar. I need to ride out to some of the further reaches of the town so I wear my split skirt to ride proper. It is comfortable and cool, and I silently thank Widow Hawks once again. The leather of the saddle, though, is hot and I can feel the heat radiating through the thin fabric, itching against my inner thighs. Swallowing my worry about the baby's safety, I know we're both safer still sitting this way than sidesaddle. The Doctor has left his horse for me, and thankfully the beast is gentle and middle aged, so I can ride him without much issue. I watch the animal's muscles move below me. The dun colored bristles are soft one way and coarse the other. He picks his way along the road, avoiding the deep ruts and moves slowly as he seems to enjoy my lighter weight, slower pace and the long lead I give him. I didn't ride much out east, though it was important every woman or lady have some knowledge of how to manage a horse. Even with the animal's leisurely gait, we are at the first house sooner than I would have liked.

Sadie Faucett responds well to my flattery, as the Doctor had advised. She is a fast talking woman, the wife of the new banker, with a brood that tumbles in and out of the house. I know she has a tongue for gossip, so my stay is long at her table before I can make an excuse to leave. Alice Brinkley and her family will be bringing a roast pig, which is already on a spit when I stop in to see Alice and be sure she has no issues providing the meat for the gathering. Nancy Ofsberger, the postman's wife, will be cooking the potatoes. Between all the other women in town, there will be a good spread. I finish my day at Kate's general store, where she is finishing the decorations. Her porch will be where the awards are to be given for the winners of the races.

"All set?" She glances up.

"I think so. And Bern has promised to set up trestle boards for the tables before the racing."

"Your man is becoming quite a helper," she teases me and I have enough understanding to blush. It is apparent the cowboy dotes on me, though I do not find him necessarily passionate.

"Well... do you need anything else tonight?"

"No." She turns back to the bunting. The sun is setting slowly and the dark hair has fallen completely out of the heavy bun she wears. It is a glossy black and picks up the ruddy light so it shines with many colors at once. I think she is the most lovely woman I have ever seen. I am always a little in awe of her, and feel that I must always be working towards her approval.

She is busy though, and does not have time to chat with me long. I tell her I need to get back to make dinner.

"Jane!" She calls as I slowly walk back down the stairs to the Doctor's mount. "Thanks for your help." She graces me with a full smile. "It was very nice to have a friend to do this with, this year."

I smile back, and ride home to the Doctor's house, filled with a small sense of triumph. He's not back yet, but it's too hot to make a big meal, so I slice up cold vegetables and a bit of cheese and hearty bread, which I have found I have a knack for baking.

I think on Kate. I wonder how she came about, as a single woman, to run the general store in town. Without a man to help her with funds, or around the shop, I am continually impressed with her ambition and her hard work. She is a leader in this town, respected by the women most of the time from what I can tell, though she does hit them rather hard around the head with tactlessness sometimes. And the men all seem to give her a wide berth, as if she is too beautiful to court. Or perhaps she put them all off, like I did before I married Henry, and now no one will have her. I will have to ask her, or perhaps I should ask the Doctor. As I muse this, he walks in, whistling.

"You're in a good mood," I comment, and he gives me a grin before glancing over at the pies. "And don't even think about it. There had better be three whole pies here tomorrow when I come to fetch them."

"Ye have my word," he vows, and sets himself comfortably at the table, reaching for some bread. "Though I want to be first in line to try them."

"There will be other sweets, too, in case they are a flop," I amend.

"Sounds like it will be quite the day tomorrow," he says, eyes glinting. I have a feeling that the Doctor likes a good party.

"Will you be partaking in the activities and all?" I ask.

"Just the dancin' and the minglin', I'm afraid. I'm not one for ridin' my animals as fast as those cowboys. I am on hand for when anyone, horse or rider, gets hurt, though."

We start to eat, and then I carefully ask, keeping my tone neutral, as I hope what I am about to ask is not gossip, but common knowledge. "I have been wondering, and I keep forgetting to ask Kate... how is it she is running the general? It is unusual for a woman to go at it alone, isn't it?"

The Doctor shrugs and grabs carrots from the platter. "Maybe. Many a widow has made it work. Kate hasn't married, so she's had to learn a bit on her feet. But she was lucky. The old owner stayed around and helped her learn the books and orderin' before he died."

"So he took her on, like an apprentice perhaps? To teach?" I ask, uncertain on how the social structure worked here in unconventional situations.

He gives a little laugh. "Oh no! Kate bought the store out from under him. The old man wasn't up to par, really, in his dotage."

"She must have had a good inheritance."

"Some, yes. Her father was livin' at the time, and helped her buy it. She wanted to be independent. She always was, though. A regular spitfire." His voice goes tender as he talks about her, and he gets a small smile on his face that I do not often see. It dawns on me that the Doctor is soft on Kate. If that is so, I wonder if she knows.

"You've known her long?"

"Since I arrived in Flats Junction with my aunt, Bonnie. Yes."

I test my newly formed theory. "You should dance with her tomorrow."

His head comes up, the blue eyes guarded. "What makes ye say that? I doubt Kate has any wish to dance with anyone. She's never been one for a spin."

"Ask her," I prompt, feeling a bit of a matchmaker. "She might say yes." I think about how she calls him by his first name, and I smile a little. "I think she would, indeed."

He leans back, a faraway look on his face. I wonder if he's ever shown his affection toward her. He is Irish, and while I see his passion in his work, he is not overtly romantic. His silly moments are very touching, and I am glad I get to see them in his own house, but I know if I was in Kate's position, the Doctor would not approach me either. It would not be his nature to be so overt and is probably why he is still a bachelor.

"Ye think so, do ye?" He smiles a little sheepishly when he catches me observing him. He covers quickly by saying, "You'll be sure to dance once around with me, then, won't you Mrs. Weber?"

"I gave you my word," I say, lightheartedly. We begin to wash up the dishes together by discussing the happy news that fireworks will be shown tomorrow evening.

Bern walks me home. He is bursting with bravado and excitement for the Independence Day races. He is an able cowboy, though I have not heard him spoken about with reverence, so I do not think he will take the races by storm as he says he might, but I listen and nod. Perhaps I lead him on with my amiable evening strolls. Perhaps he will abandon me when he learns of my delicate condition. But for now, I will bask in a little manly attention. At least I will have a dancing partner.

Without Kate's bidding, I have asked Widow Hawks to make a cornbread for tomorrow, and I smell it in the fire when I walk in. The corn has a succulent scent that is sweet yet earthy. I know it will crumble perfectly in my mouth, and that it will be seasoned with one or two herbs. She is chanting lightly. I smile as I listen, and watch her finish the bread and unwrap it to cool.

"Tomorrow you ought to wear the lavender dress. You haven't worn it yet and we need to see if it still fits you."

I sigh and agree. She is very kind to think of my fashions, as if I was her own kin to fuss over. Everyone in town is making such a fuss about Independence Day and I feel like I must do something special, too, so I don't mind the trouble of trying on the dress tonight. With her help, I slip into the fresh cloth, and we find we need to take the waist seams out an inch.

"I'll need to say something to Bern soon," I muse. She doesn't say anything in response. Since she has had children, I will rely on her for leadership on the proper way to do things, and I wish she would give me more direct answers on how best to tell people I am pregnant. Will she know what words I should use so I do not create a stigma on myself? Would she give me direction on how to gracefully keep a beau I may want to keep around?

"Widow Hawks," I start as she undoes my outer dress again. "Why did you marry a white man?"

She gives a little laugh. "I wasn't long married to him before he died. Have you learned the truth?" I blush as she looks up and nods, answering her own question. "Ah, I see you have. But I think you ask why did I leave my people, to live where I was not well liked or often respected?" She pauses, then says decisively, "Because I am a strong woman, and I know what I want. I wanted Percy, and he me, and we never doubted one another. We had beautiful children, and when we could, we married. And we did not waste much time being without each other. Life is too short."

"Why haven't you gone to live on the reservation then? After he passed?" I think of the one in the west, the only one I hear mentioned in passing conversations.

"Because I want to be near my only family living."

"Your son... daughter?" I watch her spin the needle and start to pick at the seams of my dress. I want to learn the tricks, do as she does, as I will have enough sewing of my own soon with the baby.

"My son died in childhood, but my daughter lives. You know her. My Katherine, though she goes by Kate."

# CHAPTER 9

I cannot believe how early the town rises on July 4th. Everyone is setting out, bringing out their portions of food or filling barrels with rainwater and sweetening them with sugar. The streets echo with shouts and laughter and horses whinnying. Already, it feels like it will be a hot day, but no one seems to mind. Bern sets up the trestle tables before heading to the stables, and I go to the Doctor's house to pick up my food stuffs, still mulling over my discovery from last night.

So, Kate is the daughter of Widow Hawks and Percival Davies. And Doctor Kinney knows her from his time spent in their home when he first arrived. His affection for her then goes back years, perhaps. I wonder why he has not courted her before now. Does he still see her as a young girl, one he treated as a sister in her parents' home? Or is he too shy to ask to court her, without a parlor to sit in or a father to recommend it?

My reverie is broken by the Doctor, himself, who meets me at the door in clean shirtsleeves and pants, still attaching his suspenders.

"Mrs. Weber!" He waits for me as I walk in, shutting the screen door without letting it slam. He looks me up and down and gives me a smart grin. "I don't much know ladies' fashions, but you do look very nice today."

I give him a smile in return. "Thank you, Doctor."

He follows me into the kitchen and watches me make the coffee. I wonder at his loitering, his hovering about me, when I turn around and see that he has grown serious.

"You will please to remember ye must drink water all day. It will be hot and the womenfolk can faint on us enough as it is. I don't want one of them to be you."

"You're too kind to worry," I brush off. He shakes his head and crosses his arms. I know the stance, it is a bit argumentative.

"I mean it, Mrs. Weber."

I nod in return and pour his coffee, which he takes into his study. I do hope he dances with Kate today. I'd like to see them together and to finally make a match of it.

When I arrive at the food tables nearer to midday, the women are just starting to trickle by with their delicacies. Alice Brinkley finds me, her little Pete strapped to her back for the walk into town. He is only a few months old, but already the birth seems eons ago.

"I've the men bringing the pig on the wagon before the games begin. Mitch's mother is bringing a tart and some cheese."

"Thank you, Alice," I smile wholeheartedly at her, and it strikes me that perhaps I might be able to ask her womanly questions as my time grows near, and she would answer them. The thought brings me comfort. In truth, she is more a friend to me than Kate is still, though I see Alice less than I would prefer.

"And here are the puddings!" Sadie Faucett announces, with a trio of children behind her. Each little one is balancing a bowl carefully in their plump arms.

"Bravo!" I turn to her, winking at Alice over Sadie's head.

The women are all in a good competitive spirit, and I hear the chatter of cooking secrets and childrearing advice patter through the small throng. It is a clear, refreshing sort of simplicity that I enjoy. Everyone is familiar with each other, and offers their thoughts and personal opinions freely. Most call me Jane, and I like that I know most of them, and their children's names, too. While I still miss the smell of salt air, I like the people out here more than the ones I knew in the careful society of Henry's circle.

"The races are starting!" Shouts come from the gathering crowd.

Alice is at my elbow again. She knows that Bern has been courting me lightly for several weeks now, and she leads me through the growing throng so I might be able to get a good view. At first I cannot spot him, but then I see his horse, Rusty, and then him. Bern is striking in his way. He's lean and a few inches taller than most of the other men. His dark brown hair is longish along the back of his neck and is swiped along his forehead under his hat. Like the others, he's dressed in clothes that are rumpled and dusty, with worn patches along the insides of the pant legs from always riding a horse. He seems very sure of himself, as do most of the cowboys lining up. I think perhaps I should be anxious for him, but I find I am just merely interested.

At the gun, the horses are off, and they must all complete a rather unique obstacle course before heading back to the finish. I watch in silence, while Alice cheers loudly next to me. I smile, but it is mostly just grass and dust and prairie we see as the horses and riders jump over logs and soft spots in the distance. It is a lovely view, though, of the land near Flats Junction. I find myself comparing the undulating prairie to the waves of the ocean back east. They could be considered similar I suppose.

"Oh hiyi!" Alice waves as several riders bolt past us and finish out the race. She turns to me smiling. "Your Bern took fourth. That is very good!"

"Is it?" I ask. "And he's not my Bern, you know."

Alice stops short and gives me a curious once over. "Do you wish he wasn't?"

I look away from her, at the horses and riders who have finished, Bern among them. He is taller than most of the cowboys, with swarthy skin to match his dark coloring. I suppose many women might call him dashing, same as I think. But I do not feel myself especially drawn to him, and he is more a convenience than a love.

"There you are!" Bern swaggers toward us, sweat and dust mingling on his face and clothes. He is grinning widely. "Did you see the finish?"

"We did." Alice puts forth quickly. "It was exciting!" She is so much more vivacious than me, and quick to smile back at anyone.

"Yes," I intone. "Very much so."

"Jane! Time to get ready for lunch." Kate beckons me through the crowds. Alice and I follow her to the long tables groaning with food and unwrap the last few cheeses from the Brinkley farm. Bern follows us to eye the spread and gives an appreciative whistle.

"If this is lunch, I cannot wait to see when it's time to sup."

"Mrs. Weber made pies." All of us turn around to see Doctor Kinney standing nearby, his shirtsleeves rolled up in the heat. "And I know Kate is always good with puttin' on a better celebration than the previous year. She out-does herself every time."

"Go off, you," she waves him away teasingly.

I watch the banter between them. I do not know if I can read anything between them that is particularly flirtatious, though they are certainly animated with one another.

I see Widow Hawks approach, the cornbread in her hands, wrapped in smooth brown paper.

"What is she doing here?" Kate mutters. I stare at her, surprised at her sudden rancor.

"Well, you put me in charge of the food, and I thought all the women were contributing," I stumble.

"Not her." Kate is seething mad, I realize. I know I am the cause of it, though I do not understand why.

"But she--."

"Tell her it's not wanted. I don't want her eating here!" She turns on her heel and marches away. I glance at the people who have overheard. Bern is looking bemused and unshakable, as if he has heard this before. Perhaps he even agrees with Kate. Alice looks at the ground, trying not to notice to row, and the Doctor is looking a bit awry, as if the exchange befuddles him. It certainly does me.

I look at Widow Hawks, who is trying to find a place for her food on the table. Her simplicity and how kind she has been to me from the start weighs more on me than Kate's fickle temper. I go to her and move aside some of the dishes, and say, "Good. Thank you for bringing this over. It smells wonderful."

She gives a nod, and says almost sheepishly, "Well, I've never had the chance to do much for the celebrations, you see. I'm happy to help."

There is more to this comment, I think. She is always trying to be well liked, to be included in this town, mostly by keeping to herself, though she does not help break the stigma by wearing many native adornments and clothing. Still, I know her cornbread to be delicious and I thank her profusely.

Doctor Kinney appears at my side, looking excited. "Your cornbread! I haven't had it in years!" He sneaks a piece out from the wrappings before I can swat his hand away. Widow Hawks laughs with delight.

Mitch Brinkley arrives, looking for Alice and his son and his eyes light up at the cornbread, too. "Authentic native food. Let me try it!" He also grabs a piece.

Before long, there is a line forming, and we women stand aside so the menfolk can fill their stomachs. I watch Bern go through the line. He has washed up a bit for the first round of games, and I try to tell myself that he is a good man and I should be lucky to be doted upon.

He fills his plate high as the rest, but I watch him deliberately skip the cornbread, just as Kate walks over, steps through the line of people, and deftly pulls the plate off the table, leaving an empty space on the boards.

"Oh, but!" I cannot help objecting. Alice quickly places her hand on my arm, tight and careful in warning, so I bite my tongue and stay quiet.

Kate carries the remainder of the cornbread into the general store. I can only imagine that she will toss it to the birds. I am utterly bewildered at her actions. It seems so unlike her. Out of the corner of my eye, I see Widow Hawks on the edge of the celebrations. She watches her daughter with a bowed head, resigned, as if this has happened before. Is she not the strong woman I thought she was?

# CHAPTER 10

The games are charming. Children race in three-legged heats for the prize of a nickel, and the adults laugh over charades. Little ones dodge between legs, and babies fall asleep in the drowsy heat of the July afternoon. There is no true rest for many of the ladies, as we all hustle in the background to make sure the evening meal is laid out in plenty, though I do find time to watch some of the charades. Henry Brinkley, Mitch's father, does a lively impression of a cowboy on a bucking bronco to the delight of the group, and another cowboy manages to mime carrying off a blushing bride. Bern takes his turn, as well, and makes everyone laugh with his charade of a child who has lost his ice cream in the dirt. I think, through my chuckles, that he is not so bad if he is willing to be silly like this.

"Drink." The brogue is at my back, and I half turn to see the Doctor holding a glass of sugared rainwater. I detect a bit of ale on him and give him a once over.

"Have you been at one of the saloons, Doctor?"

"Ah, no, but it is a celebration after all and some of the men have brought out their homemade beers and whiskeys. I don't mind a wee bit o' samplin'."

"Maybe you need that more than I," I tell him seriously, jerking my head at the water.

"Nonsense. You've a wee--."

"Hush!" I quickly shush him and he has the grace to look about with guilt. I realize I will have to keep an eye on him, that perhaps he does not figure how much the drink and heat both will affect him. He is Irish, after all, and Irishmen love their whiskey. I hope he does not overdo it.

I watch him carefully during supper, and catch his wink when he helps himself to an overlarge slice of my pie. He does not seem to be in any danger of being drunk, and I decide I may not need to worry about him after all. Bern, I notice, does not touch any liquor.

Kate has lanterns lit around the perimeter of the dancing space and I help clear the tables with the women to the sound of the musicians warming up their fiddles and such. It will be fun to do some dances. I think back to when the Doctor spun me around the kitchen, and I cannot decide if I look forward to a dance with him or Bern, or either of them at all. One is brotherly, the other eager for my attention, but I am not overtly partial to either in the case of romance.

I take off my apron and fold it onto one of the stairs that lead up to the general store.

"It went well, Jane. Thank you again," Kate says as she passes me to take the last of her crockery into the store.

"My pleasure. I hope to help again next year," I say, trying to keep any plead from my voice. Because I had angered her, I am not sure she will welcome my help next year, though I would so like to continue to be included in her plans. Once she had disposed of the cornbread, it seemed that Kate went back to being happy and amiable for the rest of the afternoon, and Widow Hawks has kept to the very peripheral of the festivities. Perhaps, by now, she has even gone home. And perhaps my friend is not so very angry at me. I did not know there was bad blood between her and her mother.

"Oh, most definitely," Kate agrees as she comes back out. "I'll be glad for all the help I can get." I am relieved to hear it.

"Kitty."

I swing around, surprised at the nickname, but not surprised to see the Doctor standing next to me, staring up at her.

"What?"

"Will ye dance with me?" He holds out his hand, and I look at his open face, the lines nearly gone in his anxiety, and then at her, where she stands above us at the stop of the steps. Now that I look at her, I realize that Kate does not look much like her mother, other than her coloring and height. She looks down at him and I can tell that she is much pleased with his request.

"Why, Pat," she says, almost coyly, as she takes his hand. "I thought you'd never ask me."

They walk, hand in hand, to join the other couples nearby who are forming the circles. I smile as I watch them, thinking I have done a good job of starting the matchmaking already.

It does not take Bern long to find me. He is bursting with joy. Cowboys do not often get a day off like this one. When he reaches me, he swings me around to the dance floor without abandon. When the bands starts to play the slower tunes , he holds me loosely and easily.

"I saw you at charades," I tell him. He laughs a little.

"I hope you don't think I'm too much of an idiot."

"On the contrary. I thought it was quite endearing," I say truthfully. He gives me a happy grin.

Looking away from Bern, I see Widow Hawks watching the dance floor. Her dark eyes catching the lamplight and her deep skin glowing. I hesitate, then finally decide that I must speak to him about Widow Hawks and my misstep earlier in the evening if I am to consider any kind of future with this man.

"I have embarrassed myself," I admit, and he looks down at me, inquiringly. "I thought I was doing right by Kate to have Widow Hawks make baked goods, too, like all the other women. I didn't know they didn't get on."

I look up and see a slight frown on his face. He doesn't answer right away, and at first I think he will be the type that clams up instead of discussing a displeasing subject. Finally he says,

"I know you must stay with her, for proper's sake, but most of us don't like that she stays, now that old Davies is gone. She belongs with her people and she'd do right to leave her daughter alone, to give Kate the chance to make a life of her own without fuss."

"But she is Kate's own mother."

126

Bern sighs. "Let's not harp on this subject on such a fine night, Jane." So we finish out the song without more discussion, and I am not sure why I am disappointed.

The musicians take a break, and everyone goes to find a drink or refresh their stomachs with the late food still sitting out. I see Kate and the Doctor talking animatedly, as if they are reconnecting for the first time, and I smile a bit to myself. Bern leaves to get us cold drinks. I think to have a sit, but then worry I will be too tired to get back up, and the night is still so young.

"Jane. Don't weary yourself," Widow Hawks is at my elbow, gently steering me to a seat. I go to humor her then, giving her a warm look.

"I am so sorry about the cornbread," I half-whisper. "I didn't know!"

"It is alright. It is not surprising to me. I did it for you. And perhaps to see if anything has changed. It has not. And that is what it is," she states, pragmatically.

I see Bern across the dance floor, holding two glasses. He is watching us and hesitates for the longest time before turning away to talk to someone behind him. I frown, but before I can say anything, Doctor Kinney presents himself to me.

"Time for our dance, Mrs. Weber!" he exclaims, and takes my hand. We join the other couples who are swaying to the tunes. The band starts off with a slow tune, again, and he whirls me into his arms holding me close as he did in the kitchen. I think I enjoy his embrace a bit more than Bern's, but I think it is only because I know the Doctor better.

"Are ye havin' a good time?" He asks me, his eyes twinkling with fun and, I suspect by the smell, a bit more whiskey.

"Well, I am, I suppose. And you are, too, I hope?"

He glances over my head, where I am sure Kate is waiting. "Aye. It has been good to talk freely with Kate today. We don't often have the time."

"You have a long history with her," I prompt, and he gives me a surprised look, but the drink seems to have loosened his tongue a bit.

"I have known her a long time, Mrs. Weber. She was a beautiful young girl when I first came here, and she has grown into a fascinatin' young woman."

I nod silently to this, and then quickly change the subject to discuss the day's activities. We enjoy our dance so much that we take the next one together, so we can continue to talk. Bern eventually decides to cut in, and the Doctor graciously relinquishes me halfway through our conversation. He does not look at Bern when he does so, but gives me a small wink without a smile that I do not understand.

"The Doc's dancing a lot with Kate," Bern mentions, nodding his head to them, where they rejoin the group. "That's something to see."

"It is?"

"Most men don't dance with Kate, much. She doesn't encourage it, and besides, she's..." he stops and gives me a little grin as the music picks up. "And here we be again!" We are swept away with the dancers.

But his words have me utterly confused. What is it about Kate that everyone seems to know but no one wants to speak about? It cannot be her heritage, as that is not something that could be ignored by anyone.

Another break in the music finds me seated next to Alice, who is looking wearier than I. I suppose she is tired from a long day cooking and minding little Pete, who is tucked into a basket nearby like several other infants, sleeping soundly regardless of the revelry around them. She tucks a corner of his blanket absently and gives me a smile.

"You're having fun?" she asks.

"I am. It is good to be without the daily chores. Gives one time for socializing," I agree.

"And Kate is too, for once," Alice nods across the night, where I can see Kate still talking with the Doctor. She is aglow with conversation, animatedly waving her hands. Was their friendship so diminished until tonight?

I find my own fatigue makes me less careful about my questions, and I fall into the habit of others in Flats Junction by asking almost tactlessly, "What is it about Kate that makes her so... difficult?"

Alice gives me a sideways glance. "You are her close confidant, aren't you?"

I shrug. "In a way, I feel I do not know her at all. I hear of her history from others, really."

I feel Alice give in before I hear her sigh. Relief breaks out over my chest. Finally, another little town riddle to be solved?

"With Kate being an...well, she is illegitimate and a half-breed to go with it. It is not a good combination even out here, even before the war." Alice alludes once again to the heavy skirmishes of the past. I wish there was a way for me to learn more of the actual backstory of the territories. She continues, lulling me into her story.

"Well, she was ignored at the best of times. Ostracized, taunted and teased. When her brother died so young, she was left utterly alone."

"And her parents did nothing?"

"They... had eyes for one another to be sure. And old Davies did what he could to curb what he heard. Nothing was ever really done to her outright, of course, out of respect for him and his station in town. But... what she endured anyway was enough. From childhood on, she always felt she had to prove her worth, her legitimacy, her intelligence."

"So she bought the general store? To force everyone to work with her and respect her?"

Alice nods and looks down at her lap, fiddling with her skirt folds. "She was able to overcome her pride and hatred of her father to allow him to help her buy it. Maybe she felt it was the least he could do. I don't believe she'd ever really forgiven him."

"I still don't see why she couldn't forgive her own mother." As I say the words, I am struck by my own relationships. I get along well enough with my mother, and should she ask for anything I would do my best to oblige. Perhaps my sense of duty toward her is because we now live a country apart. Mayhap I lived down the street from my parents, as Kate does, and there was past anger against them, I would not think so kind heartedly about them as they meddled in my life.

The look Alice gives me is one of incredulousness, as if I am too dense and naive to understand. And she is right. I grew up on the eastern seaboard, with restricted lessons, a lack of newspapers and nothing of my own experiences to compare to the life and people out here. I have had no preconceived notions, by fortune or providence, so to have severe prejudice against the natives is not an immediate, nor truthful response. I understand now, of course, there is a stigma against Widow Hawks, and I have heard of this recent war with the tribes. But she is nearly English in habit, regardless of her past misdeeds with Percival Davies. What is the harm in the townsfolk establishing acceptance of her? Unless... unless Kate prohibits it on some sort of backlash against her mother? Forcing her mother to... what had she said once? That if Widow Hawks lived the rest of her life in vindication it would not be enough. I see now her point, even if I do not agree with it completely.

Any further dissembling, or gossiping, is cut short as Mitch and Bern present themselves as the music picks up again. Regardless of our tiredness, Alice and I smile at one another, sharing the warmth of womanly conversation and understanding, and stand to take the hands of our menfolk.

Doctor Kinney cuts back into my twirling later in the evening, after the fireworks. This time he is obviously drunk, and I do not realize where the liquor is flowing from. I know he does not keep any in the house, so I can only suspect that something is being passed about, though very few of the other gentlemen are stumbling about. I can only see three or four of the cowboys dancing who are suspect. Though now that I look around, several of the young lads are languishing along the dance floor, sitting and red faced. Dearest heaven.

"You danced with Bern nearly all night," it is more an accusation than just a statement and I try to shush him. His skin is flushed in the lamplight, and, like all of us, he is sweating in the night heat, though it smells more like booze than anything natural.

"He was the only one who asked much," I say, placating and reasonable. The Doctor gives an annoyed shrug.

"It's not who I would have chosen as your beau."

That he has an opinion at all is surprising, though I suppose the Doctor would take an interest in the man who might steal away his new housekeeper.

Thankfully, the dance is short, and I am in Bern's arms again, though I watch the Doctor out of the corner of my eye. He dances once more with Kate, then goes to join the cowboys who are still tipping back liquor.

The music stops a bit after midnight, and Mitch Brinkley is at my elbow.

"Pardon, Mrs. Weber. The Doc's done his annual enjoyment of the whiskey. Shall we take him home?"

I follow his glance and am dismayed to see the Doctor sprawled with the worst of them. He looks in no shape to get the short distance home. I doubt that he can even walk. They are singing a silly tune, now that the musicians have stopped the music, and I blush when I hear the nature of the song, which includes a lady's skirt and something about her bosom.

"That's enough, then." Bern takes charge at my silence, and he and Mitch extract the Doctor from the group. Slinging one arm around each of their shoulders, sandwiched between them, the Doctor stumbles and starts the walk to the house.

I follow, uncertain what to do. I feel it is my place to see the Doctor settled. A shadow steps next to me. It is Widow Hawks.

"Every year he does this," she says quietly. "I am usually the nursemaid."

"I'll do it this time," I say without thinking, and she gives her head a little shake. "I can do it. I'm not too tired."

"It's not that, Jane," she says gently. "I'm only thinking of your reputation."

"My--" I stop and consider. No one knows I am pregnant yet, and it will not do to spend a night alone in the Doctor's house. She is right.

"I'll let you take care of him," she continues. "But I'll spend the night too, like I always do."

I am glad she will let me take over his care, at least. I feel it is my duty. Barely in no time, we find ourselves at the Doctor's house, and I open the door so the two men can haul the slurring Doctor up the stairs and onto his bed. He collapses, but is still awake, trying to put two sentences together. He looks disheveled and ridiculous, and I find I am more worried than upset. I did not expect this of him. Perhaps there is much of him I do not know.

"Alright then?" Bern looks at me. I glance at the bed, where Doctor Kinney is now mindlessly humming an Irish ditty.

"Widow Hawks and I will manage from here," I say, more confidently than I feel. He nods tightly and does not look at the older woman as he and Mitch leave the room and clamber down the stairs. Both of us wait quietly until the screen door slams.

"I'll bring up a few cool cloths," she says. "In the meantime, why don't you take off his boots?"

I look at the Doctor. The last time I was alone like this with any man was when Henry was alive. He was, in the end, too weak to manage much for himself, and I was a capable nursemaid. I suppose that is what I can draw on, though for some reason, the alcohol is more unsettling than cancer. At least Henry always had his wits about him, until sleep became all he could manage.

Drawing to the bed, I untie his laces and take off the heavy shoes, dusty and well worn. He starts to sing again, watching me with bleary eyes. It is a tune about a girl with lovely eyes and ample hips. I try not to listen.

"Jane, here you be. And some water, too." Widow Hawks returns, and he quiets, watching us. I wonder how much is the room spinning for him, or if he will even remember that we helped him. I hope that he really only does this one time a year, and I do not have to expect a repeat at Christmas.

Widow Hawks leaves to make some tea, and I realize I am indeed to play nursemaid in whole. I turn to Doctor Kinney, who is half propped up in his rumpled bed, watching me with a small smile on his face. Well, I reason to myself, at least he is not an angry or mean drunkard. It could be worse.

"Mrs. Weber," he says sluggishly, his brogue thick and muddled. "Beautiful."

"Drink this," I say, and hand him the water.

"Beautiful," he says again, and dutifully drinks the glass down. "Kate."

I smile as he continues. "Kate seemed to enjoy dancin' with me."

"I noticed," I say shortly, and remove his stockings. I gently press his shoulder back. "Lay down now. How do you feel?"

"I feel fine," he says, slurring the last word. "How are ye feeling, sweet mother?" His hand comes up and he haphazardly rubs my arm.

I take his hand and hold it in both of mine. "I am fine, Doctor. Don't you worry about me, now."

"But I do!" He insists, and tries to sit up again. His slurring is slightly better in his insistence, though I can smell the booze reeking through his every pore. "I don't want ye workin' too hard."

"I'm not working now. Lay down," I plead, squeezing his fingers. I free a hand from his and place a cool, damp towel on his sweating forehead. "Tell me about Kate. Did you like dancing with her, too?"

He gives a broad smile. "Oh, aye. Aye. She's just lovely, a special woman-girl. Do you know I thought she was wonderful when I stayed with her parents? I know some of the men around won't look twice at her because she's half Indian, and if she didn't have the general store they'd want her out of town too... but I don't mind. I was an outcast in Boston as a child, bein' Irish. We're kindred spirits, Kate and I."

"Of course," I soothe. "A man would be lucky to have her as his wife."

"He would. A battle for his children, though, with native blood. And Mrs. Weber," he turns to me again, "I'm awful glad there'll be a wee babe here in the house. Always wanted to fill up the rooms with little ones." He gets a bit teary at this comment and I think it's wise to have him drink a bit more water.

"I'll be right back. You need more water to sober you up."

"I'm soberin'," he insists, but his words are still fuddled. I shake my head at him, and rise from the side of the bed, but he grips me close. "Mrs. Weber, are you leavin' already?"

"Just wait here, I'll be back in a moment."

His eyes are suddenly piercing mine. "I'll wait."

He is soundly asleep when I come back up with more water. Setting the glass on the table, I pull the chair closer to the bed to keep watch in case he needs more to drink, or, worse, wakes to hurl. But I am well tired, and nod off almost immediately.

# Chapter II

"Mrs. Weber."

I wake to a hand taking mine. Blinking in the early morning light, I see Doctor Kinney sitting on his bed, still in rumpled clothes. but looking rather well for his rough night. His lips are dry and he still smells like old booze, but he seems clearheaded.

"Are you alright?" I ask, relieved he seems somewhat recovered.

"Aye, I am, though a bit tired," he admits. "But I am appalled you stayed on."

"Widow Hawks is below. I think she slept on the floor in the kitchen," I say, but he shakes his head.

"Not that. That you slept in the chair. You, pregnant." He pulls me up. "Ye must get some proper sleep. Here," he takes me across the space to his aunt's room.

"But breakfast," I protest. "And at least the coffee."

"I managed before you came to Flats Junction. And though I prefer your brew over mine, I can take on the kitchen for a day," he says, lightly. "Here you go."

He nearly forces me onto the bed and draws the thin curtain over the window. I sit and watch. I am exhausted, but I am also unsure about my employer's insistences.

"I can go down."

He gives me a stern look. "Rest first. You must. I couldn't let you work for me this mornin' after you stayed up until the early hours to manage my annual abandon. Please, Mrs. Weber."

I lay down then, and close my eyes. The soft mattress feels like heaven. I have not been on a real mattress since Massachusetts. The Doctor hasn't even left the room before I am asleep.

# CHAPTER 12

There is a rattle of a plate and I stir awake. It takes a moment to realize where I am. The light is bright and clean in his aunt's bedroom, as the thin curtain does little to hide midday sun.

"Here you be. Widow Hawks made some sandwiches." The Doctor is balancing a plate and a glass of milk on one of the slabs of wood I use for a tray.

"You've eaten, then?" I ask, sitting up. "I can certainly eat downstairs."

"Too late, brought it all up already." He hands me the plate, which is piled high with bread, cheese, and leaves of lettuce.

He goes to his room, comes back with the chair, and draws it next to me. I eat easily; it's good, more so because I did not have to make it. The bread is soft on the inside, and there is butter on some of the slices, which I eat first. It is sheep's milk cheese and soft and tangy.

"Mrs. Weber, I..." He stops and gives me a hopeful look. "I hope I did not say anythin' last night that offended you."

I finish my bite and wave his comment away. Swallowing, I say, "You were a gentleman."

"I highly doubt that," he says, looking a bit guilty. "I apologize you had to see me like that."

"You said it was your annual abandon," I remind him. "I cannot blame a man for indulging once or twice a year."

"Ye don't blame it on me because I'm Irish?" He asks candidly.

I frown. The thought had not occurred to me and I shake my head. "I've lived among many Irish and most were not drunkards." Am I unique in my lack of prejudice? I suppose he had to handle many in the east who did not care for his heritage, just as the people out west do not care for the natives. Intolerance seems to always barely simmer beneath surfaces. I prefer my simple views of people and places. It keeps me from being so emotional, which I have never been able to afford, anyway.

I drink the milk at his prompting. I find I am not horribly tired and I am enjoying my moments with him. We have a good rapport.

"I'm glad I did not say anything inappropriate."

"You mainly talked about Kate and how beautiful she is, how you liked dancing with her," I explain, and he looks boyishly sheepish, embarrassed at my words.

"I did, eh?"

"You ought to formally court her," I recommend, though I find I do not have much zeal behind the words. I say it because I know it is what he desires, and I want him to have that happiness. He is a kind man and deserves the children he dreams about. He is silent for a minute. We hear Widow Hawks in the kitchen below us, tinkering with the cutlery. Finally, he sighs.

"I am glad you were here," he says quietly, taking the empty plate from my hands. "It was nice to wake to a friendly face."

I look up at him and smile. "I agree."

He stops at the door and looks thoughtfully at me, and nods almost absently before heading back downstairs.

# CHAPTER 13

I manage to make supper without any mishaps. Widow Hawks stays with me the whole day. To make sure I am not too tired, she says, but I watch her keep an eye on Doctor Kinney as he is in and out of the house, as if she is waiting for him to relapse or collapse, but he does neither, and seems his usual self through the evening meal.

When I walk out the door with her, Bern is waiting. He is not surprised to see Widow Hawks, but tips his hat at her and at Doctor Kinney, who has followed us out.

"Thank you for your help last night, Bern," the Doctor says. His voice is neutral. Bern gives a brief nod.

"Yes sir, Doc."

The three of us walk back through town. Widow Hawks hurries her pace so she is several feet ahead of us, leaving us alone, though we do not have much to say to each other today. She stops a ways from her house, and then I see her almost break into a run.

I am surprised; it is unlike her to be rushed, but when we catch up with her, I see that the windows of the house are wide open, the hides and calico ripped away, and the door itself is hacked, as if hundreds of hammers or a dozen small axes were used to utterly damage the wood. The entire outside of the house has been vandalized.

"Oh no," I breathe. She hurries in to see if anything else has happened, but I stand, flabbergasted, with a silent Bern next to me.

"Did you know of this?" I ask him, thinking he might have the pulse on the townsfolk, to know who might do such a cruel act.

He looks away from me. I have a horrified thought that perhaps he partook in this damage.

"Bern," I say again. He looks back at me, his dark eyes heavily shaded by the brim of his hat. "Who would do such a thing?"

He sighs. "Most of the town and a lot of the cowboys don't like her here. They want her to go back to her people, rejoin the reservation, and leave us in peace."

"But she doesn't do anything disruptive!" I insist, angrily. "Do you mean to say you agree with everyone?"

"Jane," he says, placating. "I know you are closer to her than most, since you have to stay with her, but you don't know the history here. When she was staying with old Davies, her kin would come into town often to visit her. Once she married him, they cut their visits to once a year. They haven't been through this season yet, but it's always a bit wild when they do."

"Surely she would ask them to stop from anything bad," I say. "Or at the very least, Percival Davies would have done so."

"Never," he gives a little rueful chuckle, and moves his eyes away from mine. "He loved her. They were her family. I sometimes think he joined them at night around their bonfires."

"So?"

"So it ain't done, Jane." He is suddenly irritable, and tips his hat, leaving me standing there without anything more to go on.

I go into her home, and she's kneeling by the fire. I know she has overheard our conversation. I know how sound travels through the thin wooden walls of the homes here. Her head is bowed.

"I cannot leave town, you know," she says quietly. I go to kneel next to her. "Kate is my only family, my daughter, my little girl. I don't want to leave her."

I bite back an immediate response. Surely Widow Hawks sees that Kate wants nothing to do with her. Why hold on? I suppose I might understand these ties better once I am a mother. I reflect in the silence. When this babe is born, I will love it, of course. But will I do anything for it, and wish to care for it, forever? I shake my head inwardly. I cannot fathom the deep love all say exist between parent and child. I must live it myself before I can judge. "Perhaps we should tell Kate about this, then?" I offer.

"She won't care," Widow Hawks says with finality and I know she is right. "No, let it be. We will mend the window papers. The door will hold through the fall. I will see if Patrick can find us wood at the lumber yard. Since my husband died, Patrick does these things for

145

me. They tolerated me when Percy lived, but now that he's gone, I find myself unwelcome most places."

"It's not right," my voice is defiant. She reaches over to take my hand and gives a small laugh.

"Of course it is not right. Is prejudice ever so? But it is the way of people." She pauses. "Mine and yours, both."

# CHAPTER 14

As Bern predicted, the Sioux come to town three weeks later. A loud ruckus came from the streets, an echo, a whooping, and I rush to the screen door while wiping my hands on my apron to try and find the fuss. I cannot see anything at first, but as soon as I step outside, I see old Mrs. Molhurst next door on her porch, shaking her head, peering down the corner where the main street began.

"What is it?" I ask her, my voice carrying easily across the yards.

She gives me a tight, appraising look. Mrs. Molhurst has been consistently disapproving of me. Of all the neighbors, she is the least welcoming. I am not sure if she had hoped for my job to carry her through her widowhood, or if she doesn't approve of my boarding with an Indian, or if she in general does not like me. I will likely never really know. "Blackfoot," she says. Then she scurries inside.

It must be Widow Hawks' family come to visit. Well, when I am done with my chores I will go meet them, I reason with myself. For now I must harvest the second crop of beans for canning, which Alice Brinkley has promised to show me how to do, and I need to work on the laundry, which I have already told the Doctor so he can pull water during lunch.

He comes in from his rounds, and begins to bring in the pails for the soaking and sheets. He works quickly, regardless of the heat.

"The *Sihasapa* are here. Would you like to meet Widow Hawks' sisters, brother and their kin?"

"I would love to," I say sincerely. I find I mean my sincerity, truly. I care for Widow Hawks and wish to understand her family better. And maybe I feel a bit beholden to do so, as if I should help fill Kate's absence, though I should never presume that I could ever replace a daughter.

He gives me a wide grin, turns to refill a pail, and then swings back. "Perhaps you should give her time with them tonight. Kate ought to be able to find a bunk for you in her back room somehow. She's usually very busy, I know, but you shouldn't be in her way."

I do not know how I feel about Kate much anymore. She seems to think the incident of the cornbread over, and talks to me like I am her dear friend, but I am troubled by her lack of regard for her mother. Perhaps, I think, there is still another piece to the story I do not know. Or perhaps it is as simple as anger running deep. So I nod, turn back to the bread as the Doctor ambles back to the well for more water.

"You're set," he says, bringing the laundry down from his bedroom. We have a nice way of it now; he is not angry with me for trying to do too much, and I am grateful for the help. Though I am finally seasoning to the hardness of the labor here in the territories, I am just now starting to thicken in the waist and I will soon be unable to do much big lifting regardless of my desire to keep from being a bother.

I pull a small cast iron skillet down from a hook against the south wall and fry some eggs with dill to go with fresh bread. As he sits down to eat, I find the courage to ask, "Bern seemed to think Widow Hawks isn't welcome here." I think of the animals at her doorstep and the damage to her home. I am finding that I do not trust the quiet of the town so much when it comes to the topics of the natives.

The Doctor presses his lips together. He knows about the vandalism, having found a new door relatively quickly. I hurry on, now that I have found a voice.

"Or more, the townsfolk don't like the natives coming to town. I shouldn't really pry, but I hope her family won't meet with much... intolerance while they are here? I cannot expect they do much to harm anyone. "

"They don't," he says. "They don't bother to trade with Kate; she has explained she has no need for pelts or native arts. But one or two might find their way into a saloon, and the 'firewater' does not sit well with them. And they do their fires and dances, as usual, for it's a bit of a... holiday... for them to come through here."

"That doesn't sound awful at all," I say. The Doctor takes a thoughtful bite of bread.

"No. But it unnerves the conservatives," he gives a tight one-shouldered shrug. "And no one likes too much of a brush-in with the Blackfoot. They all still think about the war like it happened yesterday. And I suppose... Well... Some lost kin in the skirmishes. Not too many from Flats Junction, but even when one man is lost out here, everyone will take it personally."

I ask him to explain the viewpoint of the town to me. The news back east had always cast Custer as a sensational hero after the war and during the Reconstruction. Even I had been taken in by his wild and handsome face on the cover of Harper's Weekly. I was only twenty-three when his last stand and death hit the papers. Everyone was shocked about the turn of the battles, appalled that the natives had killed our hero. Headlines had screamed about the indignity of it all. But my mother had tried very hard not to let us be completely mindless about hating the Indians. She'd always said there was more to any story. Now I might be able to get a piece of that.

"You know of the reservation?" He asks, mouth full of lunch.

I nod. I have heard tell of it in the west, but of course I don't know much about it, or what it means, or even how it all came about.

"Well, before the army came out, this land was mainly Cheyenne and Sioux tribes hereabouts. Maybe a hundred years ago Widow Hawks' people pushed out the Cheyenne and considered a lot of land to be for their use. But when Custer came out and found gold in the *Paha Sapa* back in '74 the subsequent rush created a lot of problems with the natives. And the government wanted the gold, too. So they took more land for the territories, the sacred *Paha*--," he stops and shakes his head. "The Black Hills, so they're called by us. Anyway, eventually many of the different peoples got together, lots of the Sioux and Cheyenne especially, and decided the only way to keep their way of life was to... well... start a war."

I listen, hungrily. He is a rather good storyteller, and even though he lived through this war, he tells it so that I am not keen on either side, but see the war dispassionately and carefully. I do not have many questions, preferring to hear the whole of it first, but we enjoy the talking so much that he starts to help with the laundry. I hear of the story of the Battle of Little Bighorn, and more of the Cheyenne nation. I hear about Sitting Bull, the many inter-native wars that had criss-crossed the plains on top of the settlers coming in. I am mesmerized; it is the best lesson I have had since I left school so many years ago, and gives me more knowledge about the history out in the territories than any newspaper would care to publish. I realize the railroad that goes past Flats Junction is incredibly new, that only two years ago it had been attacked by some renegade Sioux who still wished to keep us out. I am glad I did not know half of this when I agreed to come west. I might not have been courageous enough.

"How do you know this all?" I ask as he wipes his hands casually on a corner of my apron.

"Percy Davies would talk about everything Indian over supper with reverence, and made sure to give both sides of any tale for his wife's sake. I loved the stories, and so did my dear auntie. As for the wars... well, Henry Brinkley fought out of duty to the government, but had a pretty hard time of it afterwards and sometimes I think it eased his mind to talk of it with me. He never seemed to get over the required ransacking of Indian villages what with his best friend here in Flats Junction lovin' and marryin' a native girl. I think he passed that view to his sons, which is why out of all the town, the Brinkley clan is kindest to Widow Hawks, especially these past years after the battles. Strange to think how our lives might affect any children we may have."

I agree with him, and I think over his words as I take my time over the last of the laundry. I think of my pregnancy and my unborn child. The truth of it is that I do not seem to have inherited any of the evils that the women discuss privately, or that Alice has warned me about. She speaks of tiring fatigue, persistent nausea, aches and indigestion, bowel irritation and trouble sleeping. None of it sounds particularly enjoyable, but as I have not had much other than the early queasiness and tiredness, I am counting myself lucky. I have made mention of this to the Doctor, but he thinks I am being unnecessarily strong about my condition and continues to treat me as if I am delicate.

I then reflect on the Doctor's stories. He paints a picture of a happy home, that things were comfortable and fair when he lived in the Davies' house as he and his aunt built their place. I rather like the way he makes Percy Davies sound. I think I might have really enjoyed the man. How could the banker and Widow Hawks be so blind to Kate's alienation by the town? They seemed to be attentive, at least to themselves and the world around them. Or did perhaps Kate make it worse on herself somehow as a girl? Perhaps she was too proud, or overly smart; qualities I know are never becoming to any girl, let alone one that is struggling with prejudice from the start.

And then I think about how the Doctor spoke of children, how he still plans very much to have some. I'm glad for him, if he thinks his future with Kate is possible. I know he holds her in high esteem, enough to get a bit bashful when I bring her up. I hope they are well suited. He, being a man of science, and Kate, with her hard independence and strong opinions about her mother, seems a strange match. But perhaps opposites attract. Perhaps that is what makes a union fiery and passionate. Henry and I were both suitably muted and we could only shared a small bit of tenderness. I should like to think a true romance, like the one between Percy Davies and Widow Hawks, had quite a bit of passion to keep them so happy for so long.

# CHAPTER 15

We eat a simple supper of bread and cheese, which I slice right off the crusts as we eat, and then the Doctor and I head out to Widow Hawks' home. I can see it is swarmed with bodies in hides and mixes of calico. I am nervous, but one glance at Doctor Kinney and the happy eagerness he shows puts me at ease. So far I have not been remiss to trust him. I am glad for him, that even in a town that does not care for the natives, they have been accepting of his own heritage. That is something, then.

"Will they welcome me?" I ask.

He gives me a warm look. "I'm sure, by now, Widow Hawks has told them all about you, about the comin' baby, that ye are like a daughter to her."

"She would say that?" I am taken back. While I find myself caring more and more for the older woman, I did not think she would so easily return the feelings.

"She's often said it in such a way to me."

"When do you see her so much?"

He shrugs. "Kate is often unable to drop off the goods Widow Hawks needs, so I take a box once or twice a week to her."

I fall silent, wondering why an able bodied woman like Widow Hawks cannot get her own dry goods if Kate is too busy to bring them herself. But then I think of how I have often wondered how Widow Hawks gets by. Does the Doctor manage her household and needs as a son would? Is it because he is beholden to her for accepting him into town? Because he wishes he were her son in truth? Or simply because he is a good man and sees her as his adoptive family?

We arrive at the front porch and the Doctor is quickly enveloped by some of the natives. A few ponies grazing nearby are decorated prettily, with beadwork on the blankets draped across their backs and in their manes. I recall the Doctor mentioning that horses were a sign of wealth. So, Widow Hawks' family is well off. There are strange smells of things cooking in the house that I do not recognize. There are small groups of women, old and young, small children in various ages, and a few men with Doctor Kinney, who has started to pull unexpected things from his pockets, such as buttons, a spool of fishing line, and candy for the little ones. Around this group, though, it is obvious that many, if not all, do not speak much English. Even so, the Doctor reveals he has some working knowledge of the language, and in reviewing his vocabulary with them, he seems to be in his element.

"Jane!" Widow Hawks comes out of her home with a smile. She gives me her hand and turns me to one of the old women who sits in a crumple of mismatched calico strips, hides, and even furs, in this heat. She is brown, her skin a deeply lined almond, and her black eyes are buried in sunken sockets, but she smiles, showing missing teeth.

"My mother," Widow Hawks says, by way of introduction. I am honored to meet this woman, as I have grown to care for Widow Hawks as if she, too, is my family. Sinking to my knees, I give a little bob of a bow to her as the native language washes over me. I do not know what Widow Hawks says, but her mother continues to smile at me, then leans forward and takes my hand. Her grip is strong, bony, arthritic.

I try to stand once she releases me, but instead I am held down with a firm hand by Widow Hawks. "My mother and sisters wish to get to know you."

But I do not speak their language, and so at first I sit quietly, almost reverently, next to the matriarch. There is high laughter, chatter, and yet it is not out of control and I do not feel frightened. I feel a tap on my shoulder; it is one of the young maidens. She takes up my hand and draws into it with her finger. She does not look particularly pleased about what she is drawing. The grandmother leans in to watch, and gazes into my face before shaking her head and calling out. Widow Hawks appears soon after.

I do not want to offend, so I have continued to allow the young woman to silently draw circles in my palm. Crouching next to me, she watches, and then sighs softly, glancing at her mother.

"My sister-in-law, Hantaywee, has a way with the future. She draws a moon in your hand."

"She does not look very happy about it," I say a bit worriedly. "Should I ask her to stop?"

"She will stop when she feels it is right. My mother, Eyota, says you will either have a very good pregnancy, or have need to be fertile again in your life. They know you are widowed, like me."

"Oh dear," I say. Because much of this is very blunt and open, I feel a bit exposed. Widow Hawks gives my shoulders a squeeze.

"You are doing well. I know it is a lot."

"Oh!" She pauses as I exclaim, remembering. "I am to stay with Kate tonight. So you needn't worry about me with your family here."

"I see." Her eyes flick over her kin.

"It's not that I do not want to meet them all, please," I start to explain. "It was Doctor Kinney, thinking I needed to sleep elsewhere so that you would not need to bother over me. I hope I will not be too much trouble for Kate."

Her face softens as I explain, and she glances at the Doctor before sinking back to her knees beside me.

"Stay, Dowanhowee. My family will move to the hills near the forest for their chants and fire tonight. It is the road of our ancestral grounds. You will be able to sleep here. I have thought of this so neither of you need to consider anything else."

I am relieved that I do not need to ask Kate for charity tonight. "Thank you. I am happy to stay then. Tell me, though, please, what was that you called me?"

Her eyes laugh at me and she nods to her brother and nephews. "They've given you a *Sihasapa* name, Jane. You made an immediate impression when you spoke."

"I suppose I should thank them?"

"No need. Now, to serve the food."

I finally am released of my hand so I can help her. We offer her family native cooking. I do not know what I am doling out in her mismatched cutlery, but it smells delicious. The Doctor asks to have some, too, even though we have just recently finished supper.

"I did not know you liked this type of cooking," I say, as I ladle some out for him where he sits next to the young men in a separate circle.

"You forget, Mrs. Weber, that when I first arrived, this is all I was served in the Davies' home. It's a treat to get it now."

I cannot help but admit to him, a bit proudly, "They've apparently given me an Indian name."

"What is it?"

"Don't ask me to pronounce it!" I laugh a little. He glances around, announcing he will find out so he can call me so, but I know he is teasing.

"Do they not have a name for you, since you are more kin than me?" I ask, and he nods around a mouthful.

"They do indeed, though I earned my most recent one only five or so years ago when they figured I was not going to marry. I am called Takoda - Friend to Everyone. Though, before that I was simply Lootah - Red."

"Oh," I reply. I am still a bit overwhelmed by it all, so I move away to go about my rounds with the pot.

Once everyone is served, I join Widow Hawks and two others in the house where cornbread is finishing its baking

As I watch the bread brown, I finally ask, "What is your full name?" She gives me a sideways glance, and I amend my question. "Everyone in town calls you Widow Hawks, but I know you did not marry a man with such a name."

"My name, when I met Percy, was Flies With Hawks - Chatan - because my mind always seemed to be soaring in the heavens with the birds, thinking up fanciful futures for myself. It was an apt name, and I keep it to this day."

# CHAPTER 16

The next day, I am surprised when Bern meets me halfway on my walk back to the Doctor's. While I often see him in the early part of the day, he is usually busy with his morning chores and does little more than give me a nod or a hat tilt.

"You stayed with the Indians last night?" He is almost accusatory. "I looked for you, but I saw you and the Doc leaving to visit with them all after supper."

"I slept in my usual bed at Widow Hawks' house. They all slept outside in the hills." I hope I did not sound too defensive. He shakes his head.

"When are they leaving?"

"They did not give me their plans. I do not speak their language, you know." I think guiltily of my newly minted Indian name, but realize Bern will not think this an extraordinary boon.

"Well, they should head west soon. People are not happy about them in town to begin with. The sooner they go, the less chance for trouble."

He gives me the customary hat brim touch as he leaves me at the entry of the Doctor's house.

# CHAPTER 17

In the hot sweltering heat of August, I slave over the canning jars. Alice is next to me and their little Pete coos happily in the corner of the room in a pile of blankets. Over the past few weeks, I have learned to can green beans and now the chutney. So far, with Alice's help, I am able to do this task without much fail, and the larder is filling nicely for fall. I take the time to write down her instructions as she gives them, so I might do this next summer. Her gentle babe gives me hope that I will have time to do this, even with a child of my own to watch over. Perhaps, I will be able to join the Brinkley women en masse for their annual can.

Alice is generous to give me some of her family jars to use. The gooseberries, currants and raspberries will make good sauces for the winter. The harvest is plenty enough that I will use her wisdom to salt and dry most things, but it will be a luxury to have sweet things on hand, on occasion. The Doctor does have a sweet tooth.

She tells me about the sugar and how to boil it long enough without burning so that the fruit will store well without spoiling. While I did not have much by the way of luxuries in Boston, I did not have to worry over the food the same way that I do here. It comes natural to me, the kitchen stuffs, so that I am not so much daunted by the food tasks, but rather enjoy them. The Doctor has a root cellar for storage and already I have some onions to dry down there.

"And then you do the rest of the steps," she explains as we pack another jar nearly to the brim. "Just like the others."

She watches me put the jars in boiling water and nods encouragingly. She is a sweet friend to offer to teach me these things and, in truth, without her guidance I would often be lost for ways of life in the territories. I feel closer to her more and more, now that I am reaching the middle of my pregnancy. I do not think Kate will be very sympathetic to my situation; no one knows yet about the coming baby except Alice and Mitch, the Doctor, and Widow Hawks.

"Alice," I ask, as we watch the jars heat underwater. "How are you getting along with Mitch's family what with Pete older?"

"Oh!" She smiles, happily. "Fine, now that Mitch has been back at the fields. I know they were not happy with us, taking time away from planting, but it was so wonderful to have him around to help, and to have him bond with little Petey."

"I can only imagine how much Mitch enjoyed his time with his boy," I say, and try not to wonder at the man's strange behavior. It is an odd man who will put his child before the fields out here. I still cannot fathom his reasoning, but the little one is most definitely dear to me, too, if only because I treasure his mother's friendship deeply. There is not much time with the harvest coming due to fondle and dandy babies on one's knee, but he's a smiley lad who is easily entertained. I wonder if all babes are so.

As we stand over the stove, I feel a twinge in my lower abdomen. It is light, fanciful, and I think, at first, I only imagine it. We eat a light lunch of leftover gooseberries and plums that Alice brought from her family's orchard, and continue with the canning. In the soft heat of the kitchen, little Pete falls peacefully asleep in his blankets.

I wince again. I have no way to know if there is pain as a child grows or if it is how a babe moves in the womb. But the pains are sharp and low. I bend over a little as it pierces me.

Alice is looking at me strangely.

"Jane. Are you alright?"

I start to nod yes, but then realize it is a lie. "No. I don't believe so. I'm sorry, Alice, but I need you to see if you can fetch Doctor Kinney, or send him here. Just tell him I am having a bit of a bad day, and if he can find time to stop here between his patients that would be good."

Alice's face is white. Without another word, she goes to gather up her sweetly sleeping child. Her eyes are big as she turns to me at the kitchen door.

"It's not good to have pains so early, Jane. Are you sure you'll be alright for a bit? Perhaps get off your feet."

I wave her away. I know I am not particularly good at math, but I know I am just over four months or so. Not even halfway. It is perhaps just something that is normal but in my ignorance I cannot diagnose myself. And I only will trust the Doctor's word in this. A stab of fear hits me hard. It is enough that every day I am battling the elements, the harsh work, the laboring chores. That alone is fearsome. This is different. I am frightened, desperately so, and all I want is the Doctor to come home. I don't feel well. I feel dizzy, nauseated, and sweaty.

Alice leaves. I decide, in the time to spare waiting for the Doctor to arrive, to start on supper. Perhaps it will help take my mind off the pulsing pushing in my body. Using most of the vegetables we have not used in the jars, I am able to get them boiling well and ready for spices. The pains start to come regularly and I feel fluid run through my clothes. I am too afraid to look, but finally realize I need to wear some rags.

In the lab, I find a few clean operating cloths. I take one, and go to the upstairs washroom to take care of any little stain. It is not a light smear of blood. Even in the dim light of the bathroom, I see it is quite dark, and there is more than I thought. I have already ruined my petticoats. Nothing can be done. I wrap the laboratory towel around my middle under my dresses and head back to the kitchen, where the haphazard soup is starting to simmer.

I do not know how long I stand at the stove. Time seems to lose meaning as I endure another contraction, sinking into my worries, afraid to sit, lest I ruin one of my few dresses with the blood I can feel seep through the cloths. I pray the rag is holding the gushes in, that I am not such a disaster as I feel.

"Jesus, Mary and Joseph!" the thick Irish swear booms through the kitchen. I turn around and see the Doctor standing in the doorway. His eyes are wild and his hands hanging limply at his sides. He is staring at the floor and I look down through a light haze to see small drops and tiny pools of blood at my feet.

"Mrs. Weber! " He suddenly springs into action, striding across the room as he talks, bending swifter than I would have thought him capable, and picks me up as if I was not a grown woman with a mind of my own.

"The soup!" I manage lightly.

"To hell with the soup," he growls, and marches us sideways up the stairs to his aunt's bedroom. I wrap my arms around his neck to keep from slipping from his arms. "How long have ye been bleedin'?"

"I..." I try to think. "Perhaps an hour or two. Did Alice not send for you?"

"No! I was comin' home early. Thought to help you tonight and give you a bit of a rest."

I try to answer, but I cannot because I must breathe through another bout of cramping.

"Did ye lose the babe?" I notice his brogue is more pronounced, and he is all business, laying me down, bunching up the sheets below my hips. I shake my head negative, but he is not looking, and is too busy removing my boots. I finally register that he plans to half undress me for an examination, but I am too nervous about this to protest. Perhaps this is a natural thing.

"Mrs. Weber..." He looks at me finally, holding my stocking foot. "Did you lose the child?"

"I don't know. I don't think so. Yet," I whisper. I expect to start to cry when I admit it, but I do not. This child is such an enigma, a babe that might grow up the spitting image of its father, to remind me always of my ties to Henry. It is a child unlooked for, unexpected, and brushed aside by its father's death and my new daily hardships. I cannot imagine what it would be to be a mother, to be as wrapped with my child as is Alice with het Pete .

"I have to examine you. I will have to leave ye for a few moments to gather instruments and I will send one of the neighbors for Widow Hawks. Can ye remove your petticoats?"

"I will try."

He hurriedly leaves the room. I sit up and hike up my skirts so I can shimmy out of the stockings. The rags I'd clipped to staunch the blood are drenched in hot, dark red blood and blackish congealed tissue. I give a small cry, realizing that all my under skirts are, regardless of my efforts, destroyed, and that perhaps this loss of blood is not so well after all.

He must be standing just outside the room, because he bolts in when I make a noise. He stops short, though, his eyes taking in the utterly soaked cloths at my feet. Another contraction seizes me. I hold my breath, terrified about what I ought to let my body do, and double over with the effort of trying to stay upright. As the dull pain hits, a stream of blood pours out, unstoppable, deep red and sweltering. I have not yet let my skirt down, so my naked leg is scandalously in view, but one look at Doctor Kinney tells me that he does not care about my ankles or the white flesh of my knee. He is horrified about the blood, and that scares me more than anything else.

"Sweet mother Mary," he swears again.

"Stop, please. It cannot be so bad, can it? I do not feel much more than a bit faint. The pains don't hurt so much," I explain, begging him to agree with me. And it is true. While the contractions are strong and push hard in my belly and my back and my womb throbs, it is not unmanageable and is not excruciating.

Instead, he reaches for me, and eases me into the bed, situating more rags beneath my body.

"I've got to look, Mrs Weber. I'm sorry," he says. I mutely follow his instructions, for I am frightened by his behavior. I did not truly think about what it would mean to birth a child here, let alone miscarry. My ignorance of most things in the bedroom left me with little imagination, though now that he is bending over my bare legs, reality hits all too clear. Doctor Kinney, my employer, would be delivering my baby, and seeing me in all states of undress. Another contraction hits, and I gasp through it.

He looks up at me in concern, then rustles at my midsection as I stare at the ceiling, then at the Catholic cross on the wall, pretending to ignore his rummaging along my inner thigh and quick, thankfully gentle probing. Then he is at my side, standing over me, wiping down his hands which are slick and sticky with blood.

"You're deliverin' the babe," he says, all matter of fact. "It's far too early; it must be stillborn."

"Well, that's that, then," I try to stay light, because he still seems so upset. He shakes his head.

"It's a lot of blood. I've got to watch it. But first, I'll go have someone fetch Widow Hawks."

# CHAPTER 18

Widow Hawks will arrive too late to undress me. I deliver the child quickly, while I am still clothed. Doctor Kinney is the only one in the room to hold my hand. It is an easy birth, for the babe is tiny and my body is strong with all the hard work of living here. He releases my hand to gather up the tiny bundle of limbs.

"A boy," he says softly, and then cradles the child into a clean sheet and reverently lays him on the sideboard.

He looks to me, his face unreadable, and we hear Widow Hawks running up the stairs. She stops short in the doorway, taking in the bloody cloths, our wild eyes and my state of dishevelment.

"Oh no, Patrick," she says softly, and then moves to me. "I'll get her comfortable, if I can."

"I'm not leavin' now," he says intensely. "I want to make sure she finishes up well."

I am shuddering and shaking with the birth yet, so I need Widow Hawks to unbutton my overdress. She takes the yellow calico and lays it aside, then helps me ease under the sheets. Doctor Kinney has not been watching, instead carefully re-wrapping my dead son. I want to see the tiny child, but then again, I do not.

Another contraction hits, a wave, really, still strong and long, and I feel more fluid and tissue flow out. I suppose it is normal for this to take its time slowing down.

"How are you feeling?" Widow Hawks smooths back hair from my forehead and reaches back to unpin the braids.

"Rather tired and dizzy," I admit. Doctor Kinney swings around.

"Dizzy? How much so?"

I think, and as I do, another contraction seizes my middle. I breathe through it, feeling more blood come running out between my thighs. To my embarrassment, I see the black red liquid soak through the sheet.

"Pat." Widow Hawks' voice is low, and she puts a hand on my shoulder. "Jane is still having pains."

Doctor Kinney jumps into action. "What?"

"I can't seem to stop," I sigh through another small wave. "Maybe if I walk around a bit to soothe the cramps?"

I move, my legs landing heavily on the floor and I stand before either of them can stop me. I think if I am determined to go about more normally, perhaps it will all go away. There is an emptiness in my womb, but by standing another contraction hits, and blood streams down my leg, creating an instant puddle. I cry out, and crouch, and as I do, a large piece of slimy matter slides out of me.

"I thought I'd delivered the babe!" I am panicked immediately. The earthiness and bloodiness of this seems unnatural. I do not recall hearing stories of birth like this.

"The placenta, perhaps." Doctor Kinney comes around, and stops short at this side of the bed. "By the stars, Mrs. Weber! Back in bed now!"

He leaves the room abruptly. I look at the large puddle of blood and tissue at my feet. I think I have disgusted the Doctor, but then I hear him bounding back up the stairs as Widow Hawks helps me back into the covers, clearing the red rags below me with new ones.

"We'll watch for a bit and make sure she delivers the afterbirth," he says, but he puts his medical bag nearby, and lays out several bottles of medicine and syringes.

They go about cleaning around me. I bear through the contractions without issue. They are not painful, just actively running through my middle and lower back like waves hitting the shore. I know I bleed with each. Eventually, Doctor Kinney checks under the covers and announces I have lost quite a bit of blood, but that the rest of the placenta seems to have made an appearance.

"Rest a bit, Mrs. Weber. It seems to have eased off, and your body will start to relax. We'll go grab some quick grub and be right back."

"I might try to sleep," I say. "You take your time."

They walk out together, and I close my eyes against the dizziness. A fitful sleep comes at first, but then I realize I will not be able to sleep easily with the pains that continue, sometimes quickly and sometimes not. I wonder how much blood I have lost. Raising the sheet, I am astounded to see that I have soaked through everything. Black clots of tissue still run out of me with each pulse of my womb.

Sitting in bed makes me feel suddenly faint, so I lay back on the pillows. Time seems to float; I do not know how long I am alone.

A cool hand on my forehead rouses me. I open my eyes and find that I cannot see purely. A soft haze touches everything, but I register that it is Widow Hawks' hand over my face. I cannot focus, but I know it is her.

I feel lucid, and I truly think I can understand everything. I sense there is movement around me, but I cannot tell if it is hurried or slow, worried or no. I can clearly hear words spoken around me. There are questions and I answer, believing my responses to be concise.

"Patrick! Patrick!" The shout is near, but it takes me a moment to realize that it is Doctor Kinney she calls for, and then suddenly he appears on the other side of me, tearing away the sheet.

"Jesus."

"Shall we pack her womb?"

"You know that never works. It doesn't stop anything if the body doesn't rest the pumpin' of blood. We need the uterus to contract, empty on its own accord. Mrs. Weber, are ye awake?"

I think it is obvious I am, though I find I cannot really open my eyes. My body is riding contractions now; I am powerless.

"Jane, can you speak?" Widow Hawks bends over me, taking my face in her hands. I think my eyes are open, but my vision is narrowed, a pinprick. My heartbeat feels very pure, as if I can sense every particle riding through my veins in slow motion. I am sweating, little rivers sliding down the insides of my arms and along my neck. Doctor Kinney is measuring my pulse, his hand is firm over my wrist.

"Jane," she says again, and I shift, sigh, and answer lowly.

"I'm awake."

"Don't let her sleep. It'd be a coma, and I don't think I can wake her up after that." The Doctor's voice has changed pitch. There is an acute note of anxiety under the schooled calm. I find I cannot rouse myself to have a reaction to this, as if I am under a spell, unable to feel fear or worry. My entire being is beyond all that is happening as my body contracts.

Widow Hawks sits on the bed next to me while the Doctor continues checking my vital signs. She asks simple questions about my parents, my sister, my education. I answer her softly, breathing carefully. The Doctor peels away the cover, a stethoscope pressed against my bosom. I feel the cold metal of it. The cold seems to seep in everywhere.

"My hands are cold. Freezing," I suddenly say, interrupting Widow Hawks' line of questioning.

"Hypotension, dear God," the Doctor mutters over me, but I am not really looking at him or Widow Hawks anymore. I close my eyes as the numbness fills my fingers, starts to creep up my feet and into my arms and legs.

Heavy blankets are on me, weighty and solid, though there is some warmth that immediately comes from them. It is nearly suffocating, but I cannot seem to say anything to free me. Besides, my teeth are chattering and my limbs are shuddering beyond help. Through it all, the contractions continue, regular, strong and full.

"Jane," Widow Hawks is over me. "Can you hear us?"

"Mm."

"Mrs. Weber, I have to try ergot. It's the proper time for it; I have a little. It's been banned for childbirth otherwise."

"Pat, explain later," Widow Hawks urges.

"I have to say somethin' - I've never used it. I acquired some last time I was on the coast for medicines. They said it was a good hemorrhage drug – good for emergencies. I don't like that I have to try it on her first. She should know."

I hear him rummaging along the sideboard, his words barely registering to me. "They said it should narrow the blood vessels and passages, to stem the flow of bleedin'."

"Do what you must," I say, breathing hard. The shuddering has stopped for the moment, though I am still incredibly cold.

Eventually, I feel the prick of a needle, the cold fluid of medicine flowing in my veins. He is immediately checking my vitals again..

"And?" Widow Hawks is holding my hand tightly. "*Wakantanka tunkasina*, please." There is more silence in the room, and she begs again. "Pat...will it work?"

"I don't know yet," he is tight with her. "I wish we had thought about the tea from the first, if I'd even realized she might bleed out so early on in the pregnancy. Or if I'd the proper tools for that strange intravenous therapy from that doctor from Leith I read about in the *Lancet Gazette*." He is rambling. I cannot focus on each word. "Using saline to resuscitate after hemorrhage. It would have worked, I think. Damn. Damn!"

"She's so pale. Her lips are blue. My poor girl." Hands smooth back my hair, while Doctor Kinney busies himself with my heartbeat again. "It will be alright."

I am tired still, and without another memory, I fall asleep.

I remember my dreams. I hear a man softly crying, but the sobs turn into Henry's death rattle. It takes a moment, even in my dreaming, to remember that he is dead. And then I hear a baby's cry and I think of a soft head, downy with pale blonde hair.

When I wake, it is only briefly. I am finally warm, and I am comfortable. My head pounds with pain, and I am thankful it is still night. Without being able to help myself, I drift back into slumber.

The sun is streaming in when I wake again. My head is worse this time, and I immediately close my eyes, but someone is there. I feel the weight on the bed.

"Are you warm enough, Jane?"

I nod. I am deadly tired.

"Can you eat? You really ought to." Widow Hawks' voice is soothing, hopeful, but I shake my head no, and fall back asleep.

When I wake again, the light is dim. It is either dusk or early morning. This time, I think I can stay awake longer, but find I cannot. The room is quiet, empty, and I do not even bother to raise my head. Slumber comes fitfully again, as if my body is afraid to go back to sleep. Sometime in the night, I hear soft voices.

"There's nothing much we can do but wait, Patrick. She'll wake up and eat soon."

"She needs to. She's gettin' weaker," his voice, even in half-whisper, is rough.

"But the pains, and the bleeding, has mostly stopped," she is reassuring him. "The medicine worked."

"I don't know what else I can do."

"Care for her, as you do any patient. You're a good doctor, Pat. And you've saved her."

"Not yet."

They continue to talk softly, argumentatively, but I drift off, and sleep on and off this night as well.

I wake again to the gentle brush of fingers on my thigh; it is a caress, a trail of touch. As the room swims back into focus, I feel hands lowering my knees, squeezing my ankles as if examining their strength, and I follow the sensations to where a sheet is lowered onto my legs. Doctor Kinney is covering me, his head is bowed. I see there are pale glimmers of early grey in his hair as the light hits it just so. I glance to the window and remember where I am. I am not at Widow Hawks' home, nor back in Massachusetts. I'm at the Doctor's place, in his aunt's old bedroom.

He has not realized I am awake, and continues to sit at my feet, taking a moment to stare at something, I do not know if it is the pattern of the coverlet or the wood planks of the floor. His shoulders are slumped and I see his cheeks are rough with stubble. I have never seen him unshaved. He looks rough and tumble, as if he has not slept well. It comes to me that perhaps it was my miscarriage, my bleeding, that has caused this. That it is me he worries over so thoroughly. An enormous wave of affection washes over me when I think of this, and of him. It is an emotion much stronger than I am used to feeling, and I catch my breath and blink back unbidden tears.

At my intake of air, his head snaps up. His eyes are red rimmed and blood shot. "Janie!"

He uses my front name, as an endearment, as if somewhere during my episode I gave him permission. He rises and comes to me, touches my forehead as if checking for a fever, lingering a few fingers on my jaw. "You're goin' to be alright. Everything is. I've made sure. Now, it's time for rest and recovery."

Before my eyes, he transforms into a doctor, though he is still haggard in appearance. He stands over me, listing off things to watch for; clots, blood color, fatigue and fainting. I do not think I will remember all these things. He is unwavering, professional, clinical. I think perhaps I misjudged the gentle way he just touched me, that it is not especial care, but his bedside manner.

"Paddy."

The voice comes from the door, it is a gentle admonishment in a motherly tone. We both look to Widow Hawks, where she is waiting on the doorjamb, cloths tucked under her arm.

Doctor Kinney stops talking. She gives a small shake of her head. "Let her rest a bit. She will hardly be able to remember all your direction now."

"It's important, Esther."

"I know. But let it be for a moment. Let me help her wash up. She'll be right and downstairs soon enough, now that the worst is over. And I'll stay here until the bleeding is slowed so that she can come home with me."

He gives an angry little shake of his head, too; he does not like the interruption. His words to me are gruff, "Don't overdo it now, then, Mrs. Weber. Just take it easy, even standin' could make you dizzy."

I watch him walk out, stiff backed and silent. I am confused; first he is kind, then upset with me, and I have not even spoken. Widow Hawks - did he just call her Esther? - walks in and sets the clean rags down. The top one is lukewarm and wet, and she starts to wash down my legs and arms and torso. It feels lovely.

Finally I find my voice. It sounds small even to my own ears. "Is he angry?"

She stops her massage and looks me straight on. "Jane. No. He grieves for the loss of your little baby, as if it was his own flesh and blood. And you mean a great deal to him, you know. He finds your help indispensable. He thought he was going to lose you."

I frown at her description of his worries. "I'm sure he could advertise for another housekeeper."

She resumes her washing and gives short tut. "Perhaps so, but what are his chances of finding another he gets along with so well, or who fits in with the town readily?  Regardless, you think him heartless if you do not realize how much he cares about you."

"I know he is not heartless.  He is a good man," I placate, not wishing to delve further into the Doctor's character at this moment. I am too tired.

"He is," she says, and follows my lead, filling the room with her companionable silence.

# CHAPTER 19

I sit in the golden sunlight of the late afternoon. I hear Widow Hawks in the kitchen. She insists on making supper, that I am to stay off my feet and rest. I want to help. All this time in the west has made me prefer less pampering, but I am still bleeding, and I am faint when I stand for too long. I ache for a full bath, but she is worried to put me into the tub without permission. It is too soon, and the warm water could easily start the bleeding hard all over again. There is a rumble of a voice in the house; the Doctor must be back from his rounds.

"Where is she?" I hear him through the open windows. There is more muted chatter, and then he darkens the sunlight, and I look up at him. I do not have on a bonnet, but I do not care, and he stares down at me, unreadable and dark against the sun.

"You're doing alright?"

I shrug. "Just tired."

He crouches next to me, careful, as if I am breakable. "Ye look awful pale. You're still bleedin'?"

I nod, and trace the pattern of the wood on the chair. His hand comes to cover mine to stop my half-hearted picking of the grain. It is as if I am newly awakened. I have long realized he is a tactile man, very much because he is a doctor, but I also know I respond to his touch now, as if my being has become readjusted to my world and emotions surge through me quicker, stronger. I delight in his touch, more so than I recall. Long have I buried parts of my nature as a woman should, but I find I am less inclined to rein them in after the trauma of the past few days.

"Mrs. Weber, I'm so sorry about the child."

"It's not your fault." He is so dear to me and I do not like to think he blames himself. "Really, from what I understand, this is natural."

"No," he shakes his head. "You nearly died. I should not have let it go so far."

We are quiet. I reflect on this. He is right. I know that I was close to death, and that the recovery might be longer than I can comprehend. The thought of what I might have lost - my friendships to him, Widow Hawks, Alice and the others - it makes me weak to think of it. There is so much purpose to my life yet, so much I want to try and see and experience. I know at the time I was fading so I did not understand the loss of my life and what it would mean to me. But I do now.

"I was thinkin'..." he starts quietly, then finishes in a rush. "We need to take care of the wee babe. It's too hot to wait. There is a small Catholic cemetery here. My great aunt Bonnie is buried there, along with a few others, and he could rest next to her. If you don't have a preference, that is."

I glance at him. I know he's Irish Catholic, and I am a non-practicing Episcopalian. The idea of my little son, who I did not meet nor even see, to have company in the afterlife is comforting. It nearly matters more than what earth he sleeps under.

My other hand covers his, grasping it strongly. My chest feels tight, and my head still pounds and aches, but I know that I need to touch someone, and am desperately thankful for his sensitive ways.

"I'd be honored," I whisper, and then we are quiet together, reflecting, perhaps, the easy way of life and death, as the prairie grasses undulate in the hot August heat, spreading out before us like an endless sea.

# CHAPTER 20

Widow Hawks and the Doctor decide I can have a bath, as it has been two days since I woke from my death daze. We are still staying at the Doctor's house; me, because he refuses to let me leave yet, and her, because she refuses to tarnish my reputation. I am grateful for them both, as I am still incredibly weak. Doctor Kinney spends one evening hauling water up the stairs for me. I do not mind that it will be a cooler bath, as the August heat is nearly unbearable today.

Widow Hawks takes me into the washroom, and helps me with my clothes. I am to bathe completely nude to wash away any remaining blood. She is right in this. As I strip, I see I am crusted with blood in places. Dried, pale streaks of it still run down my thighs.

The dark curtain is drawn, but she sits next to me, ever wary of me fainting. Those two seem to have a pact between them, that unless I am sleeping, I am not to be alone. We are quiet but for the sloshing of water along the metal sides of the tub. I look at her, where she sits serenely and brushes down my dress. Below, I hear the Doctor rummaging in his lab, the echoes of his tinkering audible all the way up the stairs.

"Why are you called Esther?" I ask.

She looks up and smiles. "My husband was English, but his father's side was Welsh, and he liked the name. And it was a Bible name. So I was called Esther Davies until his death. And then people started to use my old name, in a way."

"Which do you prefer?"

She shrugs indifferently. "I am all of them, so it is no matter."

I look again at her, at her lined face and gentle eyes, and I reach out a wet hand to touch hers.

"Thank you for being as a mother to me."

She nods, and I press on. "I'm sorry Kate does not treasure you as a daughter should. I wish I could do or say something to change that."

She shakes her head, resigned and yet still content. I do not know how she manages the balance.

"Kate wishes to be seen as something she is not. I am proud of my daughter, and how she has made a strong life for herself. But she refuses to recognize her situation, that her half-native blood is both intimidating and sympathetic to the townsfolk. She's been a success. They see her as one of them as much as their prejudices allow. And she dislikes to have me in town, as a reminder to anyone of her ties to my people. I suppose someday I must leave her, must drop away to let her be. Perhaps then one of the men might marry her, though I do not know if she wants to be married."

"I think Doctor Kinney might," I say softly, and am surprised at how difficult it is for me to say these words aloud, as if saying them makes them true. And why should that matter? He has cared for Kate for many years, and if she is what he wants, he ought to have her. And now at least, I think I understand why Widow Hawks and Percy Davies did not intervene on Kate's behalf in youth. They needed her to grow strong and defiant, half-breed that she was, so that she might survive and even thrive.

Her head comes up at my muse on marriage for Kate, and she gives a rueful smile. I am reminded at how much of a mix she is, both Indian and white, and how beautifully she transitioned between the two worlds for the love of her man. I am again amazed at her strength to do so.

"You must see that my daughter's bitterness runs deep. She has no use for people, really, especially her own family. Do you think that is a good match for him?"

I look down at the water, which is pale and tinted a soft pink with my blood. I think of him touching my legs and my thigh, of his fingers on my face, and I feel a surge of emotion that is unexplained, full and tight. No, Kate is not a good match for Doctor Kinney. I would be saddened to see him tie to her. Both are dear to me, but they might grow unhappy together.

I sense Widow Hawks watching me, and she is, her eyes dark and opaque in the lamplight. Her hand comes to take mine.

"You'd suit him, Jane. More so ever than my daughter, who does not cherish history and is filled with intolerance of her own race. If you'd let yourself, you might find you could love him."

I think it is the unbalance of the miscarriage that makes me so emotional, for her words fill my own eyes with tears, though I do not know why I cry. Is it because she is so kind, or because she speaks a truth long subdued within me? Or is it because I nearly died, and now, newly awakened, I see my world differently, or am I more apt to take a chance? I do not know what it is, only that she has touched on something that makes me weep.

"Oh, Jane." Her arms come up to caress my shoulders and I abandon myself to softly crying as if I were a child and she truly my mother.

There is a step behind the curtain, and my head comes up with hers. It is the Doctor.

"Everythin' alright?" There is genuine worry in his voice. I wonder how he knew I cried, for I was not sobbing loudly. And then I wonder how much sound carries below, where he works in his laboratory.

"Yes, Patrick," Widow Hawks answers for me, for my own voice is still too soaked with tears.

"Okay." I can tell he is still uncertain, and does not leave immediately. "Do ye need more water? How is the bleedin'?"

"It's nearly stopped." She peers into the water and makes a judgment. "I would say she could come home with me tomorrow."

"I--." He pauses. I can imagine him, standing in the greasy glow of light next to the wash bowl. His mind is thinking, his eyes on the floor, his long lips trembling a little as he decides what to say. There is a part of me, newly unbridled, that wishes to see him, touch his mouth, tell him that he is fine to speak out to me, that I will not mind whatever he says. I am overpowered with these feelings, and it does not help that my head continues to pound every moment. Perhaps it is all just that, and nothing more.

"I'd like you to stay on here another few days, if ye can," he finally amends, and I know he is talking to Widow Hawks. "It's just... best if I can keep an eye on things."

I wonder why it matters? He can certainly stop into Widow Hawks' home any time he wishes to check on me, as I am now his patient. I do not like to be an imposition. It occurs to me that he likes a busy house, with things happening, voices chattering. He would have liked to have a child tripping about the floors, regardless of whose it was, or why it was there.

I find my own voice. "Tomorrow is the burial. We can go home afterwards, and I promise to stay abed at Widow Hawks' house for several days before I come back to work. I don't like to outwear my welcome."

He does not rejoin this. Instead, he leaves, and I turn to Widow Hawks, who is looking at me with a sad sort of smile. We finish the bath, and I fall into an easy sleep.

# CHAPTER 21

Kate finds out about my miscarriage. I decide that a small town has no real secrets. I should know this, as I lived in a small town throughout my youth. I know that after the baby's death, Alice spoke of it to her family, and they had no reason to keep quiet. It was apparent many townsfolk knew when several showed up at the burial.

Kate is enough a friend to tell me that there were whispers of the earliest sort, wondering if perhaps my child was the Doctor's. Thankfully, his reputation was sterling enough that the idea didn't take full hold on town imagination, and I had both Kate and Alice to thank for quenching those rumors from the first, else my time in Flats Junction might have come to an immediate, scandalous halt. To lose the friends and life I have built here would have been more crushing than the miscarriage, and I feel indebted to both women beyond measuring.

"So you don't mind that you nearly died in childbed, then?" she asks, as I buy a bit of precious brown sugar to go with the early squashes. As it is midway through September, I am happy that my garden has caught up and I am getting a harvest slowly, but surely. It has been several weeks since I lost the babe, and while I still tire easily, Doctor Kinney will let me do most of the house chores without fuss.

I shake my head. "I don't. There is nothing I could do about it anyway, you know that."

Kate raises her eyes to heaven. "I'm glad I haven't had to worry about it."

"You might, someday," I tell her.

"The men here don't want to marry a half-breed," she says lightly, but there is weight to her words, and it draws me up. Therein lies the crux of her issue with anyone; herself, her mother, Doctor Kinney, the townsfolk. She is so aware of her status as a part-Indian that she cannot see past her own skin. I am silent while I reflect on this. These types of revelations are swift and sudden on me, now, as if nearly dying has made me see people clearer.

I find myself pushing the issue, just to hear her speak on it. "I don't think Doctor Kinney cares much about your heritage. He might embrace it."

"Just what I need!" She gives a hard laugh, then stops, giving me a strange look. "Well, what if he does start to court me earnestly? He has not shown much interest in years, but lately he has been attentive."

I shrug, but I start to wonder if I might repay her kindness about stopping those rumors here and now. "Then that is good, right? You have a beau, and a possible future in marriage. All is not lost."

She is quiet as she wraps up my packages. Her hair is down today; it is one of the first crisp days of the season, and I too am glad I can leave my hair in a braid instead of worrying it up with pins. I watch her long fingered, strong-nailed hands tie string, and then she looks up at me. I cannot tell if the look in her eyes is shrewd or honest.

"Suppose he does want to court and marry me. Should I?"

I do not know if the question is rhetorical, but I find myself answering a bit sternly, as if she should not even consider saying anything but yes to the Doctor. He deserves whatever happiness Kate can bring him, though I now doubt that any happiness would last.

"I think he might, though I cannot speak for him." I think about what she is asking, and finish up decisively. "And if I were in your place, I'd choose him over any man in town."

"What of your own beau?" She is fishing for information about Bern Masson. He is starting to walk me home again, though our words are stilted and careful. Our conversation now reminds me very much of my marriage with Henry. Cautious, sterile, but ordinary, as if passion is not allowed because it is unseemly. I wonder if it has always been so and I have never noticed it, or if my fresh views of the world makes it hard to have trite conversation easily.

"What of him?" I run my finger along a soft pink calico that is new in. It would look lovely on Kate should she wish to make it up for herself, and I say so, but she is not to be distracted.

"He's courting you, isn't he?"

I glance up at her. "Is he? Is that what it's called?"

She shrugs. "You're a widow. You can't expect much more, and you don't have a parlor to sit in on Sunday or a father to ask."

I frown. It paints a cold picture of love and an uninspiring prequel to marriage.

"Well. He hasn't asked me anything formal yet. I'm not to worry, I should think," I say evasively. "What about you?"

"You mean, should Pat ask if he might court me?"

I shake my head, pushing myself to ask the question. I need to know her mind. "No, Kate. Should he ask you to marry him."

She has the grace to blush, and she does it prettily, the high color making her eyes light up. I could not measure to her beauty ever, and I do not expect to, nor ever find the need. Her spirited, fiery personality is captivating. It is why I wish her to be my friend, and why she is tolerated among the townsfolk, even with her native heritage. It is probably why the Doctor has pined for her for so long, even when she has been aloof to him and all the other men.

"I think I might say yes," she says slowly, almost bashfully. "He is handsome, and kind, and I should be accepted even more to the town."

"He would take care of your mother, too," I remind. "Take her the food she needs and manage the house."

Her smile leaves, and she presses her mouth together. It is a sore spot, one that I still cannot completely understand. "He wouldn't need to, I expect," she says. "I am sure once I am married, mother would be able to get on with living elsewhere, go back to her people." The idea is said slowly, thoughtfully, as if she has not realized this before.

"I should think she'd like to stay and see grandchildren," I reason, and Kate's manner turns sour quickly.

"Anything else, Jane?"

I sigh. Her moodiness does not bother me any longer. Since feeling the coldness of death in my arms and legs, I find many things do not bother me quite as much as they used to, so I shake my head and leave.

Walking back to the Doctor's house, I reflect. My pace is slow, and I look at the dusty ground. September is dry on the prairie, though the trees in the distance still are lush and tall and green. What a strange, half-desert area this is. I have actually grown to enjoy it.

Kate does feel something for Doctor Kinney. He ought to pursue her, to have his heart's desire. As I approach the screen door, I think about the idea, and, like so many things these days, I feel emotions well up. I know that I wish to be his instead, but I have spent too many weeks as his sisterly housekeeper to ever ask him to love me differently than he does.

I make a hearty stew with the early fall produce. It is difficult, because I have to pause and wipe my eyes on my apron. Now that I am dwelling on these thoughts, it is hard to push them off. I must repay the Doctor's kindness for the burial of my son and saving my life by giving him his own. But I will not spend my years in Flats Junction, watching two people I care about, both in different ways, marry and live happily. I am maybe stronger than some women, but I am not unemotional, and I have means of my own if I must use them.

My thoughts turn over and I start to think in steps. I will help Doctor Kinney see that he ought to woo Kate. It is not what I would wish for him, or me and I know Widow Hawks does not approve, but it is what he wants. He softens when he talks of her, or with her, and he has no other prospects. And once I see he is earnest in courting her, I will leave. But I need not return home to my elderly parents, worry their minds about my status and my care. There is freedom in being a widow, yet, and I have no child to burden me now.

"Smells divine, Mrs. Weber!"

I have been lost in musings and I do not hear him come in until his voice is right over my shoulder, peering into the pot. I try to give my expected little response, and he leaves to wash up. When we sit for supper, I look at the light from the windows, casting shadows in the kitchen and along his face. I love it here, and want this to be my home. But I am not brash or outspoken, and I will not chase after a man who does not love me, nor need me to stay.

"You're quiet," he states around a mouth of stew.

I look down at my spoon. There is no good time for my words. Without looking at him, I say, "You ought to court Kate, Doctor Kinney."

He is silent, and I have the courage to look up at him. He is staring at me strangely, as if my idea is utterly foreign.

"Haven't you always yearned for her, since staying with the Davies'? I think you should. And I think you'd find her very receptive."

"Mrs. Weber..." He leans back. "You're a mite involved in our personal lives." I cannot tell if he is angry or not. Then he leans forward and searches my face earnestly. "Ye really want me to do this?"

I nod, and look back down at the food. I am not much hungry these days as my feelings for him have slowly built in my chest, tightening it so it is hard to breathe sometimes when I think about his large hands and his booming laugh. He wants me to eat to build up my strength again, so I dutifully try, but tonight I have no appetite at all.

"Hm." He does not say much more, and instead of helping me with the dishes as usual, he goes to his study. I fear I have unsettled or irritated him. Or perhaps, I have given him hope.

We do not say anything the rest of the night, and Bern is at the door for me at the usual hour. We walk into the late sunlight. With fall approaching, the light turns orange earlier, and the shadows grow blacker.

As we near Widow Hawks' door, he turns to me to bid me goodnight and I put out my hand, saying quietly, "You do not need to come round anymore."

He drops his fingers from his hat. His black eyes are in shadow, but his grim mouth tightens. I cannot tell if I have made another man angry tonight. Bern is still a bit of a mystery to me. I do not understand why he has spent weeks courting me, and why he continued after my miscarriage. We do not speak words of affection. And I know I do not love him.

"What are you saying, Jane?"

"I'm saying that I don't think we ought to continue on like this, when I have no intention of marrying you."

I am more confident than I feel, for he is not a laughing man, and I know he will take my rejection to heart more so than he will let on.

"Do you think you'll get a better offer?" He is not rancorous, just curious, as if he wonders how someone else could have started to court me without his knowledge.

"No," I say. That is a truth indeed.

"Then why not make some sort of a life here?" He wonders, and I put my hand on his arm lightly, to stop him from questioning further. It is the first we have touched since the Independence Day celebrations, and it feels odd to put fingers on the worn denim of his shirt.

"Because it would be a sad life, Bern. We would not find much to make our life together interesting, and we would eventually resign ourselves to misery, however we bear it. I have done it once before, and I do not want to do it again."

"How long have you felt this way?" He asks. He is right to ask, and he deserves an answer.

I sigh. "I don't know. I know I've not ever felt deeply for you, though I thought I might, someday. I tried." This is not entirely true. I never actively looked at him other than as a distraction. "But I don't. I am sorry."

He is quiet for a long time, looking at the ground, before he nods. "I thank you for your honesty."

Touching his hat to me one last time, he turns around and walks away, a long black shadow in the setting sun. I think I should feel happy, but I am simply tired and exhausted, and go into Widow Hawks' house, where it is dim and dark.

Dear Aunt Mary,

I deeply apologize to so unexpectedly impose on you, but I find myself in need of introductions in Gloucester. My experiences as a wife include nursemaid and cook, and I have furthered my skills in housekeeping, cooking, and gardening since widowhood. I do not plan to trouble your domestic situation, but will need your expertise in finding a suitable cottage for rent.

I look forward to hearing from you as soon as you are able to reply, and I will be on the first train out after receiving your favorable letter.

Thank you for your help. I am eager to spend time rekindling our relationship as it was when I was a child, visiting you at the seashore.

Until then, I am your loving niece,

Jane

# CHAPTER 22

I bring my laundry, and a bit of Widow Hawks', to the Doctor's for washing day. She has very little I can rinse out, much of her fall wardrobe consists of hides and furs that I do not dare try to clean myself. He has brought up the water in the morning after breakfast, and I spend the better part of the day soaking, beating and wringing out all our clothing, sheets and blankets. I have decided to have Kate send out for some fabric for new sheets. My bleeding ruined an entire set of the Doctors'. The package should arrive soon and I can replenish his linen closet.

The late September breeze is still warm in the afternoon. Everything here is yellow with the light after lunch, and yet the evenings are colder every day. I wait for a letter from my Aunt Mary and stop at the post to check if it has arrived while on my way to Widow Hawks' home each night. The postmaster gives me an appraising no, as if I am awaiting some scandalous news, but so far nothing has arrived.

The Doctor courts Kate most nights. I do not need to make him supper, for he eats with her on the front porch of the general store. Many of the townsfolk stop to say howdy to them, and some evenings, as I walk home, it is like they are setting court, for all the bodies that are drawn to their cozy tableau.

I miss him, desperately. He has breakfast with me and we are companionable, but I admit I try to hold myself apart, so that I am not drawn into his warmth overmuch. He still tries to pull me out, especially at dinner, and sometimes I laugh because I cannot help it. And I am so happy during those moments of the day. I stare at his face, delighting in the slant of his cheeks, the wrinkles around his eyes, and the languid brogue. His words wash over me, and I cannot help but finally be lost in what could be, if the world were different.

I do not admit this to anyone, but seeing the Doctor with Kate hurts my heart, my stomach and my head. It is not for me to choose what matter of a person he marries, or whether a pair will be well suited together in the years to come. It is not my place to speak up any further to my employer. He seems to now have a spring in his step, and he whistles when he leaves to see her at supper. His happiness is beautiful to see, regardless of how I am devastated by it.

Some nights I lay awake and wonder why I survived, why against all odds I lived through my miscarriage, if only to live a life so alone.

I feel Henry's ring twist around one of my soaked skirts. Pulling my hand out of the water, I inspect the band. It is dented with use now, and spins around my finger due to weight I have lost. I slip it off and set it beside me on one of the garden rocks so it doesn't come off in the suds.

Standing at the laundry, a secret part of me imagines that we are all family, living happily together. I pretend my son is alive, and he is not Henry's child, but the Doctor's. And all is well.

There is a shout on the street. I glance up, but do not stop my tasks until I hear yet another cry, and then a woman's scream, and then horses whinny, and I smell it on the breeze.

Smoke.

Wildfire.

Hay-fire.

Something hot and acrid. A fire now on the prairie will raze the town. It is a death knell.

I spin, thinking to carry water to whatever it is, but then I realize I do not know enough to help, so I pick up my skirts and run out, through the backyard, the kitchen, the hallway, and I let the screen door slam behind me as I join the small groups of people sprinting down the streets.

The blaze is high, hot, and fast, and I see men are already trying to contain it by shoveling around the fire so that it cannot jump further, though there are not any homes nearby enough that might catch easily. There is far less damage than I had imagined at first, but it is enough for me to stop in the middle of the street and watch in horror.

Once the men finish saving the rest of the town, they stand back as Widow Hawks' home continues burning. It is this refusal to douse the house with dirt or sand that spurs me into action again, and I begin to run toward the building, toward the bowed head that stands apart from the group.

"Mrs. Weber!" There is a yank on my arm. The Doctor, looking both aghast and furiously frantic. "Stop runnin'! There is nothin' ye can do now. And you are weak enough as it is!"

He holds my upper arm in a tight grip and marches us hurriedly down the street to join Widow Hawks on the outskirts.

"Why is no one helping? Why are they not putting it out?" I ask, appalled and frightened. The fire is lifelike, hungry, angry. The timber of the house, the dried baskets, herbs and hides do not have a chance.

"They do not wish to do so." Her voice is resigned, but not beaten. "And they do not want me here anyway."

"Who did this?" The Doctor has left us, and is pacing in front of several of the men, who stare at him blandly, their faces streaked with soot, sweat and dust. They don't care about the home turning to charcoal remains of a life; they are only satisfied if nothing else catches fire. The heat radiates off of the building, waves of air are visible, wafting around us.

One of the men gives a crass shrug and spit. "Aww, Doc, we know you're soft on the Indians. But now maybe there'll be no need for them to come back to town. No place to stay, as it were."

"That doesn't answer my question, Hank."

He is a fool if he thinks anyone will own up to this assault, this terrible action of anger and intolerance. I know the Doctor thinks he is powerful here in Flats Junction, but in the end, even he is an outsider, and does not share the same quarrel as some folks do with the natives. Even though the settlers of these lands have won the battles and the wars, it is as if they do not feel completely well with

their victory until all of the tribes are gone from their sight. Some of
the men standing about are mere overgrown boys, who could not
possibly have fought in the war, and have no real quarrel with Indians
other than what their parents warned them, and prodded them, to
feel. I know prejudice exists everywhere, but where I come from in
Massachusetts, it is not quite so blatant. It does not include
annihilation.

Already the evening grows darker, and the flames become orange in
the early night. It seems it starts to roar less, slowly, as though time
stretches out and contracts, and before long it is night. Still I stand
next to Widow Hawks as she stares at it all, burning to ruin. There
were other things in that home, memories cherished from the man
she loved for decades; love letters, a bridal veil, gifts and books. All
gone and ash.

Mitch Brinkley arrives, finally, with his father, three brothers and
brother-in-law. Their wagon is full of sandy dirt and they throw it on
the small flames. The fire hisses, dying, until the embers themselves
are buried in blackness.

They swing their lanterns over us. The other cowboys melt away,
assured the town is safe. I cannot think that one of them is
responsible for this, but then, perhaps they watched only to be sure
their own handiwork did not do more damage than they wished.

"Will you be alright?" Mitch asks the Doctor, who nods, taking one
of their spare lights.

"I'll take the women to stay at Kate's for a bit while we sort out the
mess."

Mitch glances over to us, and says casually, "We'll go with you.
There's enough mischief afoot tonight."

The Doctor does not bother to argue. We follow him. I am numb with anger and shock and betrayal. This was hatred, with no purpose other than to cause pain on another. Would the people of this town even care to track down the perpetrators, to bring this to justice for the sake of an Indian woman? If not for her, at the very least for the memory of her husband, or her daughter?

Kate is standing on the porch. She has had a clear view of the flames this entire time, and I know why she has refused to come to her mother's side; it is her selfishness, and her fear.

"Kitty," the Doctor pleads in a low voice. I hear it because I am on the stairs already. Mitch and his family are with the creaking wagons and shifting horses below. "You've got some room. Can ye make up a bed for your mother and Mrs. Weber?"

"Why? There's room with you." Her answer is clipped.

"Because it is your mother and she has suffered tonight. I expect she'd like to see her daughter and you know Mrs. Weber cannot stay with me alone."

Kate gives a shake of her head, her lovely hair cascading in slight waves. Even in the dark, she is lovely and proud and unyielding.

"My mother should take herself to the reservation."

"You know she does not want that. Her home is where you are."

"I'll not take her in," Kate's voice is a whisper, angry and fierce. "I cannot have anyone thinking I am partial to her, that I would put my native birth first."

"That is not the point here, Kitty." His voice is soothing. I cannot see his face in the oil lights from below. "Your mother needs your help."

"I will not help her. You should know better than to ask this of me. She does not help me by staying on, reminding everyone about my native birth. Perhaps she will finally realize that her place is not here. I'm sorry, Pat. I can't do it."

They stand there, as if measuring each other's mettle, and, finally, the Doctor gives in. I wonder if she realizes that she is in danger of changing how he views her, that he will be appalled at her lack of familial duty. But maybe I am mistaken about the man. Maybe family is not so important as he used to think. I have changed much in my months here. Perhaps he has too.

"Kate is too tied up with goods this time to make room," he says in general. "We'll make do at my place for now, and we can decide tomorrow what to do next."

The Brinkleys see us to the house. I light a few lamps, enough for us to go upstairs. It is unspoken, but I plan share the bed with Widow Hawks so she does not need to rest her old bones on the floor. The three of us walk up the stairs in some state of shock, and she goes immediately into old Aunt Bonnie's room. I watch the Doctor come up the stairs with his light, and in the dancing shadows I see that he is downcast. He mourns for his adoptive family, for the loss of Widow Hawks' home, and the evil of some of the cowboys, whoever they may be.

"Doctor Kinney," I say softly, laying a hand on his arm as he moves past to his bedroom. He pauses and glances down at me, but does not meet my eyes. I wish I could touch his face and we could face this tragedy together. Instead, I try to soothe him. "I am sorry you had to quarrel with Kate on our behalf."

He shakes his head. "It should never have been an argument. Good night, Mrs. Weber."

He pulls away from me, and I turn to the other bedroom, where I undress in the light. Widow Hawks is already in the bed, with her back to me. I feel tears in my eyes, and wonder at her staunchness. How can I cry for her loss when she bears it so readily?

I put out the light, climb into bed, and put my arms about her shoulders. She is strong, with a boniness that comes with age. Her hands grasp mine, and the power in the hold speaks to me, and tells me that she is hurting. Eventually, I fall asleep. I do not know if she does.

# CHAPTER 23

In the morning, at first I think it is a dream, that my hair does not really smell like smoke, that I am still simply recovering in the Doctor's house, that time has not pushed forward. But then I hear the rattling of crockery below, and it is not Widow Hawks' gentle hand, but the Doctor's rough and tumble way of making coffee. She is gone from her side of the bed even though the light is watery, pale and early.

I go down to the kitchen, realizing that the clothes I had been washing the night before are still half in the washbin in the yard. The soak probably did them more good than harm, but just the same, I pass out of the house to check. Everything is laying about in a haphazard place, tasks unfinished. I sigh. Now is as good a time as any to wring things out and let them dry. Pulling the washboard toward me, I swirl my hand in the chilly water and gaze at my garden. It has done well this year, and I wish I would be able to stay and cultivate it more in following years. But this will be Kate's realm soon enough. It will be her green patch, and her washbin. It was never really mine to begin with, so it is not really a loss for me.

"Stop." The Doctor is behind me, holding steaming mugs full of coffee. "You know I don't want you hangin' up the heavy things yet."

I sigh, and take one of the cups from him. He does a decent job with the brew, and I sip it slowly, watching the bits of morning haze and fog shift on the grassland around us. He stands next to me, comfortable and at ease while my whole body tenses without my doing. I fear that if I am not on guard around him, I will give in and will grab his hands and kiss his mouth and he will be shocked and repulsed and will no longer wish to spend such moments in friendship together.

"Where did she go?"

"Esther? She went down to the rubble, to see if she can glean anythin' from the ashes. I doubt she will, but there's always a chance."

"What now?"

He gives me a sliding glance. "You mean, what happens to those who did this?"

I nod, and he gives a long, sorry sigh. "I'm not the lawman, and even if I were, it would be hard to get people interested in talkin', even if they knew somethin' about it. She's Indian, pure and simple, and folks don't think our laws apply to them. It doesn't help that memories here are fresh of the wars and many think of natives as shirking the law anyway. It's a huge mess, is what it all is."

I feel my body grow hot with anger. "So nothing will be done?"

He shrugs and looks into his coffee. "I'd like to see something. I'll be making general inquiries when I can, but I know my place here isn't quite so revered as all that. Unless someone outright admits or brags of it in a moment of drunken pride, I doubt we will ever really know who did it. If old Davies was alive, there'd have been hell to pay. If Kitty wanted justice, some would probably listen."

"Then she must! For her mother's sake! You ought to talk to her about this. You're her beau-" the word trips from my mouth, and hangs between us. We have not discussed their relationship since the evening I forced the issue, even though it is obvious what has happened.

He gives a bemused smile as he looks down at me. "Speakin' of beaus, I noticed ye walk home alone when you go by the general."

He's trying to be lighthearted, to reflect attention from his personal life, and I suppose he is in the right. As my employer, he does not need to answer to me about Kate. I gulp down the rest of the coffee, nearly scalding my throat. Bern has not come by in several weeks now.

"Yes. I--that is to say, Bern and I decided it was not necessary to continue on."

"Why? Are ye not interested in settlin' down? You're young yet, and could still even have children. I have made sure of that."

"I know, and I thank you for it," I say, and I smile up at him. "But no, I do not wish to settle down. I've been married once before, and it was not... easy. Henry and I had a simple marriage, expected and with purpose, but I could not tie myself down like that again."

"I can understand that," he agrees, though I do not think he truly could, and finishes his coffee, too, while insisting on helping hang the heavier clothing before he goes on his rounds.

After he leaves, I stand in the quiet, and a winking next to me in the sun reminds me of my wedding band, which is still on the garden rock. I bend to pick it up, inspecting it. It seems a shame to give it up, for it is a stout piece of jewelry and could be pawned if I ever fell into penury. Putting it in my pocket, I turn back to my chores.

# CHAPTER 24

She comes back, soot stained and weary. In her hands is a small cherry wood box that is streaked black, a corner so charred it breaks away as she opens it.

"My wedding band, a hawk's feather, and the pearl buttons from the first pair - only pair - of gloves I ever owned," she says softly. "I would have taken the photo of Percy over any of this."

The box lays on the table between us at the Doctor's house, forlorn, half empty, a strange collection of sentimental items that survived the flames by chance of being buried under the iron stove, which is blackened and choked and twisted beyond use, but the only thing still standing. She is as emotional as I have ever seen her, more affected by her loss now than while it was happening in front of us.

"What will you do now?"

She sighs and sits, leaving the box open, and picks up the feather. "I know my daughter would have me go to the reservation, west and north of here, by the Grand." She pauses, and looks at me serenely; I do not know how she buries emotion so well. Even I, before I became more attuned to my inner feelings, could not be as stoic as her in all this. "I think I will stay here for a time, help you and the Doctor."

I look down at the well worn grooves of the planks. Everything in this house is mine, I know the creases that collect the most dirt, the drafts around the doors, the stairs that squeak particularly loud. I know where the Doctor keeps all his files, and how to find a case at the moment it is needed for reflection. But I will not stay. Even now, he does not come home for supper, choosing instead to dine with Kate even though they had a fight last night. I cannot bear these lonely nights, and refuse to watch while he leaves his bachelorhood. Besides, what will become of me when he marries? He will not need a housekeeper.

Widow Hawks is watching me; I wonder how much conflict shows on my face. Slowly, she reaches across the boards and grasps my fingers.

"I do not mind the loss of my house, Jane. Do not weep for me. The memories most dear are still in my mind, and that is all that matters."

I nod silently, then turn to the stove to make us a light supper, mostly of squash from the garden. We eat in silence; something that is usual for us when we're together now. My appetite is still diminished, and for the first time, she notices acutely.

"What troubles you? Do you not feel well?"

Pressing my lips together, I stare down at the simple meal, and put my fork down. I push my fingers into my eyes, willing them to keep from crying, but it is no use. I am much too passionate. My miscarriage seems to have let loose torrents of feeling, and I do not have the language to explain it.

"Jane!" She stands and comes around to the bench I'm sitting at, and her hands cover mine, pulling them away from my face so that I have to look at her. "What is it?"

I sigh inwardly, then realize the truth is better than anything else I can say. "I will be leaving you, and I will miss you."

"What?" Her shock is genuine, perhaps even more so than when her house was on fire. "When will you go?"

"As soon as my aunt writes of a situation that will suffice. I expect her letter any day, and then I will take the next train out."

"But why?"

I give her a small smile. "It is as you said. I suit the Doctor and I should love him. And I do."

Her eyes immediately grow warm, but she seems to innately understand my dilemma. As a mother would, she draws me near, embracing me lightly, whispering to my hair, "You soft girl. I'm so sorry."

I try not to weep on her, because she has lost so much so recently herself, but I cannot help it. My tears turn to sobs, and I cry for the future I have lost, the chances I wasted, and the words I'll never be able to say. Even with her arms around me, I feel empty and alone, as if crying forever would not make things right for either of us.

# CHAPTER 25

The sun is golden today, as it sets in the west. The long grasses of the prairie are gold as well, and soft pale ivory and brushed copper. The colors are vibrant here, in the tiny cemetery at the western edge of Flats Junction. Grasses grow thick along every small stone and marker, except the clay and sand filled mound, freshly finished a few months ago now for my little son.

I kneel next to his small cross, and I absently pull renegade weeds from his grave. No one will think to come here when I leave, and he will turn to dust without prayers over him. There is some comfort that his bones will not be lonely, as I have been, and at least he rests near a Kinney.

"My dearest boy," I whisper, as the wind catches my voice and pulls it away from me. "I'm sorry I never was able to hold you properly, and that you left my body early so you could not even breathe one breath of air. You would have loved it here."

I brush the dirt in swirls with a finger, and feel tears pressing against my eyes, but thankfully, for once, they do not fall. I'm quiet for a while. I hear a dog bark in the town and a wagon creaks by, But no one hails m. Perhaps it is an unwritten courtesy that you do not call out to someone mourning at a grave. The wind stops and slows for a bit, and in the silence of the grasses, I say, "And I love you, my little one, though I never met you, and though I know I could not have given you everything you deserved. Your father and I did not love each other, but we would have taken care of you so diligently, had you each lived. I'm sorry I must leave you. Please forgive me."

"Where are you goin'?"

I nearly jump out of my skin with surprise. The graveyard, even in daylight, is a bit disconcerting. It is the Doctor, probably on his way to Kate's beyond for supper, and he is standing nearby, arms crossed, his broad mouth half trembling with words, and the light shines into his face so that his eyes are truly blue and pure. I do not have the energy to stand and tell him my news, and I glance at the letter folded in my hands. I've just gotten notice, and I will leave when the train comes back through in two days.

"My Aunt Mary has found me work. I'll be gone on Wednesday to make sure I have time to set up a cottage before I start cooking for one of the great houses in Ipswich."

He drops his arms, nearly gaping at me.

"And why would your Aunt Mary write you about a job when you've got a good one here?" He is indignant in his surprise. I can see he is nearly angry. I sigh, clear my dress and slowly stand, careful so that I am not too dizzy when I do.

"Because I need to have a purpose, Doctor Kinney. And I know that once you decide to stop courting Kate and marry her instead, I won't have a thing to do here. There will be no reason to stay. I need to make my own life."

218

"Aye, but there's no reason it can't be here. I've a practice here that could use help." His voice is low and his gaze is locked with mine.

"I'm easy to replace. I think you might find an avid helper in Widow Hawks. She is capable, she helped you save my life. She has nowhere to live. It works out right proper." The ill-put English slang slips out as I try to fend off my unease. This is not how I had planned to tell the Doctor of my departure.

"If ye are doin' this because you don't wish to impose on my charity, I have no issue with you both stayin' on with me."

"Doctor Kinney," I shake my head at him. "You know that it is an impractical arrangement and eventually the townsfolk won't like it. And you know it will not work once you are married."

He gives me a hard stare. "You seem so sure I'll marry."

"Won't you?"

I brush past him, heading back to his house, irritated I have nowhere to retreat from the argument. He follows me though Kate's store is in the opposite direction.

"So where will ye go?"

"My aunt has found me a cottage to let in Gloucester. I'll be on the seashore again." The idea gives me some hope. Surely only good can come of living by the ocean once more. It will be homey and I will be able to start over with the introductions my Aunt Mary has found. Perhaps eventually I will forget the Doctor, and will find a beau.

"Gloucester. Jesus," I hear him swear lightly under his breath. We stand outside his door. I know Widow Hawks is napping upstairs as she has done now for the past few days, and I think the slamming of the screen door will wake her unnecessarily, so I am determined to see him off. He stares at me, as if deciding if an argument now is worth his breath.

"Well, Mrs. Weber," he says. "I did not expect this of you, though I cannot find fault in your reasons even if I think them premature."

"Then I'll get to packing tonight, so I might say some goodbyes tomorrow."

He does not meet my eyes, and he walks away, back down the small yard into the street and toward Kate's welcoming porch. The evening chill descends quickly as the sun continues to set, but I do not go in and pack. I watch him walk away from me, his lightly striped shirt sometimes grey in shadow, and other times washed a brilliant white in the late sun streaks. I hope I will have a memory of him always, regardless of what my future is.

# CHAPTER 26

"But you could cook out here," Alice Brinkley urges me to reconsider my move back east. "I'm sure that Sadie Faucett would love to be the only one in town with a cook."

"No," I shake my head, though I smile at her earnestness. She is soft again, and I wonder if she is already pregnant, even with young Pete only a handful of months old. It would be the way of it, and I know she and Mitch do not waste time talking when they are alone. To have so much young love all pent up, and a way to spend it! What a life that must be!

"Well, I still don't see why you should rush off when it's not even settled between the Doc and Kate. Their courting could go on another year or more."

"That would still mean I'd have to look elsewhere to make a way. There is an opportunity now. You understand, Alice? I don't wish to be redundant."

She sighs and presses a small wrapped cheese my way for the journey. At least this time I will not be with child on the train.

We give a teary good-bye to each other, and we promise to write. I will miss her cheery ways, even though I did not get to see her as often as I would have liked.

As I walk back, I look at Flats Junction, spread out in dun colored sunlight. Half of the homes are familiar to me. I know the families and children who live in them. The other half I know only by sight. Everyone has been kind, welcoming or at the very least, cordial to me. It is obvious that without trying hard I have found a little place for myself, and at one time could see setting up a home of my own, where I might look after myself and the Doctor as would be fitting. The edges of Flats Junction meet prairie suddenly, and the dusty land shows small holes filled with the little dogs, but the lushness of the tall trees on the horizon keeps one from feeling too desolate. It's cozy. And I think that it is a very lovely town. I know my nostalgia comes with my leaving it. Truthfully I am still appalled that no one searches out the arsonist who burned Widow Hawks' home. It is probably the best that I go.

Kate is out on the porch. It is not quite October yet, and the night is still warm enough that she and Doctor Kinney can court in the open air. She is setting the table. I find solace in the idea that he will be well looked after.

Every time I think of leaving him, pain runs through my chest and stomach. Could I tell him I loved him even if pressed? I doubt it. The rejection he would give me would be even worse than the relief of honesty on my part.

"Kate," I say, as I stand at the bottom of her stairs, just like I did the first morning I arrived in Flats Junction. She gazes down at me, but her eyes are not shrewd this time. She seems in a good mood, and comes down to where I am, taking my hand in hers.

"I'll miss you," She gives a small laugh. "Who will help me run all the festivals in town now?"

"I should think that you'll manage splendidly," I say. I cannot bring myself to speak out more, that she will eventually have Doctor Kinney at her side always to help with whatever projects she undertakes. He is a good man and will stand by her, proud and happy, regardless of her mercurial swings.

"Well," she gives a shake of her head. "I'll make sure the Doc is fed and cleaned up."

"I know you will."

She smiles at me, and I do not see tears of sadness at my departure. She is genuinely happy to see me leave, as if once I go, she can more fully take a place in Doctor Kinney's home. I'm not stupid. I do not need to fight a losing battle, but there is a part of me that is disappointed. For several months now, I have thought of her has a friend. One with whom I do not always agree, and sometimes her behavior appalls me, but a friend, regardless. I see now she has never really thought so much about me.

"Mrs. Weber!" The Doctor comes behind Kate and interrupts us, so that Kate backs away from me. I see his hand come up and touch her shoulder. They glance at each other in a comfortable, familiar, way, and she starts up the stairs.

"Supper is nearly ready."

"Cornbread tonight?" He asks hopefully, and she gives him an exasperated look.

"You know I don't do any of that type of cooking, Pat. It'll be a stew."

I look at her and realize that she will never give him the type of food Widow Hawks makes, that I would have learned from her for him, so that he might have foods he likes sometimes. But that is his choice. He should know that his sweetheart has no intention of ever doing anything remotely Indian with her life. And it is not my place to say anything.

"I was just giving my goodbye." I nod at him, indicating he can follow Kate, take a seat on the porch and wait for her to bring out the meal. For all that she scoffed at domesticity when I miscarried, she's fallen easily enough into the patterns of it.

He looks down at me and does not smile. "You really mean to leave tomorrow, just like that?"

"I must," I say quietly. "And I will miss you, Doctor Kinney." It is all I can say and then I leave him, and walk back through town. The postmaster comes out to bid me goodbye, and so does Sadie. I have made a few very kind friends in my time here, and I am an object of sympathy since my miscarriage. No one knows how lonely I really am, how much I hate to leave them all, how much I mourn the loss of the richness our friendships could have bourn out.

Without caring, I let the screen door slam behind me. There are no smells from the kitchen. Widow Hawks is not inside. I can only imagine she is back at the burn pile of her house, or outside in the backyard tending the garden a bit. It is my last night in this place and I find myself wandering the rooms. They are quiet, silent, as if waiting for their next adventure, the next womanly hands to touch them. The faucet in the lab is shining, the floors are swept and scrubbed. Upstairs, my small bag is packed, the clothing is carefully folded up. I do not expect to need the split skirt in Gloucester, but I will take it nevertheless. I'd asked the Doc about repaying him for the clothing and he'd brushed it off, angrier than ever, and I did not dare offer the idea again.

I wander into the Doctor's bedroom. It is not so sacred a place to me now. I have washed the man's clothes, cleaned his bedding, scrubbed the floors and window. His parents half-smile serenely down from the portrait on the wall. I stare at them, and I know now I like the look of his mother's eyes, because they remind me of him.

"I love him," I tell her softly. "I hope that he is truly happy, perhaps even more than I could have made him." My voice falls into silence again, and I go to bed early, so I might wake in time for my train.

# CHAPTER 27

In the morning, I do not bother to make coffee or tea. Widow Hawks will do so. We did not speak much last night, but said our goodbyes simply. She pressed her forehead to mine, promised to write a bit, and held me tightly as we slept in the small bed together. I've grown used to her next to me in the sheets, a surrogate mother. I am a daughter to her, now, closer to her than I have ever been to my own parents.

As I dress, she wakes and watches me. We do not speak. Now it is not a silence that makes me uncertain or uncomfortable as it did those first few weeks together. Now it is because nothing needs to be said. It is a native trait I've learned from her without meaning to do so. I enjoy the full quietness it gives us.

"I will write," I tell her again. "And I will miss you so much."

She smiles at me, accepting of this as well, as is her nature. I pick up my bag and walk down the stairs, trying to keep my shoes from making too much noise as I do not wish to bother Doctor Kinney so early.

The town is quiet, unearthly so, though I know it will pick up as soon as the train comes in. No one can really sleep through the whistle of the steam and the bellow of the tracks. Even now, I can hear it making its way through the prairie though it is not quite in sight. The platform is empty. I am the only person making a journey, though I hear wagons creaking through the streets. Some farmers are bringing fall produce to be sent down the rails and sold at the bigger towns along the way.

There is a hoot and a whistle and a rush, and the black engine comes around the bend of the green hills, heading easterly. I cannot believe how recently I came here, and how quickly I now leave Flats Junction. Now that I am on the brink of the next journey, the time here seems both longer and shorter than the reality. So much has happened. I have learned depths of my strength, of my abilities and my tolerance. I am wiser, worldlier.

The train screeches as it slows, and then comes to a full halt, waking most of the town with this last bone crunching sound. There are shouts of men beside the platform and a general scurrying. I take a step toward the passenger car, and I hear the brogue shout through the noise.

"Mrs. Weber!"

I turn and watch him hurry toward me. He does not have his hat even, so he must have sprinted out without pause. I can see he barely has adjusted his clothes; the train's sound must have woken him moments ago. There is a moment of foolish, ridiculous hope that rises in me, that he has come to stop me, to keep me here. But I know I could not do this, even if he asked. I could not watch him court Kate and marry her. I must move forward.

"Mrs. Weber." He comes in front of me, gazing down with something between devastation and hurt across his face. "Did ye mean to leave without sayin' good-bye?"

"I didn't want to wake you, Doctor Kinney."

He runs an agitated hand through his hair, still tousled from sleep. "Are you sure you're well enough to travel? No more dizzy spells?"

"I can manage it," I say placidly. "I did before."

"I know it," he puts stoutly, then stops fidgeting altogether and looks hard at me. I am too distraught to really look at him, and I feel him inch toward me, as if he wants to give me a hearty embrace good bye, but there are too many people on the platform and below it, and such warmth would be unseemly in so public a place.

"Well, then," I say. "I have told Esther I will write. You might learn of my adventures through her if you like."

"Mrs. Weber." He says my name again, then stops and says, so softly, that I can barely hear it over the steam and shuffle around us. "Jane."

My head comes up and I wish I could kiss him, but I do not bother to try. I nod, and turn my face to look at the train.

"Janie." There is nearly a plead in his voice, as if he does not really want me to go, but will not beg, or ask me to stay when there is nothing to offer.

The whistle blows. It is my signal to leave Flats Junction.

"I will think of you, Doctor Kinney," I say, and I smile at him tightly for my smile is not very sincere. "I wish you very much happiness out here." This I mean truthfully. "Thank you--for saving me, for giving me work when I needed it. Thank you."

I turn away, going into the train and finding a seat among the many empty ones. I go to the opposite side of the car so that I do not need to watch the platform. I like to imagine that I can think about him standing there watching the train leave, when in all actuality he probably walked away as soon as I boarded. This way, I will never know.

# GLOUCESTER

## 1882

# CHAPTER 28

I like the little cottage I live in, and my employers, though exacting, are kind. Time here in Massachusetts seems to slip by a little quicker now, and I eagerly wait for spring when the beaches will warm, the ice floes will melt, and I can walk the sandy stretches and listen to the waves.

My Aunt Mary, while elderly, is thrilled to have family in Gloucester now. I know all her friends, and have met some of their granddaughters. Rose Albin, a lovely girl, several years my junior, is not yet married and so we make time for tea once a week.

The Chesters, who own the large home I work in, are patient with me. Though I have cooked in their large, shiny, tiled kitchen for six months now, I am still perfecting some of the fancier dishes. They are newly minted in their money, having inherited the estate from Mrs. Chester's father, and are desperate to make a go of it properly, hiring a kitchen girl to help me with the cleaning and a small group of maids. I am glad when they eventually hire an older woman as a housekeeper; I should not like to be in charge of such a large place, or a staff. I have enough on my hands, now that spring is coming, as

Mrs. Chester also wants to start having formal teas and pretty luncheons.

I go to the larder. It is always packed with things I consider delicacies; candied gingers, unusual spices, fruits and jellies. When I was married to Henry, sometimes I would purchase such pastries, but it was rare as we were not overtly wealthy. And my time in the territories made me all the more used to a rougher way of eating.

But now I enjoy making unique dishes with the specialty ingredients. Monday is the first tea, and while I will have off on Sunday as I do every week, I want to make sure I am prepared.

As I reach through the bags of tea, cones of sugar and sacks of flour and pull what I need for a pastry, my hand knocks the coffee and the bag splits open, enough for the smell of the beans to waft through and I pause. It smells so very much like the brew I would make for Doctor Kinney each morning.

Tears come without warning sometimes, and this is one of those times. I stand there, holding the coffee, and my shoulders tremble as I close my eyes and try to hold in my longing. I don't speak of him to anyone - my aunt, my new friends, and my acquaintances at the Chester house - as if by staying silent, he will disappear eventually from my memory except during soft faded moments in summer gloaming, and then I will be able to think of him fondly, without missing him quite so much.

"Mrs. Weber?" It is Beth, the kitchen girl. "Are you alright?"

I straighten, but am not able to turn around yet. "Yes, yes. Just planning out Monday's tea."

She leaves me be and I go ahead with organizing the menu again.

I'm grateful I need only be in the great house from five in the morning to ten at night. From what I hear, many women are stuck in the kitchen for even longer hours or even live with the staff. My employers pay me well, considering my shortened time, so that I am able to afford a tiny place on the beach in Gloucester. It is small, one large room that contains the kitchen and sitting space, all of which has a window overlooking the ocean, and a porch along the front. There is a washroom that leads into a bedroom. The renters before were a married pair and the bed is enough for two, so I sleep in the middle. Some nights, early on, I would wake, thinking Widow Hawks slept next to me, but those dreams have since stopped.

After lunch is served and then cleaned, I go to the market. The stalls are always open, come rain, shine or snow. Tonight I will be making a vegetable puree and potato soup to go with the meat, and I need turnips and parsnips.

I walk the stalls. It did not take long for me to meet most of the keepers. Some are elderly sisters who know my Aunt Mary and who I am to her, and they offer me their chickens and eggs for a good price. The butcher is a round happy man who reminds me of my father, if he were larger, too. The dairyman has a son who is widowed like me, and while I have not talked to him much, I recognize in him a pain that I never felt with the death of Henry. He truly loved his wife. Perhaps I would be as distraught had I married Doctor Kinney, and he had died instead.

Ada Baker is waiting for me with the vegetables. She and her daughter Jean have the best produce and do a roaring trade every week.

"Will we see you tomorrow?" she asks warmly. Sometimes Aunt Mary and I sit with them at church, and then Jean and Rose might both come to my house for tea in the afternoon. It is strange to hold with genteel traditions, such as a sermon every Sunday, when for so long I did not even look at a Bible. I think of my time in the Dakota Territory as long, even though it was less than half a year. The life I had out there seemed so much more colorful, richer, than what I have here, though I do love the winds off the ocean, the salt in the air, the crying of gulls midday, and the cool colors of the houses, the sky and the salt marshes.

"Of course," I say, and take the turnips into my basket. Jean comes around the corner with the parsnips and smiles at me. The ladies in these towns are usually so cold to outsiders, but Aunt Mary paved the way long before me. She hinted at my miscarriage as if it was a strange illness, and I think some of the women assume I still miss my husband. So I am a bit of an enigma here, and because Aunt Mary is an institution in herself in the small town, I am accepted more naturally than if I came in a complete stranger.

"We've got in the first spring asparagus," Jean announces. "I'll bring a bit for tea tomorrow, then."

"Thank you," I murmur, and move on to the dairy stall for cream. Mr. Chester, while not large, is tall and likes his food full of flavor. I think a bit of cream in the puree might be an unlooked for treat tonight for my kind employer, and I wish to please him as well as his wife.

"Mrs. Weber," I get a nod from the dairyman as he reaches under his stall, where an icebox keeps things chilled, even though it is not very warm outside yet. Andrew, the son, comes around the corner hauling a large cheese. He sets it down carefully, and gives his head a shake to the little hands reaching up from below to pick at a curd that fell off. His wife left him a son and daughter to care for; the daughter is at school, but the little boy is still at home with the men and his grandmother.

"On the house tab, as usual?"

I nod, give a small smile to Andrew, and head back up the road to the house. The roads are winding, twisted, cobbled in places, though a few are still mostly dirt and mud. Everything leads away from the wharves, where the dark water is home to fishing boats. So I go up the hill, with the ocean to my back and the wind in my face. Everything here feels heavier, older, wetter. I am not sure which I like more, the coolness of here or the new dustiness of the territories. Nostalgia, for one, always hits when I am away from it.

Beth, my kitchen girl, is waiting for me at the trestle table. She has heated the stove for supper and set water to boil. She learns quickly, and I am pleased with her. I will have to say so to the Chesters when I next get a chance. My new tendency to daydream is always cut short when I enter the kitchens. Always so much to do, so many things to attend. It is a good busy life.

"Mrs. Weber, I was hoping I might help with the tea on Monday," she asks breathlessly. I see her eyeing up the jam I have put out. I give a laugh.

"You can taste it when it's all set. If there is enough pastry, we can make petites for all the staff to try. I don't think Mrs. Chester will mind."

She comes over and helps me unload the basket and starts to clean the turnips. I pull out the mill to grind the puree once the vegetables are soft. It is a luxurious kitchen, to be sure, with plenty of space, many surfaces, and the stocked larder, but I miss the simplicity of the Doctor's. I am sure it is, once again, just nostalgia.

"Mrs. Weber?" Beth breaks into my thoughts. "Where did you learn to cook?"

"I'm mainly self taught," I say, concentrating on putting the mill together. "I cooked for my husband, and then for a Doctor in the Dakotas, and now here. Time helps us all learn."

"I'd like to be a fine cook like you, someday," she says, wistfully.

"We'll make sure you leave with an education," I tell her, and find myself warm at the idea. I could find purpose in that, teaching a young orphan a skill so she might always find work. It is not unlike having a daughter for a few hours in a kitchen, teaching her how to make her way as a wife. I smile fully at her. "You will be making the main dishes in no time, then."

"Really?" Her soft violet eyes sparkle with excitement. "I mean, I've only just started a few weeks ago, but you think I might do so well?"

"Anyone with two hands and a mind for reading directions can cook. It is a bit of an art, but not a difficult one."

She is so happy with this idea, she falls to the vegetables with renewed care. I smile at her young, narrow back. Yes, I will find a life here. It is possible.

# CHAPTER 29

Aunt Mary sings off-key, but she does it with gusto. I look down at her. She is tiny, like a delicate bird, and she wears overlarge pearls in her ears, her one glory from my uncle, long since passed. The wide brimmed hat trembles with her warbling, and she has her eyes nearly closed, as if singing is an utter delight. I envy her abandon, her freedom in her age. Like me, she has no children, so my appearance in Gloucester gives her new life and vigor, and she is blooming again with activities and notions.

My mother was disappointed, but understood my plain reasons for refusing to come home. I did not wish to return to Rockport and live under a roof where I was a dependent again, and while I would have found purpose in managing their needs, Mother always did understand my nature and could easily sway my father in line. She might have liked the constant care I could give them as they aged, but I could not return to my past. It would have been too easy and too suffocating. My sister thinks I am rash, and also stupid for remaining unmarried. She does not have my interest in living fully. But Aunt Mary likes the simple method of life, the undulating of the sea, the quaintness of the village affairs, and she understands me well, so well that I have only fond memories of her during my youth. She does not pry into my past much, and seems to surmise enough on her own with my sparse responses.

The tune finishes, and we all file out of church. Ada and Jean Baker slide out before us, chatting happily with Mr. Baker and Jean's beau, Clark. Rose is on the arm of her betrothed, their heads bent, still planning a wedding that has been the talk of the town for months. Her grandmother, a close friend of Aunt Mary, is not helping matters by continuously adding new ideas and frills to the day.

My eyes pass over the crowds. These are good people and they are more welcoming than I was expecting. It has been a relatively easy six months, now I think on it. I am lucky. And if I do not think about Doctor Kinney, I am that much better off.

As I nod and follow my aunt, I catch the dairyman's son watching me. He has his young boy on his hip and the girl in his grasp, and he is staring, as if measuring me. I have not spoken to him much, as his father runs the business ably yet, and I never met his young wife before she died, but he seems a gentle man. As he catches my eye he gives a grave nod of his head, acknowledging that I caught him, and follows his parents out of the church.

I frown. I do not think I want attention from any man just yet, though I realize it is my only chance to move ahead, and perhaps have a baby of my own. Else I will dwell on my dusty past forever.

# CHAPTER 30

At my little cottage, I prepare the tea for Rose and Jean, who arrive soon after church, flushed with spring chill and giggling over their menfolk. They are pretty things. Rose is slim and tall, and Jean is robust, and also quite tall, and they make merry friends. I will be sad when they are each married and unable to come around quite so easily.

"Come in, come in!" I open the door wide, and they walk into the kitchen, where the window gives a beautiful, wide view of the water. "You know where to put the wraps."

They trip in and out of the bedroom and then help me with the tea, chattering away as if they do not need to breathe. I enjoy their talking; it is refreshing to have it wash over me so that I do not need to think. It is my Sunday evenings, alone and quiet, that are the hardest to fill.

"Did you see Andrew Angus making eyes at you?"

I do not realize Jean is talking to me until they are both quiet, and I look up from my cup, surprised. I did not think anyone noticed.

"I don't think it was quite like that," I amend, carefully.

"He has kept his head down with his children for nearly a year now. I'm glad you caught his attention. He needs a nice woman to make him happy again."

"Does he? I thought he was still pining for his wife."

"Oh, Janie, you ought to consider it!" Rose puts in. The two of them are love matches, so they think everyone is as well, that love comes naturally.

"I do not think I am cut out to be a wife again," I say, and offer the biscuits in hopes of making a change in the subject. Jean takes one and bites off a corner.

"You'd be grand at it, and you know it. Are you really happy being a cook at the Chester house? That's what you want?"

"I don't think it is really about what I want, but what is. This is my life, and I'll find happiness. I've found you two."

Rose humphs. "I still say you should at least consider him. I've known him all my life and he's a very dear soul."

My silence prompts them to tackle the latest of Rose's wedding decisions. They know me enough that I won't speak if I don't wish to divulge any further. I've finally been able to master my easy emotions by not talking much to anyone, especially on topics like these.

# CHAPTER 31

Andrew Angus, the dairyman's son, asks Aunt Mary if he might court me formally a month later. I do not see why, and I ask him so bluntly at our first uncomfortable sitting in her parlor Sunday afternoon. Aunt Mary, as my chaperone in Gloucester, is home with us. As we are both widowed, she does not see the need to actually sit in the same room and graciously excuses herself at my bald question to sit as a shadow in the adjoining room.

He has the grace to flush a bit, the high color making his blond hair turn almost pink, the dusting of freckles disappearing for an instant. He leans forward, the starch in his shirt crinkling.

"I suppose because I realize there is no other way to really get to know you, Mrs. Weber. And whether or not we decide to marry, I'd rather see for myself first if we'd be a good match and go from there."

His honest answer makes me smile. It is much like how Doctor Kinney would respond, and a tiny seed of wonder wells in me. Perhaps I am not destined to be alone after all, though it is too soon to hopefully speculate.

# CHAPTER 32

I learn his children's names: Anna and David. Suddenly I have two surrogate daughters; Beth in the kitchen, who has a knack for bread like I do, and Anna, who shadows me whenever she can. I like that I can mould her a bit, that she is eager to please. School is out in May and she comes with me several mornings of each week to sit in the kitchen at the Chester's, learn some basic cooking, and watch. It is a gift to Andrew, who otherwise has his hands full helping his father run the dairy farm and the market, and keeping an eye on little Dave.

As I drop her off at the stall one afternoon, she scampers off to help her grandmother in the back with the cheese wrappings, Andrew brings me my order instead of his father. I am surprised he jumps ahead to speak to me.

"I must thank you for your time with Anna," he says, handing me the milk and eggs. "She speaks about you often every night, and what you show her and tell her about the world, even beyond the kitchen."

"She is a good girl," I smile. I still hold my words tightly to my chest, even though I do not think Andrew would judge me for the love I hold for Doctor Kinney. In fact, I think he would understand it completely. It is one of the reasons I am slowly taking a shine to the man.

"She is a good girl, and much like her mother." Even after so many months, Andrew still gets a bit emotional when he speaks of his wife. I know he stops by her grave every Sunday before church. I've seen him there, head bowed and his children close.

"I wish I could have met her."

He actually shrugs at this. "Yes, you would have liked her well enough, I suppose."

I look at him, and wonder if the hold his wife has over his memory is finally waning. It would be a step toward building a life with me, anyway, if he can be so stoic about a mention of her.

"Well, anyway, she has a lovely little daughter," I say, and put the rest of the cold goods in my basket.

"Perhaps you might still have a daughter," he says, and I stop short. He plunges on, and does not even blush at his romancing. "I think you'd make a very good mother, anyway."

Now I am blushing, so I move away before his father comes back out and sees us standing there, like two young ones falling in the first flushes of love.

# CHAPTER 33

My mother gives me a smile across the tray and cups, she is glad for my visit. I try to spend a Sunday afternoon here and there with my parents in Rockport. It is not so far a distance from Gloucester so I might accomplish it and stay for tea before going back to my cottage.

"So your Aunt is still well?" She asks me. It is a routine question. Aunt Mary is one of Father's relations, and Mother is always careful to be proper and ask about her. Father himself would care to hear, though he has continued to busy himself in his study this Sunday instead of joining us. It is no matter. I love my parents, but my father has forever been a kind, distant presence in my life, so I am glad to have the more intimate time today with Mother alone.

"She is, of course. I don't think she'll ever change," I say, and take the offered cup.

My mother pours herself the brew and daintily adds a small sliver of sugar and drop of milk. She has the prettiest manners, and both my sister and I have always tried to emulate her as we grew older and entered society. She led by example rather than harsh forcefulness, which was a good practice for willful young daughters.

"And how is Sissy?" I return the question, asking about my sister, who is typically engaged in any number of societal outings in Boston.

Mother sighs, but not unhappily. "She is busy, of course. I'm sure she would love to see you sometime, now that you're back in the States."

"Perhaps at Christmas," I reason, hoping to delay visiting her. My sister and I were never very close. As we became older, I realized we didn't quarrel as often, but we also had little in common. She and I view life very differently. It is also another trait of my mother's to see this, and to understand and nurture it accordingly. It is why I never was pushed to marry young, why I was allowed to chose my own beau and husband carefully, and at my own leisure. But my sister was always on the hunt, for beauty and men and social standing, so my mother dutifully supported that as well. It is the type of mother I hope to be, should I ever have children. Tolerant. Perhaps that is why I am tolerant of others so much, as well.

My thoughts are on children and family, so I unexpectedly offer up a tidbit of gossip on my own life.

"I have a beau, now."

My mother's cup comes down with alarming speed, though she has the presence of mind to set it on the china saucer with care. Her eyes widen. "You do. For how long now?"

I think back. "I suppose he began to court me in the later spring. It is very proper, and Aunt Mary is a good chaperone."

My mother sits forward. She is not eager for details, but wishes to know as much as I offer, and I find myself staggering to say more, now that I have let out the secret.

"Is he well off?"

"He is a merchant," I explain slowly, thinking how to describe Andrew. If I were to talk about Doctor Kinney, I might be able to paint a vibrant picture of broad brogue and kindly manners, but truthfully I know so little about Andrew. Our stilted, careful conversations are usually overseen by several people, and I have only known him in the privacy of Aunt Mary's parlor for a handful of hours over the weeks. "He is a dairyman," I elaborate.

"Ah." She will try not to judge this. I know it is not so prestigious as a lawyer or a businessman. But I have already married one such as that, so my social obligation to make a good match has been mollified. Perhaps she will not even tell Father unless it becomes more serious in nature. He will frown a bit at me marrying a dairyman and becoming a farmer's wife, but he cannot stop me at this point in life.

"He is kind," I reason. "And he has been widowed, like me. And it would be the type of active life I like."

"That is true. My Janie, who never does the expected or easy way of it," she says gently. It is both an acceptance of my nature and a soft wish that I were a bit more complacent with my lot instead of seeking some sort of unique situation. But she does love me, and does support me, and of this I am grateful. If there is something that is good from leaving the Dakotas, it is that I am nearer to her, so that no matter where I am, I have a mother to whom I can speak. That is a comfort in itself.

# CHAPTER 34

I wave good-bye to Andrew as he leaves my Aunt's home. He gives me a little smile, lighting up his green eyes, more brilliant because of the cloudy day.

The storms roll in more often now that October has started. Whittling away the summer in Gloucester has been wonderful. The sea is balmy, the waves are soothing, and I have a little romance with the dairyman's son.

I like him. His children are sweet, his parents welcoming. Aunt Mary is beside herself, hoping for a wedding to plan with her friends. We have courted six months and he is, as my friend Rose has said, a dear soul. We do not touch, and are quite proper as is expected and I miss the easy tactile way I had with Doctor Kinney, but that was something altogether different. We were as brother and sister, until I fell in love with him, and had a danger of reading too much into his nonchalant touch.

Andrew rounds the corner as the wind picks up and disappears up the hill. The sky is filled with clouds and is turning pale purple and gray I think I will go to walk the stretch of beach in front of my little

DOCTOR KINNEY'S HOUSEKEEPER

cottage when I get home, as I like to do before the rain hits. I love the smell of the sea as it is cleansed with new water from the rains, as if the beach is washed itself. It is a pure salty scent, free of fish and grit.

"All is well?" Aunt Mary gives me a hopeful grin as I go into her kitchen, where she sits knitting for the ladies' group at church.

"As always," I bend down and give her skinny shoulders a little hug. She absently pats my hand.

"When do you suppose you might fix to marry that nice man?"

I sigh. She asks the question at least twice a week. It is her age that makes her eager, too, as I know she'd like to have a wee one to hold before time takes her away. "I don't know. That is to say, we've discussed what I'd do, leaving the Chesters and coming to work for the family farm. I wouldn't mind the work. It sounds rewarding. He hasn't asked me yet, anyway."

"Well, he's asked me."

My heart stops. "He has? When?"

"After church, two weeks ago."

"Well, why so long ago?"

She arches her eyebrow at me. "So eager for him to ask? Because he's still not certain you'd say yes, Janie."

I inhale. She's right. I don't know what answer I'd give Andrew. I like to think I would be grateful for another chance at happiness, even if it is a quiet marriage. I think I might grow to be very fond of him, even though I do not ache for his touch, or feel overwhelmed with his nearness. Never matter, I will reach the moment of truth soon enough, when he asks me to share a future with him, however long or short it might be. He would be a gentle husband, more sensitive than Henry had been.

"My dear, it's time you let go of whoever you are pining away for." Aunt Mary's words bring me away from reflection.

I give her a careful look. "I have not ever said I pined for anyone."

She chuckles and puts down the needles. "You don't have to. I've seen a lot in this small town, and it's always apparent when someone is worrying over someone else. Besides, there's no other reason for you to hesitate over Andrew Angus. Someone from out west then?"

I do not dwell on the fact that I haven't yet heard from Doctor Kinney. I hear enough from Widow Hawks - Esther - about town life, and the gossip from Alice Brinkley. As far as a few weeks ago, when I received my latest missive from Alice, the Doctor was still carrying on with Kate. I wonder at his hesitation for moving ahead with her. I had expected a marriage proposal much sooner than this, but no matter. My friends in the territory both know of my beau, and now I will be able to write my own happy tidings, should I accept him.

"Well, perhaps Mr. Angus will ask me next week," I say to her, and then bend for another kiss to a dry cheek before heading out to the cottage.

Time has slipped well these months. Rose is married now, and Jean is in the throes of her own wedding planning to young Clark. I have a good purpose; teaching, cooking, courting. And I am near the ocean. There is little for me to want. This is a peaceful, fulfilling life.

Sand finds its way into the black shoes I have taken to wearing again. The boots I used in the Dakotas sit forlorn and unused next to the split saddle skirt in my closet. It is too soon to part with those relics, but I suspect I will dispose of them when I decide to permanently plant my roots in Gloucester. Here, in my home state, I am used to the grittiness of sand, of the heavy air, and the salt that seems to somehow sit in my hair at all times. There is mud instead of dust, and the oldness and stone of the buildings are so different from the newer planked wood of the houses out west. Everything here is both sharp angles and soft fog at all times, a strange mix of elements that I find both familiar and tiring. It reminds me of my past while comforting me in what I have always considered a place of home.

The wind is strong, almost horizontal, and the clouds streak purpled blue and soft dark grey across the sky, skittering over the black water and white capped waves that crash into the beach. I stop walking and hug the shawl over my shoulders, my hair whipping around my shoulders. I do not need to wear bonnets against the dust here and I let my hair down when I see Andrew, so he can notice the dark luster against the pale, muted colors I now wear.

I think on him. I do not desire him, but there is a stirring of romance when I think of his kind ways and gentle heart. If I think about Doctor Kinney too much, I will start to feel weepy, so I focus instead on what my real possibilities are here on the coast. I could marry, and move to the Angus farm, and help my new family with their way of life. I needn't stay in service all my days, and perhaps Andrew and I might have more children. The thought of laying in bed next to him does not thrill me, for I do not hold any serious lust for him, but I have had a marriage bed like that before, where passion is put aside for expected convenience.

Of course, I could always rebuff him if he does ask for my hand. As a widow, I have earned the right to stay alone forever. But then I will always be lonely, and with Andrew there is a chance I might fall in love with him a little, and be a bit less alone.

Yes, I will marry him. The decision is made slowly but decisively. The mind can wander without actually thinking while the pound of the waves lulls, and then a final choice can be picked up without the brain being too crowded with thoughts. The same small seed of wonder unfurls again within me: perhaps I can find some happiness yet, with another.

I think about the pale pink calico I saw at the mercantile up the road, that reminded me of the pattern and color I saw at Kate's so many months ago, and I decide I will make that up for my wedding dress. We can marry in the spring, when things are all new and fresh, and I will move forward, with as good a resolution for my life as ever.

My steps pick up again. I will walk this beach until the storm overpowers the water and hits land, and then I will run inside my cozy cottage and watch through the windows.

As I walk carefully, balancing around the wind and my skirts, I see the gait of the passerby on the road ahead and I pause. Is it Andrew, coming to find me after our Sunday sit in, unable to wait to ask for my hand? I find myself with a dry throat. It is time to accept my future.

The dark clothes are unfamiliar in the dim light. At first, I think I have misjudged, but it is, in fact, Doctor Kinney walking down the dunes toward me. His stride single-minded and quick. I would not have thought this was possible, perhaps I am still harboring my old fantasy. Surely, I would have had word that he was on his way.

As my steps halt, I wait, and when he is at arm's length, I look at him intently. All I think to do is reach out, so that my arms loop about his neck, and suddenly his are holding me, too, so tightly that I am lifted off my feet. The smell of him; his medicines and long traveled dust still cling to his suit, and I bury my face into his shoulder, trying not to weep.

"Janie!" His voice sounds smaller than I remember in my daydreams, or perhaps it is because the wind captures it and throws it against the roar of the surf. I refuse, at first, to even speak, in case doing so will break the spell. I fear that I will find I am not in his arms, am still alone, near my little cottage, bearing the ache of a love that is unrequited.

"Doctor Kinney. Is it you?" I wonder, still holding to him tightly. His arms are strong, but he sets me down so that I need to release him, and the space between us yawns open. His eyes are warm, almost wet with feeling, as he stares down at me.

"It's me," he says, happily, as if no time at all has passed, that it has not been a year since I've last spoken to him or touched him. "But as I am no longer your employer, ye could call me Patrick."

I shake my head in disbelief, "What are you doing here?"

"I am pickin' up medicines in Boston over the week and attending a short lecture at Cambridge on latest tests. It is close enough to Gloucester."

My heart feels like it will fly out of my chest. But before I say more, the rain starts in pellets, driving with the wind, so we take one look at one another and race up the beach in a rather undignified manner. He follows me closely to the cottage and we get in just in time before the big droplets begin in earnest. It is a proper late afternoon storm, but it will blow over by evening, so I put the heavy iron kettle on without a thought and light the lamps. The rain is loud, but comforting on the window, and Doctor Kinney goes to the glass to watch it all.

He gives a low whistle. "Now that's a view worth leavin' Flats Junction for!" I go to stand by him. "Look at those waves! It's been a      long      time      since      I've      been      here."

I find I am speechless. It is as if I have suddenly entered my own daydreams. I'm overwhelmed, desperately wishing he confesses his affection for me, or that he will say something wildly romantic. Am I foolish to hope so? Likely. But I am hardly able to fathom his appearance. He fills my rooms and I am utterly aware of his nearness. I can smell the same medicinal scent on his clothes, and I see the way his hair waves back. I want to touch him again, though there is no way for me to do so without being entirely wanton. This is so unexpected, so surreal, that he is here in my own little house.

"Have you already been to Boston?"

"No." He turns from the window to me. "First, I thought I might see you. And then, yes, tomorrow I'll head back into the city and take in the lectures and get the medicines."

"So you're only here for today?" I am touched he goes so far out of his way to make time to see me, but I know enough not to hope against hope that it means much more than that. "I am so glad you came!"

His eyes are warm, a clear blue, and his face looks the same as I remember. He gazes down at me, so near I could simply reach out and run my hand along his shoulder. Time has done nothing to cool how I feel when I am close to him. It is undeniable.

"I had to come, Janie."

"You did?" The kettle whistles and I turn from him to take it off the stove. "You are lucky to find me here, yet."

"You're leavin' again?" There is surprise in his voice, and I find I cannot face him while I admit my future plans.

"No, I'll stay in Gloucester. But Aunt Mary just informed me that the man who has been courting me has officially asked for my hand."

"Mrs. Weber!" He is immediately behind me, turning me to look up at him, his urgency unexplainable at first. "Jane. You haven't said yes?"

"Andrew hasn't asked me yet, so no, I have not given an answer."

"Well, you'll have to tell him no," he demands. His tone so final. "You're comin' back with me as soon as ye can resettle things out here."

I laugh a little at him. "You think it's so easy? I've built a life here. I'm not thinking of leaving it."

He sighs, and looks back out at the window. "Esther said you might need convincin', but I didn't think it might come to this, that you might be marryin'."

"Widow Hawks spoke to you of me?"

"Oh aye. We read your letters together over supper. Or that is, we did." His forehead creases even more into a frown. "She's gone off, you see. To the reservation. She said it did not matter that I think of her as my family. She's decided her place now is with her people as her daughter won't have her at all. Kate won't even speak to her own mother." There is amazement and resentment in his voice as he says this, as if it is a new idea he's just discovered.

"Then who received my last letter?" I ask, already knowing the answer. I wrote of my growing attachment to Andrew most recently, not knowing he meant to marry me. Doctor Kinney read it, and he admits to it without preamble or excuse.

"I didn't think you'd mind. Ye said I might get news of you through Esther's letters."

"You certainly did."

"You're not angry with me about that, are ye?"

I could not be truly angry with him had I wanted to be, and I cannot help myself. There grows in me a bit of hope, even while I push against it, that he came to see me, to stop Andrew from marrying me, to whisk me back home to the Dakotas so that I am with him always.

"No, Patrick. I'm not." His name falls out of my mouth with effort and it is a bit foreign to say it. "But the tea will keep. I think you ought to take a rest from your journey. The sofa will suffice, perhaps?"

His eyes travel over my simple seating, and I can see the idea of laying down sounds delightful to him.

"You know me too well. Will you wake me in time to get to the inn for supper?"

"I'll wake you for supper, but you'll eat with me. I want to hear all the news from Flats Junction."

"You will make me one of your meals?" He goes to take a seat and stretches out with a groan. "I didn't think I'd be so fortunate."

"I'm glad my cooking still pleases you."

I plump a pillow and hand it to him, and he stuffs it behind his head, staring up at me. There is a change in his face, as if he sees something he did not notice before.

"My word, Jane. Do ye have any idea how beautiful you are?"

I think he has been too long in the company of men on the train car. I shake my head.

"You are flattering me just so I agree to return to the Dakotas with you to keep house for a bit. I'm no old maid or bent hag yet, but I know beauty when I see it. Kate, not me."

He eyes are already closing and as he drifts to soft slumber before me, I hear him mutter Kate's name, as if the reminder of her made him dream of her from the start. How can I compete with that? It is not even worth a try.

# CHAPTER 35

I sneak glances at him as he sleeps, while I pour myself some tea, and quietly warm up the leftover soup I brought from the Chester's. There is enough for two, especially when I add in some bread and put a squash in the oven.

Outside, the storm is howling. It will get dark quickly due to the time of year and the rain clouds that stretch across the sky. I wonder when he had made the arrangements at the inn.

I sit at my little table and look out over the black waves and angry sky. Doctor Kinney's arrival sets loose my heart, which has not stopped pounding since he walked across the beach toward me, when, for a fleeting, wild moment, I dreamed he was coming to claim me. I'm flattered he wants me back to cook and clean for him, but I don't know if it's the right thing for my own mind. It would be torture. And then there is Andrew, who has courted me so prettily, and who I have grown to care about as a very kind friend.

The problem is that being near Doctor Kinney again has reminded me how passionate I feel about him. I cannot help myself from wanting to be near him, wanting to touch him and be touched by him. It is a kind of almost violent desire I thought I'd never find, and to deny myself that and turn to a quieter type of marriage is much harder to do. Now that I remember how such a love feels in the flesh, how can I say yes to Andrew knowing I will be living a lie?

I cannot help how I feel. I cry a little and bury my face in my hands, willing myself to stop this silly emotion and be strong. It will be alright. He will leave and I will not see him again. The thought is not comforting, but it is true.

"Mrs. Weber." I hear him sit up on the couch. "Jane."

"Yes." I raise my head. "Would you like some tea?" Anything, so he doesn't see my red eyes right away.

He swiftly rises, his movements quick, precise, so unlike Andrew's simple, slower ways, and his hand is on my shoulder.

"Are ye alright? It's been so long, but you've recovered well?"

I smile a little. I do not think of my little boy, buried so far away in a Catholic cemetery, half as much as I do about Doctor Kinney, and I do not think of my health at all.

"Oh yes, I have. Thank you."

I push off from the chair, keeping my back to him, and pour him tea. The soup is nearly heated, I note, as I hear clattering behind me. The Doctor is setting the table, as he did when we ate together out west. I try to keep myself from thinking how wonderful the arrangement is, and how easily we move around each other in a house.

"Jane's cookin'. I can't wait."

I glance at him, and he pulls up, catching my eye. "What is it? You've been weepin'!"

"Seeing you brings back so many memories and reminds me of my friends in Flats Junction."

"Good!" He plants himself in front of me. "Then you'll come back."

"Patrick," I sigh. "You cannot ask me to leave this life I've built. It was hard enough to start fresh."

"I like to hear you say my name," he admits, ignoring my refusal to agree to his scheme.

"That's all very well. But I won't go back. Tell me instead of Alice and Mitch. They have the two now."

He pulls out our chairs and we sit. After giving me a long look, he dives into the food and the news. "Aye, and she's just confirmin; that she's pregnant with the third. And Sadie is expectin' again."

We talk about everyone; the postmaster died of a heart attack, but his wife is happily managing the office, and her elderly father is watching the little ones. The Brinkleys have added a hundred head of cattle to their farm. A buffalo was found wandering the street one morning in summer, and there were no fireworks this past Independence Day. I drink in the news, more colorful and funny when I hear it spoken. I watch his face, trying to commit his words to memory. A heaviness sits inside my chest, because I have missed him so desperately, and I know this will be the last time I see him.

We do the dishes companionably, like we used to, and he asks me about my work at the Chester's, and Aunt Mary, and the townsfolk, and how I fill my days, and who my friends are. He grows quieter as I tell him about Rose, Jean, my aunt's dear friends, tea parties, the Chester pantry, Beth's lessons in the kitchen, and then of the Angus farm, and Andrew's kindness, and his sweet children.

As we finish the last of the tea, eaten with a few biscuits I found in the back of my larder, long forgotten for an earlier tea with my friends, he looks out into the deepening sky.

"It's been long since I've been back. It feels good."

"Back to Boston?" I ask, running my finger along the rim of the teacup, trying not to look at him fully.

"That," he nods. "And Gloucester. I was here, once, in my youth with my auntie and her employer. In fact, my old friend, Doctor MacHugh, the one who placed my ad and found your letter. He used to live in this place in his childhood."

"You kept in touch with him, then, after so many years?"

He smiles a little, thinking back. "Aye. It was a peculiar set of days, to be sure. Hot. His father was ill. It's how I got my first start as a doctor, in truth."

I want to ask him more, but as he is not the many courting me, I don't wish to pry into his past. Besides, it will only make me cling to his words dearer, as we are linked again in another way. I will ask what streets he walked, and what he did when he was last here, and every time I walk them I will think on this. I do not need more reminders of what will not happen. Besides, it is getting late, and he should go before this situation is any more unseemly.

He leaves my cottage to head back to the inn. I am relieved he does not press his case in continuing to ask me to return to Flats Junction. He is too much a gentleman to do so, though a part of me wishes he would vehemently protest about my staying in Gloucester, that he would demand I go back with him because he needed me for myself. But that is a silly girl's hope, and nothing more. And I know it.

"What time is your train?" I ask. "I'd like to see you off in the morning if I might, before I need to be at the Chester's."

He looks up at me, where I stand on the porch. The rain has ended, but the wind is still strong, and I can just see him in the lamplight.

"The early one, at four."

"Good," I nod. He nods in return, and then turns and melts into the darkness towards the town's brighter lights. I go inside and I do not sleep all night.

# CHAPTER 36

We meet on the platform at a few minutes to four. The air is chilly, damp, and cool, and the fog lays heavy so the train is a few minutes late. He wears his stetson, a hat that looks so out of place in the east, but it makes him look as I remember him.

My heart feels heavy and overwhelms me at first. I love him very much, and this has done nothing to help me overcome my emotions so that I might move forward.

"Please give my best to Esther, whenever you see her next. And tell Alice hello. And Kate too, of course," I say, the usual niceties falling heedlessly.

He turns to me I hear the train coming now, and suddenly there are more people on the platform than I would have liked, because I want him all to myself when I say farewell for always.

"Will ye really stay? And marry the man who courts you?" His eyes are grey this morning, as if he is tired, too.

The train comes in, loud, obnoxiously so, and I wait for the noise to clear, and the bustle of bodies to start.

"I don't know if I can marry him," I say carefully. "But I can't go home with you."

"Home. You call it home. Please, Jane. I don't know when I'll have enough money to get out here again, and I know I won't be back before you're married when it will be too late to convince you."

My head lifts. "You've been saving to come see me?"

He nods. "That and for the medicines."

I sigh. The whistle blows. He must board now, but he is still loitering. This good-bye is even harder than the last, because it takes away the hope I have carried that he would come after me. He has, but he did not come to take me away in the fashion I dreamed about. It is wonderful to see him, but devastating to realize that my fantasy is just that.

"Thank you for coming," I say, as the whistle blows again. "I know you want me to go to Flats Junction with you, Patrick, but I won't."

"Can't or won't?"

For one brief moment, I find more strength inside than I thought I had. I look at him and I do not weep. "You have to board." The sooner he is gone, the better, so I can end his senseless pleading once and for all.

"Ye won't come with me, Janie?" He sounds desperate.

"I won't go, only to watch you finish courting Kate," I say in a rush. "You cannot ask me to help you woo her, to dance at your wedding, and bounce her children on my knee, as if my loneliness would be filled simply by watching your happiness. I can't do it."

"All aboard, sir!" The conductor is behind him. Doctor Kinney is staring at me, his face raw and unreadable. I do not believe the situation is as dire as all that. He will find another housekeeper if he needs one, truly. I am dispensable. I always have been. He is edged closer to the train as the last few people rush by to swing into the car.

"Jane--"

The whistle sounds the final call and the steam rushes out in an angry hiss, and I know he has to get on before it's too late. I watch him board as he turns to look back at me from the stairs. My eyes finally fill, and I don't bother to brush away my tears. He takes a seat near the window, and I see his face through the glass, looking down at me, and then away. Then the train pulls out and rushes past, and he is gone.

# CHAPTER 37

I pull the pastries out of the oven for Mrs. Chester's tea. I must concentrate carefully. I feel as if I am in a half dream; did I really say good-bye to my dearest love only hours ago? How could I have let him go without telling him of my heart? I know the answer: it is because I could not bear it when he would pat my shoulder and arm, and be sorry, because he loves Kate and she loves him. I am the unrequited woman, and I know I am not alone, but that does not make the pain in my chest go away.

"Can I fill them?" Beth asks, looking at the pastry shells. I nod, and show her how to do it. She is too young to realize that I am troubled, and I am grateful I do not have to explain myself.

I make a fish salad with fresh whitefish from the market and I send Beth to the stalls to get lettuce, though that is slim pickings in October. There are raspberries on top of the pastries and I arrange a plate of quickbreads made with pumpkin and cherry.

When the food goes up, I sit at the table and think over the rest of the week's menus. The fall produce is bountiful and I will be able to make hearty food. There were recipes I used last year this time when

I'd first arrived that did not do well, but others were good and Mr. Chester requested them again, so I pull those out and set to writing down the lists.

It does me good to keep busy like this. I suppose I would be just as busy if I married Andrew Angus. But can I, now? It would be a lie to say I loved him when I love another, and apparently still do just as strongly as I did when I last left him. It is not comforting to know that I cannot move forward, even though I have been trying.

# CHAPTER 38

The week slips by. I realize that tomorrow is Sunday and Andrew will find me at Aunt Mary's parlor again, as always, and perhaps he will ask me to wed him. I was so certain of my answer a week ago. I was sure I would be happy enough.

Ada Baker and Jean are busy in the market stall. They have many different squashes out and eggplants and late blackberries, and of course the root vegetables. I will be making a soup for the Chester's lunch and supper for Sunday, and so I pick up the meaty beets and zucchinis, weigh them in my hand and nod.

I glance up, my eyes wafting through the market. I see Andrew at the dairy stall, but he is looking surly, as if he has been having a rough morning. Perhaps I ought to stop by and try to liven up his day, but as always I am never quite sure what to say with him. Our rapport is still shy as it ever was.

It is harvest and the market is busier than usual. My sleepless nights and daydreams of the Doctor have me seeing him everywhere, out of the corner of my eye. Every man in a dark traveling suit might be him, but I know it is not. I turn to Ada, who is staring at me shrewdly, her hands on her hips. I am pressed close to her; the swell of people in the walkways is heavy and she shakes her head at me.

"Was he the man you've pined for all these months?"

"What?"

She juts her chin. "You were seen on the beach last week in the arms of a stranger. From the sound of it, I'd guess he was the one you've been remembering so desperately."

I close my eyes briefly. So that is perhaps why Andrew was looking so angry. I am grateful it is so busy today, that holiday groups and families are out strolling, filling the market so my voice is not so audible.

"Yes."

"Who was it?"

"A doctor, from the Dakota Territories."

"He came to take you away?"

"Not like that," I shake my head. Jean comes out and stands behind her mother, listening hard, a small smile on her face. I do not mind finally dissembling to her either, and I wonder how much Aunt Mary has already heard. Surely she would be able to put it all together, that I had fallen for my employer out west.

"He... he is wooing another woman in Flats Junction and wants me back as a housekeeper. I decided not to go."

Jean leans forward. "What about your own heart? Don't you want to be near him, no matter what?"

"Of course I do!" I am surprised at how vehement I sound. I take a breath. "Just as you wish to be near Clark always, so do I with the Doctor. But I could not do it. What woman can watch the man she loves marry another? What kind of life would that be?"

"So you won't be saying yes to our Andrew when he asks for your hand?"

"I don't think I can. I'm destined for a life apart."

Ada's eyes grow soft. "I doubt that, Janie."

"You're very kind. But I love a man who does not care for me, and intends on marrying another."

"You poor, soft girl." Ada's hand reaches out. "I wish you could find happiness."

Her kindness threatens to make me weep. Jean comes over, the small smile still on her face. She is trying her best to cheer me up. "I'm sure it will all work out, Jane." It is an easy and trite thing to say, especially by one who is heady in love with a man who has asked for her hand. She weds Clark in a few months, so I turn the conversation to that wedding, deflecting conversation away from the workings of my heart.

# CHAPTER 39

Andrew comes on Sunday to Aunt Mary's parlor. His hat in hand, he sits on the edge of the plush chair with his sharp elbows on his broad knees. He is tall and strong, and his blond hair is combed back yet from church. We are quiet, and I pour some tea out for us, but we don't touch it. I know enough of Gloucester to know that he has heard of my beach-side twirl with Doctor Kinney. It was not much, but it is enough to set tongues wagging. He sighs, and then looks up at me.

"I am sure by now you know I have been courting you, hoping that we might grow fond of each other and perhaps decide to marry."

It is his fairness that draws me to him, the way he speaks as if we would decide everything together. I smile sadly at him. His tone speaks to me of his mind, but he plunges on.

"I thought we might reach a reasonable understanding. I like you, Jane, and I was thinking you felt the same."

I reach out a hand, but stop halfway. As is proper, we rarely touch and to put my hand in his now would be misleading. "I do like you, Andrew."

He nods, as if expecting that. "But we are not in love, are we?"

I am surprised he includes himself in the comment, and I agree. "No, you're right. We are not. I don't think you should ever love me the way you loved Elizabeth."

He gives a little smile. "You're right, too. I was hoping I might learn to love you, just as much as that, though. Or at least, be happy together so that I am not alone, and my children have a mother."

"Your children are dear," I say.

"And you still love the man you left out west," he states, and straightens up to look at me fully. "I don't think it is fair to ask you to care for me when you are still pining away for another. You are only luckier, in that your heart's desire still lives."

"Is that easier?" I ask painfully. "When he is as good as dead to me? I doubt I will see him again. Besides, he is off to marry another."

Andrew gives a rueful little laugh. "He is a fool to have even looked at another woman if you were offering yourself."

My mouth opens. I suppose I never did really present myself to Doctor Kinney as an interested woman, but it would never have been proper. He stands, and I go with him. "I should like us to be friends, I hope," I tell him.

"That would be very nice, Jane. I don't think we ought to hold out hope for anything else."

We walk to the door, and he leaves after giving me a little bow. I turn around to see Aunt Mary standing on the threshold of the kitchen. She knows that we will not be marrying, and she gives me a sad little smile, understanding all.

# CHAPTER 40

My Sunday afternoon is quiet. Jean was supposed to come for tea, but that time has passed and I realize she must be with family yet, discussing wedding details or making bows. There is a lot of work on weddings here in the east, where frills are just as important as the vows, and the older women in the family fall into the making of many crafts. It is all prettily done, and, as I enjoyed Rose's nuptials, I look forward to Jean's. I am happy enough for my friends that I do not feel jealousy often, nor deeply, and I am grateful my nature is kind enough for that.

Another October brew comes rolling in from the east. I see the clouds swell, slowly coming toward the beach, which quickly turns grey and tan and black. I like the wind that comes with the storms. It smells wet, heavy and salty, like tears and rain mixed. As it picks up, I close my eyes, thinking about what I can do to keep some semblance of reason in my life. I will be a good cook, and perhaps I might take in some classes to learn more delicacies. There are places Mrs. Chester might send me should she wish for fancier dishes. I will teach Beth, and be like a little mother to her. I will be lonely, I'm sure, but my cottage is cozy, and it is really all I need.

As the afternoon darkens, I go in to light the lamps so I can see when it is time to make supper. Finally I have gotten used to cooking for one person. It is a talent in itself. But I am glad I have had time alone; not many women have these types of freedoms - they go, like me, from parents to husband. Perhaps I will regret this freeness someday, when I am old, and wish for a partner or children or grandchildren, but if I am still employed by the Chesters or some other great house, I will be busy enough.

I heat tea water and go to the window, watching the storm. It will have to be enough. I will write to Alice Brinkley, and tell her good-bye. To hear from her will become too painful, and I do not think I can get any more letters to Widow Hawks now that she is gone to the reservation. Kate must be so pleased to have the last obvious token of her heritage gone, and to have a man who adores her ready to ask for her hand. I only hope she will not be stubborn and turn him down to stay her course of fierce independence.

The tea is done and the storm has not yet hit, so I go back out to the porch. If this is heartbreak, I think I can stand it. I did not mourn Henry much because I did not love him, and while I am disappointed I will not have a partner in Andrew, that is all well since I would have been sad, eventually, knowing what was missing in our marriage.

And now I can pretend, sometimes, when I am alone like this, that I am a widow again, that I was married to Doctor Kinney and that we had years of memories and passionate embraces. I close my eyes again to remember his arms around me on the beach, his rough, large hands holding mine on the platform of the train depot. I can build on these memories. Many women do, and I am not unique among them.

I sigh, looking back out on the waves, taking in the slate color of them. There is the ocean, at least. I turn back to go inside, even though there is time yet before the rain hits, but I am too sorrowful to stand here alone, like a sailor's wife wishing a husband home, safely.

At first I swing by the porch entry, knowing it is just my tiredness and my fantasy that he might come back, but I stop short.

He is there, in his dark suit, with one foot on the porch step, staring at me. I do not know how long he has been there. I was so caught up in the wind and my own thoughts I did not even hear him.

I do not think I can manage it all over again. I cannot say good-bye to him one more time, but he comes toward me, solid and real, unstoppable. My first inclination is to touch him, reach out and hold him, but that would not help. I hold onto the porch railing to keep from buckling foolishly.

"You came back?" How many times must I refuse him? He has to be brought to understand that I will not subject myself to the pain of watching him with another. Once I had thought I was a strong woman, who would not take the easy way out of a problem, but in this I am weak, and I will run away from it all to save my sanity and what shreds of happiness I have left.

He stops in front of me, drinking me in, as if we had not just parted ways a week ago. I cannot understand him. He is usually so stoic and accepting of other's choices and fate. He must leave me be.

"I had to come back. I had reason. What you said... it gave me hope."

I think back to our conversation at the train station, and I recall I did not tell him anything that might be misconstrued that I would accompany him to Flats Junction. I shake my head.

283

"I think you've come all this way for nothing. My answer still stands."

He takes another step forward, and I try very hard to hold my ground. I can smell him again and I take a shaky breath in and out, not sure I can hold his bright gaze without weeping.

"I realized you did not know. Kate and I have parted ways. I am not courtin' her, I have not been for weeks. Ye need to know that."

The wind gusts and his hair blows with mine. When I am with him, I forget to school myself of my practiced detachment.

I reach up to brush the hair out of his eyes, and I say reprovingly, "You should not have done so. You've loved her a long time, Patrick. She was accepting your suit. You had always wanted that."

He captures my hand, holds it solidly in both of his. I notice how his eyes are a brilliant blue against the grey of the sky, the black and grey of the water and the dullness of the sand behind him.

"No...not always..." His lips tremble, the way they do when he wishes to say more, when he is intensely passionate about something, but I do not trust that he holds so much emotion on my account. He hesitates, then brings my fingers to his lips. The tactile way we have always had between us is now torturous for me. I have gone months without his touch, and now the easy manner we have makes me desire him even after such a little, simple show of affection, however innocent he means it.

"Please," his voice is low, rough, his face lined with apprehension. "Come back with me. I will bring you here as often as we can manage it, I promise ye. I will rent a cottage, and we will vacation on the seaside and watch the storms. But I need you home. It is... it is not even home without you there."

"You miss my cooking and cleaning? This makes it a home?" I refuse to hope that he is revealing his heart. I think I know enough of him to understand that I am not the center of it.

"Confound it, Jane," he says irritably, shaking his head at my caustic attitude. "I am tryin' to explain to you that I love you."

The words come out, catch in the rising wind and ring through my ears. I am mistaken. Surely he does not love me like that. His Irish eyes meet mine and I see he is in all seriousness. He does love me. He does not really think I will love him back, that I will devastate him with rejection. When did this happen? How long has he loved me so?

"You love me," I repeat, daring him to confirm it. Because I am not resisting him with words, he releases my hands and puts his arms around my waist, drawing me up against him.

"Love of my life," he says quietly, sincerely, and then he kisses me. It is--oh! It is what I have always dreamed of, and yet it is so much more than I had hoped for. The kiss is not tentative, it is full and heady and alive. His mouth tastes like a man, but more a man than I've ever known. He takes to me like my own desire. I feel the strength in his hands as he squeezes my back, and then captures my face. I do not realize it until his thumbs brush against my cheeks that I am crying through our first kiss.

Finally, we break our lips apart, and he is flushed and smiling widely, his arms still firmly locked around me. Bending forward, he kisses away the tears.

"I think ye cry out of happiness, Janie?" He teases lightly, before giving me a swift soft kiss on the lips, and then resting his cheek on my hair.

I nod, and then pull away to look up at him again. Does he really mean this? That he loves me? Loves me enough to come back, yet again, to fetch me? If he does, then my life is made.

"How did you think to come back?"

He smiles again. "When you said good-bye last Sunday and you told me that you couldn't go back to watch me marry Kate. I realized you didn't know - how could you? - that I had decided not to wed her. I realized you were pained with the idea of me marryin' another, and the only reason that could hurt you is if you cared for me, yourself. Finally, I knew your heart."

"Then you didn't know?"

"Know what?" He is baiting me, though he does it with a twinkle in his eye. I blush, and admit to it all.

"You didn't know I loved you? That I do love you?"

"Janie. I have hoped for many many months that ye might, someday. I can hardly believe it's true as it is."

The rain suddenly hits. I hear it pelting the beach and we turn as one to go into the cottage, though he does not release my hand. Inside, in the warm dim glow of the lamps, we sit side by side on the couch. Above, and at the windows, the hard rainwater drums, encasing us in a cave of privacy. It is highly improper that we are yet again alone in my home with no chaperone. My neighbors know I am a widow, and some have reputations that are less than desirable. So far I have not given anyone warrant to speak so damagingly of me, but a beachside twirl, and now a man in my home, would be enough. Still, I find I do not care at the moment.

"So you've come in today?" I ask, and he shakes his head.

"No. Yesterday."

"Why did you wait to come see me, then?" Was he searching himself when he arrived, wondering if he loved me enough to come back to my door?

He gives a little sigh, and then smiles sheepishly. "I'm afraid I was caught out by some of your friends. As in Flats Junction, it's obvious when someone is an outsider. Your Jean Baker saw me aimlessly wanderin' the stalls at the market, hoping to see a glimpse of ye. I didn't have much of a plan, I only knew I needed to talk to you again. My mind had been playin' our conversation many times over while I was at the lectures. I borrowed a bit of money from a colleague and came back as soon as I could."

"And Jean saw you?" I prompt at his pause.

He gives me a little wink. "She had a good inklin' of who I was. I admitted that I was looking for you." He pauses. "She's a shrewd one. She told me that I was the one you've been pinin' for, and I did not believe her. My own hope was so weak that it did not seem that I could convince you that I care for you, and not Kate. Her mother, Ada, I think it is, had a scheme, and I'm sorry to say I went along. I couldn't help it."

I think of Ada's merry character, and would not put a trick past her. "What did she propose?"

He has the grace to look bashful. "They had me hide behind the stall, enough so that you might not spy me out, but I could overhear. And ye admitted you loved me. I'm afraid after you left, Jean found me a bit red eyed and weak kneed from relief."

My sensitive man. I put a hand on his cheek, battling with feelings that I do not entirely understand.

"How long have you loved me?"

"I don't know," he says. "Probably for nearly all the time I've known ye."

"But you didn't want to court me," I remind. He places his hands on my shoulders and looks me directly in the eyes.

"Jane. Believe me when I tell you that you took my breath away the first time I saw you, standin' at my door. I could not believe you were to be my housekeeper, that you would be in my home, at my table, every day. You were too young and beautiful to be widowed, to come out and care for a bachelor. I was overwhelmed with you."

I take his hands, wishing to get more of his earnest honesty. "But you still pined for Kate, Patrick. You wanted her."

"Ah, yes," he sighs honestly, and looks down at our joined fingers. "Yes, I did in a way. I had spent so long rememberin' her for the sweet girl she was when I first met her that I refused to see how hardened she had become to her own roots, that she would turn her back so entirely on the mother who loves her. Her desire to be seen as someone she is not, to have her past and heritage be forgotten, and that she would do anythin' to be seen as non-native, even at the cost of her family... it is a fundamental difference I could not overlook." His eyes meet mine. "I cannot love a woman that would do such a thing, who will be so intolerant."

"So, I was next best?" I offer.

"Janie," he admonishes. "Ye were first."

"First?" I scoff lightly.

"Yes," he insists. "You were more real to me than anyone, tangible, reachable. Kate was a phantom, an untouchable woman who I fantasied would be an excellent partner for me. She is driven, independent, and I got along well with her from the start. But I never pursued her actively. Maybe because I knew it would not be a good fit. Widow Hawks certainly thought so. So I did not think Kate was ever really an option, not until you tried to persuade me so. And then I only courted her because I thought you were interested in Bern Masson, and would not consider me at all."

"You mean to say you pined for me?" I am incredulous that only days into my arrival in Flats Junction the Doctor, Patrick, had been falling in love with me.

He nods, and brings my fingers to his lips again. I close my eyes against the sensations. When I open them, he is leaning closer. "I thought ye were quite wonderful from the start. I expect I will always think so. It seems that I might love you a little more each day."

"Patrick," I battle back my practiced simple ways with words. My sweetheart is eloquent enough, and I must try to communicate in kind. "I hope you might. I know I will."

Now it is his turn to lock gazes with me. "And what about you, my girl? You've loved me long?"

He has declared his intentions, so I suppose it is only fair I do too. I look at his beloved face and touch my forehead to his shoulder. When I look up at him again, I see he is still waiting, hopeful, expectant. "I have... I suppose I knew I cared about you a good while at first. It was only later... after I nearly died, that I knew I loved you, truly. And ever since."

He kisses me hard, and long, and I find myself overcome with desire, lust, want. I have laid in bed for months thinking and dreaming of this moment, but I realize the heat I feel is many times deeper and more overwhelming now that he is here, in reality. He is fumbling with the buttons on my dress, blindly trying to expose some of my flesh. His obvious need for me is wonderful and I help him with the tiny hooks and bands of a bodice's neckline. Once it loosens a bit, he rashly leans in to kiss my neck before staring at me. He seems a man enraptured. His breath is coming short and he captures my face in both his hands, kissing me softly, tenderly.

"Marry me," he whispers. "Please, Janie. Marry me."

"When?"

He pulls away, his blue eyes searching mine, as if incredulous again. "You mean ye will?"

I give a little laugh. "Of course I will. I have never been so..." I stop and blush a bit, for this emotional disclosure is still new to me. "I have never felt so much passion about another man. I wish to marry you, love you, help you... have your children..." I trail off, thinking of how I almost died, and how upon waking up, how much more I felt, and how I had fallen in love with him once my eyes were opened. I find his gaze again. "Oh yes, Patrick. I desperately want to marry you!"

I suddenly come to the realization, after my outburst, how exposed I am with my neck open to his eyes, and try to demurely put a hand to my throat. The heat of passion certainly makes me less prim than I expected of myself. But perhaps no one has ever lusted after me enough so that I would be so eager like this.

"Why are you hidin'? Your bosom is legendary, Jane." He takes my hand and pulls it away.

"Indeed?" I give a nervous laugh.

"Oh, aye!" He is drinking me in, as if thrilled he can now look at me openly. "The cowboys always gave me tease, that I should have a lovely housekeeper with a bosom enough for two men to lay their heads. They would wonder how I did not try to court you myself from the start. Only Bern had the guts to try and woo you away."

"He didn't manage it. Nor did Andrew. I realized I loved you, and a commitment to any other man was pointless," I say, and I find my voice is filled with tears. I was so lonely once I had realized I loved a man deeply, finally, and loved someone who I believed would never care for me in return. But that is now untrue. "Paddy, how much I love you!"

My admission grants me another hard kiss, passionate and titillating. He moans, "Sweet Jesus," and lays his face in the crick of my neck. The faint tickle of his cheek and hair is delightfully sensual. I am amazed that this is how stimulating this is, how I utterly desire his nearness and touch. I want him to continue touching me. This is what I missed in my first marriage, this heat, this conversation, this need. I will not mind tying myself to this man and this delight with a promise and a ring. There is enough life for me in simply adoring him. My hands come up unwittingly, and stroke his face and hair, and hug him nearer.

We sit like this a long time, enough that our passion cools so that we do not devour each other any more unseemly than we already have, though just thinking about his hands on me is enough for lust to course all over again through my body. How long did he hold this hearty desire inside for my sake, because of my unemotional view of him? How silly of me not to notice this earlier, how odd that I felt so alone in my love for him and was so blinded by Kate's beauty to think that my own was not enough.

His head comes up, tousled and flushed. I think he has mastered his desire for me to get up and make us some supper, but instead he bends down and runs his lips along my neck again.

"How did you learn to make a puddle of a woman?" I gasp. His eyes are clouded with desire, but the unmasked want makes them even a brighter blue. He gives a little smile.

"I have dreamed of what I would do to ye, if I had you alone and you'd let me, by some miracle, touch you."

"Patrick," I blush. "You've thought a long time then."

"Nearly since the first day I saw you. I've been buildin' ideas since then." He gives me a bit of a wicked grin.

Now that we are not so near each other, the windy chill of the storm outside seeps in, and he quickly goes to fix the fire without another word.

As I heat the water for a turnip and potato soup, he comes over to the small stove, takes one look at me and shakes his head. Snaking an arm around my waist, he pulls me tight to him.

"Ye'll not get much supper done, I'm afraid," he admits, and I look up at him, delighting in his nearness. "I will be too distracted and I won't be able to stop kissing you." He bends down to plant a kiss at my temple.

I give a soft sigh. If I let myself go, I could be entirely wanton, and I want to do this right by him.

"Patrick," I say, touching his hair. He stands looking down at me as if he is the most fortunate man in the world.

"So, you really will marry me?" he asks again. He actually seems amazed at his good luck, when it seems to me it is I who the lucky one.

"Yes," I smile at him. "Gladly and with a full heart."

"Then you'll wear this." He dips his hand into his pocket, and pulls out a simple band.

I stare. "When did you think to get that?"

"This mornin'. After I heard you say you loved me at the grocer's market. I went into Ipswich to buy it. Will ye wear it?"

"Of course. Yes!"

He picks up my hand and slides the cold metal on where it instantly warms, and he kisses my palm. I look at my hand clasped in his. I can hardly believe that I will be able to hold onto him whenever I want. If I think back to all the times he brushed against me; doing laundry, wiping the dishes. I know now he did that because he couldn't help it, and I love him all the more because of that. The need to be near another is overpowering.

"Kiss me again," he requests, and I drop the spoon and turn into his embrace. I do not think I will ever get enough of this.

I kiss him, but behind me I can hear the soup begin to bubble, and I pull away, though he leaves his arm about me and watches me scrape the bottom of the cast iron pot to turn over the vegetables. As we eat. I listen to the fire crackle in the hearth, and I look out at the rain and ocean. He seems attuned to me and reaches across the table to finger the band of gold.

"I meant what I said, Janie. I'll bring ye back here as much as we can manage it. I would hope..." He trails off and looks at me strangely. His voice is suddenly rougher. "I would think we should let our children know the sea, as you did growing up."

"Patrick. What is it?" I stare at him as he struggles to keep a composure. I've forgotten how expressive he is, how much more emotional he feels things. It is this empathy that makes him a fine doctor, and a tolerant man.

His strong hand pulls at mine, grasping it tightly, and, finally, he clears his throat and looks up at me.

"You don't know how much I worried when you miscarried. There's only so much medicine can do at times like that. I was scared, more so than I'd ever felt before. Ye were dyin' in front of me, and there was nothing I could do but wait. I did not realize how much I loved you, even then. Your death would have brought me to my knees. It was the most horrible day, and night, of my life."

I thought I'd heard a man sobbing. Had that been him, at my bedside? The thought is too dear, too sweet, to ask.

"I lived, though. And yes, Paddy. I'd like us to have children."

He is quiet again for a moment, gazing at my hand, rubbing it with his thumb. I can see he still has a thought to say, for he is never one to mull too long once he decides to speak. I am surprised he waited so long to press his suit to me, but I suppose I was not interested at first, and then it was I who was too shy to show any feeling. What man would reach for that coldness?

"I..." he sighs and meets my eyes. "I am relieved you want children. You know... when I first found out you were with child, I thought it would be wonderful to have a babe in the house, someone to dote on and watch grow. And then as you started to show--"

"I barely showed!" I protest.

He shakes his head. "I noticed. I watched you. Ye did start a bit, Janie. And you were so lovely..."

He pauses, then plunges ahead. "I began to think of that baby as mine. And I dreamed that we created a wee life together. It was... imaginary, I know. But I liked what I saw in my mind's eye. I wanted that."

"We'll have that," I promise.

"What do we need to do to get you gone from here?" He asks pragmatically. "Do you need to give notice?"

"Yes, traditionally I do. Several weeks, to let them find another cook. But I've been teaching my kitchen girl for months. She possibly could do well enough until they find another."

He glances at the clock on my small mantle. It is late on a Sunday evening, not exactly the time to go calling on my employers. I know what he is thinking. He wants to take me home.

"I can stay at the inn another night, but that's all." He hints to the fact that he will run out of borrowed funds, but he is matter of fact about the next. "Still, I'm not leavin' until you're on the train with me. No more good-byes like that. I think the next one might kill me."

I laugh a bit tremulously. "I think my Aunt Mary might be very happy to fill her guest room for as many days as needed to get things settled."

He laughs, a deep, sweet sounding rumble. "I can't wait to meet your Aunt Mary."

We have so much to dream and discuss, but we are quiet instead and listen to the rain, which is slowing down now, and are content to just be together. My heart is finally full.

# Chapter 41

I go to Mrs. Chester first thing as the sun rises. Today it is not stormy, but instead the sun is crystal, white, and bright. I smell the briny fresh saltwater, refreshed by last night's rain as I walk into the great house. Mrs. Chester is in her morning gown, writing a note to a friend in town, her hair pinned up prettily and her toes folded over daintily. She is a very lovely woman, and kind, and I have been fortunate she is so easy a mistress, willing to take me on with such little experience. It was probably helpful I did not make many wage demands.

My hands twist nervously. I have not mastered the easy stance of seasoned people in service.

"What is it, Mrs. Weber?" I instinctively pause at the title. It is the first realization that someday soon I will have a new name.

I look at the floor, and then into her clear face. "I am... I've been offered marriage, ma'am."

Her gaze flicks to my fingers. The new gold of the band from Patrick glimmers in the early soft light and she gives a truly delighted smile.

"Why Mrs. Weber! How splendid for you! I am glad you've found someone to make you happy." She stops short and squints at my face. "You do, indeed, seem very happy. Love becomes you."

"You're not cross then?"

"How soon do you have to go?"

"As soon as I am able. I--I have been teaching young Beth. I thought if you might be able to find someone in a fortnight or so you'd be fine off with her."

"You'd like to be married soon, then?" She arches her eyebrow, and I flush. Yes, I cannot wait to marry him.

"He's a doctor, ma'am, and needs to get back out west. I'd like to go with him when he leaves."

She gives a little sigh. "Well, I don't like the speed of your departure, but I have no hold over you. It's a good reason to be a little relaxed with the rules, anyway." She laughs a little. "You will have to be sure Beth has all of Mr. Chester's favorite recipes."

"I will. Thank you ma'am, truly. I'll have her settled in a few days, then."

She nods, and turns back to her desk. That was easier than I thought it might be, and I head to the kitchen with a light step. Beth is waiting there for the morning's list, and I break the news. Her eyes well with tears.

"Oh no, Mrs. Weber! But I'll miss you so much!"

I hug her shoulder with an arm. "I know, and I will miss you, too. But we have gone over so much, and this may be your chance. Please Mr. Chester and his wife and they may not hire a new cook at all, but give the post to you."

Her face pops up. She is a bright and ambitious girl. It would be grand for her to land the position so young.

"See?" I soothe. "Let's plan to do that for you."

# CHAPTER 42

Patrick is waiting for me at Jean and Ada's stall in the market. His face absolutely lights up when he sees me, and I feel myself blossom in return. I ache to run into his arms, but it would be entirely unseemly.

"How did it go?" He asks, as I loop an arm through his.

"Wonderfully so. We can leave before the weekend."

"Now that is good news," he says contently, then looks around the marketplace. "Do ye have time to go to your Aunt's now?"

Jean gives me a little wink. She has been listening. "Go. This order will take quite a while to fill."

I smile thankfully at her. Oh, how I will miss her! I fall into step with Patrick and we walk the short distance to Aunt Mary's little house.

When she opens the door, her narrow bird-like face erupts in wrinkles and a huge smile.

"There you are! Finally you've come for her!" It is a classic greeting, to have her say so precisely what is on her mind.

Patrick has the presence of mind to take off his hat and give a half-bow of his head.

"Doctor Patrick Kinney, at your service."

"Come in, then." She opens the door wider, and we file in. I am happy to introduce her to my love. I know she won't wrongly judge him. I'm still reeling with happiness that he is here, that he loves me, that I can leave with him in a few short days.

"Tea?" She asks, and sits in front of her service in the parlor. Only yesterday did I sit here and dismiss Andrew's suit. Now, I am an engaged woman, and Pat and I sit across from Aunt Mary. There is an odd space between us until he swallows, gives up, and takes my hand. She glances at us as she pours.

"I am sorry I did not have the presence of mind to ask your permission," Patrick starts. I know these formalities are a bit beyond him and he is nervous about it all. "I was uncertain that she would even say yes, and I admit I was distracted with worry about the whole business. I've never married, and things are less involved out west."

"Oh yes, the Dakotas. I've heard tell." Aunt Mary sips her tea carefully, but her eyes are very bright as she stares at me.

"I..." He looks at me. I know he wants to pull me closer, but doesn't dare in front of my aunt. He takes a breath and turns back. "I love your niece, and I have for some time."

"Why'd you let her get away from you, then?" She asks a bit shrewdly.

He smiles a little, as if the memory is painful. "Because I was a fool. And because, as you may know, Jane does not express herself overtly. I never had so much as an inklin' she might care for me as well."

"Oh, I'll give you that," she agrees and shakes her head gently at me. "You'd do well to remember this man loves you, and will want for your attentions and nurture."

"Yes, of course, Aunt Mary," I say, and blush a bit, like a silly schoolgirl.

"And be sure you say to him how you feel, so he doesn't wonder."

"Listen to your aunt. She gives good advice," he teases me, and I laugh a little.

He sees an ally in her and leans forward. "We'd like to marry."

"Of course you do." She looks at me. "And what will you do about the Chester's?"

"I've already asked leave."

She spreads her hands. I can tell she is excited for me. "Well, when can we have the wedding?"

"As soon as we might." Patrick is pleading with her, though I know he doesn't need to do so. She will humor us, no matter the speed. "Perhaps on Friday, if that is alright with you."

"So soon? There will be hardly time for a cake."

I look at Patrick. I can tell he does not care one whit about a cake, or flowers, or bows. In truth, neither do I. My first marriage was heralded with a bit of fanfare and it did nothing to help find love and happiness.

"Aunt Mary, we just care about the logistics. Keeping Pat here in Gloucester until we are wed and can travel together, for instance, and settling up my cottage, getting the license."

He gives me a grateful glance, and squeezes my fingers.

She frowns a little. I know she wanted to enjoy a bit more fuss, just like her friends do, and I have a suspicion they will throw just as much compacted energy into this quick affair as they can anyway. Then her face clears and she smiles.

"I'm sure we can make it work. In the meantime, you'll stay here with me," she directs this to Patrick.

"Thank you... Aunt Mary," he says, and the title makes her chuckle.

"You'll want to wire her father," she instructs. "And we'll want to go to Ipswich for a dress for you, dear." She looks at me and I shake my head.

"I don't need a dress and there won't be time to make one up."

"Nonsense," she scoffs. "I do not have any children, and I've always wanted a little family wedding. I've got enough by to do something for my favorite niece."

"Thank ye," Pat speaks for me. I can tell he is touched as well as I am.

"I don't know what to say." I suddenly am very excited to wear something pretty for him. "I feel so fortunate on all corners."

We stand. I need to get back to the house for the meals. Now that things are settling, I find I am eager for the week to move forward so that I can be done in service and finally married. I want to go home. Flats Junction will always be home now.

"Stay back, Patrick." Aunt Mary puts a hand on his arm and looks up at him merrily. "You can help me open up the bedroom. Go get your things from the inn. Jane can come tonight for a spell."

I smile at them. They look like two kindred spirits already, but as I move to open the door and head back to market, he breaks from her arm and moves to me. Unapologetically, he puts a hand about my waist and gives me a quick full kiss in front of my auntie. When he breaks it off, he presses his forehead to mine and then releases me. "Have a good afternoon, Janie."

"I'll see you tonight, Paddy," I say softly. Out of the corner of my eye, I see Aunt Mary looking very pleased. And as he goes back to her and I leave, I hear them plotting his stay. She will be in her element this week and I'm glad I can share this happiness with her.

# CHAPTER 43

Wednesday, my last day at the Chester's, I write my sister and my mother. I tell them about Patrick's two arrivals in Gloucester, about his declaration of love and his proposal. My letter to Mother is long. I finally dissemble what I have held so close to my heart, and I know she will understand, though she will be sad I thought to keep such heartache from her. I wish I might see her again before I leave, so I wire her as well, though I do not bother to do so for Sissy. She will only be disapproving of how quickly it all is happening, but still I am glad to share my news.

The caretaker of the cottage comes in the afternoon to discuss the key drop and what furniture needs to be covered with sheets for the next tenant. I head to my aunt's home. Aunt Mary and I will go into Ipswich to look for a dress.

When I let myself in, I hear the two of them chatting in the kitchen. The voices echo, and I pause, taking delight in hearing how well they get on. I will miss my aunt desperately, and have thought to have her come out west with us, but I know she would miss the sea and her friends. It would be too much to ask of her.

"But you're certain she really pined for me all this time?" Patrick's low voice carries through the doorway. I shake my head. I doubt neither of us can believe our luck. "I really couldn't figure it. If I'd known she cared for me, I would have stopped her from leaving Flats Junction. I nearly did anyway, but she held herself together so well I didn't think my beggin' would amount to much."

"Well, you were courting another." My aunt's voice is reasonable. "Did you know you loved Jane when she left?"

"I'd like to say yes, but I was too uncertain about many things to make a clean decision right then. I just knew I was cut to the quick that she left me. It was my... a surrogate mother... who made it all a bit more clear."

"How so?"

I wait, too. I want to know how he came to his decision to chase after me and I don't know if he will reveal all this if I were to ask.

"Well, she decided to take herself to... a reservation. She's Sioux."

My aunt is silent. I know she is digesting this. The idea of native savages is one that is well documented, sometimes incorrectly, here in the east. The notion of a native woman who was genteel enough for a Doctor takes time for her to understand, and I know it only paints a more vivid picture of the wild west where I choose to live.

"What does that matter?" She manages. "How did she help you to see your choices?"

"Esther asked me if I cared for Janie, and by heaven, by then I knew I loved her, so I admitted I thought of her often. And she disagreed with that simple explanation, and accused me of lovin' Jane, and that she was a far better match for me than any woman in Flats Junction or beyond, and I ought to fetch her. And she was right."

"You find many women are right," my Aunt says cheekily, and he chuckles.

I take this as a cue to come around the corner. "Who's always right?"

"Women," she announces. "Something a doctor should remember."

"Oh, I'm quite aware of the wiles and minds of ladies." He pulls me tight to him, comfortable in front of my bit of family in the cozy kitchen. I am poured a cup of hot tea.

"Warm up," he rubs my shoulder. "We're off to Ipswich, then."

"You're coming?" I am surprised. "I didn't think that was done."

"I've got some shoppin' to do," he says. "And now that you're free of the Chester house, I plan to spend as much time with you as Aunt Mary allows."

"You'd think you're not planning to marry and spend the next several decades in each other's company," my aunt laughs, and we join her. "Well, then, you finish your tea, Jane, and I'll go get my hat." She leaves without ceremony, giving us time alone again, which she does artfully and often and I am thankful for her attitude.

She is not even out of the room before I take his hand. How will I show him that I really do care for him as he does me?

"Oh, Janie," he breathes. "Friday does not come fast enough."

"I can't wait to marry you," I agree, and look up at him and smile. "I want to go home."

He squeezes my fingers tightly. "I'm a bit excited to travel with my wife and show ye off on the train as mine."

I laugh again. "I'm rather excited for that, too, and also to have you completely to myself." I blush a little, but plunge ahead, determined to take my aunt's words to heart and tell him how I feel. "I am desperately wanting to have you in my bed, my love."

He inhales sharply, and bends down for a kiss, as if my admittance means much to him. Then he looks at me, as if debating to talk, before saying quietly, "I'm a bit nervous about that myself, Janie."

"I think I'm all healed up," I dismiss, but he shakes his head. I am disconcerted we are talking about all of this, but I constantly remind myself that he is a doctor and open about the body. That he saw my own limbs in near nakedness.

"It's not that. It's the act itself. I'm afraid I'll... not know what to do... and ye've been married before."

"Paddy," I touch his cheek. "You must understand that I did not love Henry. I did not lust after him, and his illness often prevented much of anything. What we have already shared pales anything from my first marriage. I'm scared, too. I'm frightened by how much I want you and how to go about that."

His honest face breaks into a grin. "Thank the saints!"

"And what are we thanking for now?" Aunt Mary comes around the corner finishing up her hat. She has taken her time on purpose.

"For my Janie." He releases me and flashes me a devilish grin behind my aunt's back as we leave the house. He makes me feel desirable and young with his unabashed happiness.

# CHAPTER 44

There is no aisle to walk down at the courthouse in Gloucester. My pale dove gray dress has lace and satin on the bodice and along the hem, and my aunt and her friends pulled together a few late fall flowers for my hair and a little posy for my bouquet. They have a small spread of food waiting for us at Aunt Mary's parlor, and Jean and Rose and their beaus join my aunt as witnesses. It is not much, and I almost feel guilty that Patrick does not get to experience the whole wedding extravagance I know Aunt Mary would have liked to do for us, but as I stand next to him, and he holds my hand and stares down at me while we echo the vows, I know he only cares that I am marrying him, and to hell with any ribbons and bows.

My mother and father have arrived for the nuptials. It was a breathless surprise, and I only had a moment to tell my mother's shocked face that all was explained in a letter she would soon receive. She can see I am beyond happiness, so she is mollified for the moment, though I can see she aches to know more. My father says little, his dark eyes taking in the tableaux, but he is quiet enough knowing I wed a doctor. In his mind, that is even better than marrying a businessman.

When the justice says we are wed, I am filled with so much happiness I do not know what to do with the emotion. He is smiling at me with glittering eyes, as if he would weep if he could allow himself to break down, so I reach up and kiss him, and he pulls me tight to kiss me back. My family and friends follow us out to the little luncheon, where more of my aunt's friends are waiting for us. The Angus family was invited, but they do not attend and I do not blame them, though I am sorry I will not have a chance to say goodbye to Andrew and his children.

Patrick does not know many of the people here, so Aunt Mary was gracious enough to keep the party small. He keeps a hand on my elbow or my waist as much as he might, and it is all I can do to remember that the older ladies would not take kindly to me kissing the groom whenever I liked. Are all newly weds, in love matches like ours, so happy and bursting? I did not think this would ever happen for me. I feel as though I might wake to have this all a dream.

I'd thought we would take the evening train out, but Aunt Mary had other plans. She will go stay with the Bakers tonight, and we will have her little house to ourselves. I want everyone to leave now, but instead, I make the usual conversation, and watch Patrick discuss the west with Jean and Rose's men, who seem genuinely interested in the gold that is often discovered nearby Flats Junction.

"Jane." Jean is at my elbow, balancing a glass of champagne. "I'll miss you so much."

"You ought to visit," I tell her, warmly. If it weren't for her charade in the market stall, perhaps I would never have become Mrs. Kinney. "We'd love to have you."

"Perhaps that is where Clark and I should honeymoon in the spring." She smiles and takes my hand. "You know I'm very happy for you."

"Thank you. We will write," I promise.

I make the same offer to Rose, and then as the late fall afternoon wanes, people depart en masse. Mother comes and embraces me, her eyes wet. She knows this means I am leaving again, and that a wide distance will spread open between us again. I share her sadness, but I am too excited about my future to dwell on it.

"I'm very glad for you, Janie," she says quietly to me as she and Father prepare to head back to Rockport. "I expect you will explain everything in your letter."

"Everything," I promise her, and hug her again. In a way, spilling my heart in a letter to her is best. I was more eloquent on paper in making my story than if I were to tell her over tea.

Aunt Mary and her friends wipe up, and both Patrick and I help them. They think he is only drying dishes to hurry them out, though I know he genuinely enjoys people and conversation and so much of that happens in the kitchen.

"I'll see you off at the train tomorrow, my dears," Aunt Mary says, picking up her satchel at the door. "And there is cold chicken for supper in the larder."

The moment she shuts the door, Patrick comes up behind me, wrapping his arms around my waist and kissing my neck. "You look perfect and lovely," he murmurs into my hair. "But I want to see less lace and more of you."

I turn in his embrace and cock my head at him. "You've seen plenty of me, you know."

He knows innately what I refer to. "That was different." He pauses, and then admits sheepishly, "At first, when I took your heart rate and it was early on, I had to try very hard not to stare too much." He looks at me straight. "But then ye quickly started to fade on me and I didn't much care about anything except keeping you alive."

We kiss, as if reaffirming life, and I find myself nervous and yet utterly desirous, and we do not even wait for the sun to set before we make our way to the small bedroom where he's been staying.

My Aunt is not a flowery person, so the bedroom is decorated as most austere, proper New England homes ought to be; pale blue walls, painted wood, bare furniture and a cast iron bed. Patrick pulls the curtains, though no one can see in through the garden and trees in the backyard. I look at him; his loose frame, strong arms, vivacious health, and I feel need drop down through my shoulders, stomach and loins. He is mine, not Kate's, and he loves me.

"What is it... Mrs. Kinney?" He comes to me. "You're a mile away."

I laugh. "I am indeed Mrs. Kinney. Jane Kinney. My heavens. I never thought it would happen."

"And I'm a married man, now," he says happily. "It was worth the wait."

He falls to kissing me again, and we are pressed tightly together, the hardness of his body against the softness of mine. Finally he pulls away.

His hands have been wandering up and down my sides and around my waist, and he asks with barely masked eagerness, "Might I see more of you, Janie? I have been achin'..." He pauses. "I have spent many nights dreamin' about seeing you just so, because I could not imagine that you would ever be mine to touch. And now to have ye like this, I'm afraid that I've become even more needy. I don't want to stop."

"Well, it's a bit early in the night to think of this, but yes," I say with more confidence that I feel. "Yes, please, untie me."

The corsets come away and my ample bosom springs out, and I see Patrick's eyes feast on the sight of my skin. I try to cover myself a bit demurely. Henry and I only ever had intercourse in the dark, so to have someone see me in this half golden shadow of late afternoon lamplight is disconcerting. I forget for a minute my love is a doctor, has seen many a body, and even my own in the most intimate way.

"You are glorious." He frees my flesh completely, and eventually picks me up and lays next to me on the bed. I am unable to stop touching him, and I am suddenly glad we do not wait for the dark. More time with him is everything I want, and I want to see him entirely. I've never seen a naked man before, but I desire it with him, and I say so, forcing myself to be emotionally vulnerable.

"Ye want to see me?" He grins. "You first."

I undress carefully, hesitantly, shyly. He is watching me, his eyes bright and soft. When I get to my last layer, I pause. It seems my boldness still has its limits. He gets off the bed and comes over to me.

"Janie... I am a bit out of words. You are more lovely than I imagined." He reaches up and unties my hair, slowly pulling out the pins. When it falls out and down my back, he rakes his fingers through the strands, pulling my head up and kissing me as if he never plans to stop. I hope he does not, until I find myself unable to end it here, and I am untucking his shirt and loosening his tie.

When I pull off his undershirt, I see that he has a light dusting of red brown hair across his chest, and his skin is pale as I would expect of the Irish in him. I lean forward and kiss his shoulder, where it rounds into his arm. I taste his cheek, running a finger to his navel. I feel a heady tingle through my whole body. I run the back of my hands along his skin, amazed at his vitality and strength. I am amazed by the man in front of me, that he should wish to touch me just as badly.

I drink in the strength of his legs, the broadness of his chest, the sinewy lengths of his arms. I want to touch every piece of him, and I stretch out next to him, intertwining my legs with his, marveling that he is mine, that he desires me, that his hands are everywhere on my own body, grasping, tracing, kissing.

"Patrick, my love. I never want to leave you... or this bed," I say playfully, running a finger along his jaw and down his neck.

"No. You'll stay with me always." He loops his hands low on my waist, pressing his palms into my hips. "No more leavin' after supper, no Bern to take ye off for an evenin' walk."

"Did that bother you?" I ask, pulling back a way, our bareness rubbing deliciously together. I never knew the act of love could be preambled with so much desire and that I would want a man's body so much.

He nods. He is so honest about his emotions. I must learn from him. "It was very difficult to say nothin'. I wanted you to stay my housekeeper... not go off and marry some cowboy because he was the only one who made a pass. And then I wanted you for myself in an entirely different way."

"What way?" I know the answer, but I gasp a little as he turns the tables, and flips me under him, pressing me into the mattress, grinning down at me.

"I wanted you this way, here in my bed, in my arms." He bends down and kisses me hard. We stop talking so that we can focus on each other. Soon enough he is holding me, and I can hardly breathe because I want him so. I must have him. I ache for him so much that when finally we are joined, I spiral up and down, unable to stop from crying out. It is no matter that I am so wanton, because I feel his body responding likewise, so that we lay panting in short order.

"Sweet mother," he lightly swears, burying his face in my bosom. His voice is muffled. "Is it always like that?"

"I wouldn't know," I say, clasping him. "I have never made love with a husband I love, who I desire so unendingly. I would hope it is so."

His head comes up and he chuckles. "Me too."

I do not think we get more than a few hours of sleep before it is time to rise, get our clothes on and leave for the train. I feel that I do not even recognize myself at moments; communicative, emotional, very much in love and full of lust. I plan to make this last. I enjoy myself much more now that I am freer with my own self; tactile, talkative, and allowing myself to really be happy.

# CHAPTER 45

We head to the station, with my belongings in a large satchel he carries and the rest in a small bag I have. I wonder if everyone who sees us can tell we are newlyweds, and a few who know me in passing, hail me, some using my married name and some without. Aunt Mary is waiting for us. She is too old to cry over our departure, but she tucks a lace hanky in my pocket and gives Patrick a little kiss on the cheek. She is glowing, as if she is the one who got married.

"My sweet neice," she says fondly. "I am so happy for you. Many blessings!"

Then she turns to Patrick and gives him a strange, shrewd, once over. It is a look I have never seen her give, and then she nods, once, and says off-handedly, "It was a good choice."

He frowns a little, and I jump in. "I think so too, Aunt Mary."

Then she smiles, and the moment is gone, as if she has made her final judgment on our entire situation, and clasps Patrick's hands in goodwill, telling him to take care of me, of our off-spring, that she will write.

I cannot stop thanking her and she waves me off, as if I am the one who gave her a gift.

I will miss her and I know there is a good chance I will not see her again, so I am weeping as the train pulls out, and I wave to her until I cannot see her any more.

# CHAPTER 46

We arrive in Flats Junction on the afternoon train. There is snow on the ground here. Patrick says it can come early in October sometimes, but nothing is frozen yet, and the road and platform is dirty.

The minute I step off I hear, "Mrs. Weber! Jane! You've come back!"

It is Kate. She is coming toward us, her eyes bright and happy. I wonder if she knows anything, and by the tensing I feel in Patrick as he picks up our belongings, I know she does not. For all she understands, perhaps, he stopped coming round and then disappeared to lectures and medicines. I stoop to pick up the box of vials myself, the gold wedding band clanking against the wooden frame.

"And Pat." Her voice is more guarded. "You've returned as well."

"Aye." He picks up my satchel.

"Then you've found Jane and convinced her to come and keep house for you again? Good! I've missed my friend."

She seems to not mind that he had stopped courting her, and for a brief, wildly unclear moment, I wonder if he misspoke to me, that he never ended their courtship.

"Let me help you." She picks up the last of our bags, and slings the satchel over her shoulder.

We glance at each other and fall in line with her. I understand his hesitancy. There doesn't seem to be a good way to explain that we are married. Many of the townsfolk thought the Doc would wed Kate, especially once it was immediately clear that the babe I miscarried was not his.

"Jane!" Sadie Faucett waves heartily from her family's wagon. I see Mitch Brinkley, but he is juggling his two little children while Alice is in the post office. There are so many dear, friendly faces here, I am overwhelmed and happy that this is my home. It is even more so much the better, because tonight we will be able to sleep again in a bed, the second time since we are married, and I cannot wait to get Patrick alone. Such thoughts are still new to me and I will blush if I linger on them. I refocus.

Kate is running commentary on the past several weeks, full of her usual news and gossip. "The Indians were seen passing nearby, but none came to town. Shouldn't wonder, there's no reason for them to make a stop. And Alice thinks she's having twins. And your neighbor, Anna Pavlock, thinks she has gout."

We walk, stiffly formal, the three of us, regardless of her chatter. Down the main street and over to the Doctor's road I am only half listening. To think this will be my home for always. The permanence of it is deeply satisfying, and I smile and nod at anyone outside, barely remembering their names sometimes, though they seem to remember mine as they call out a howdy.

We approach the Doctor's house and Kate opens the screen door. It creaks a bit now, I notice. She places our bag inside, and turns to us, her face bright. I realize that she thinks Pat has just gone away for a bit, and perhaps thought about her, so perhaps she'll try to get him back. Her entire body quivers with this energy and I find that she is just as beautiful as I remember. I look at my husband, but he does not seem to notice. He is too busy peering into the rain barrel and checking on the garden at the side of the house. I see it is mostly a tangled mess of old weeds.

"So, Jane," Kate says, kindly. "I am not sure if you know, but Widow Hawks has left town for the reservation."

"I know it. I wish she'd consider coming back."

Kate gives a swift laugh and flicks her hand. "Why? She has no home and you are here to replace any work she might have. I am glad to see you, Jane."

"I'm glad I am so welcome," I say, carefully. Kate stands for a minute. I see her giving the Doctor sideways glances, but he comes up the stairs, opens the screen in her face and takes the large bag in. He disappears into the dimness of the house. Kate suddenly looks a bit nervous. I do not blame her. Patrick's attitude is one of indifference to her, and I am sure part of that is because he is no longer pining for her, and the other because her disregard for her family so disgusts him. It would be disconcerting to anyone.

"Janie," he comes back to the door, opens it slightly, holds out his hand, smiling a little at me. "Give me the bag, I'll take it up to the bedroom."

"Oh!" Kate's exclamation makes him pause. "Jane doesn't need to stay here, Pat. I'm sure I can find her room. I mean, there's no where else other than the inn now, and that is expensive." She turns to me with a friendly air, as if offering a favor. "We don't need your reputation turning right away." She says this easily enough, but I know she is glowering inside. She is reminding me that it would not take much to start tongues wagging if I were to stay at this house, unmarried and unattached with no chaperone. She reminds me of her power in this place even though she herself never really seems to do much with it. Suddenly, my welcome to Flats Junction doesn't feel quite so wonderful.

"Well," I say, carefully, stepping up so I am at the same level as her on the porch, though she still towers over me. "I thank you, Kate, for the offer."

"Yes," Patrick interrupts, and gives her a smile, but I can tell he wishes her to be gone. "Yes, that is very good of ye, Kitty, but no need. Mrs. Kinney and I are perfectly happy sharin' the house and a room."

"Of--" She stops halfway through her nod. Her gaze swings wildly to me and then him, still standing in the darkness in the house. I'm suddenly sorry for her. Her bitterness is a loneliness that she is starting to wear. I watch as her face actually registers sadness and anger. "That is... Jane." She looks at me and her eyes find my finger, where the gold glints in the afternoon light.

"Yes, Kate. We've married," I say, gently. I will not apologize for my marriage, and even though she has proven herself a flighty and

326

unreliable friend, I also don't wish to hold a grudge. Flats Junction is too small a place for such anger on my part.

There is a moment of silence. Then her old shine comes back and she tosses her hair. "So that's how you brought her back, Pat? You bought her off with a ring?"

"Oh, aye." I can tell his remark will be cuttingly, damagingly, sarcastic, and I jump in, a hand on the screen to silence him.

"Yes, you're right. He brought me back as his wife, as I'd come no other way. But that was not a compromise. I love him with all my heart."

She snorts, a delicate sound, but one of disbelief anyway. "Distance made the heart grow fond, I suppose?"

"Jane is the reason I went east, Kitty. I need her--love her."

She scoffs again, then looks between us. Her shoulders tense and I see she is more hurt than angry. Without another word, she walks off, and I know her feelings will be vented on anyone unlucky enough to walk into the general this evening.

"Come in, Janie." Patrick's voice is gentle, and he opens up the door wider. "Come home."

His words make me close my eyes, and I follow him in, and the familiar sights and smells of the house fill me up. I have missed the drip of the faucet, the smell of prairie grass and dust, the creaks of the wood. He does not give me much time for remembering, because he picks me up as a bride, and carries me up to his - our - bedroom. We devour each other as we have so desperately wished to do the entire train ride out. Afterwards, he draws us a bath, and we take turns washing the travel grime away before falling to the mattress again for well-needed rest.

I fall asleep, thinking that my return is too surreal, that I will wake and find that it is not his arms around me, or his leg between mine. I am almost too afraid to really sleep well. Still, the travel has made me exhausted, but we are awakened in the wee hours of the morning by a pounding on the door.

It is one of the cowboys. One of the horses is sick at the Olsen ranch, so my naked husband ruefully pulls on his clothes and heads out after a quick, hard kiss to me and my left breast.

# CHAPTER 47

He does not come back to bed, so I rise with the morning light, pull on a serviceable blue calico, and go downstairs to make the coffee. The kitchen - my kitchen - is just as I remember it. It seems Widow Hawks and the Doctor kept things in order as I left it. Hard to believe it was a year ago already.

"Mrs. Kinney." He comes in, cheerful as the sun, no matter how exhausted he looks, and I can tell he is delighted to call me such. His eyes are bright and happy, and his arms come out of their own accord and grab me around the waist, pulling me in for kisses and a squeeze.

"Paddy," I laugh. "Breakfast is ready."

"I'd like to say forget breakfast; I'll have you instead," he quips gamely, nuzzling my neck. "But I'm half starved. What'll it be?"

"I've got flapjacks started. First batch is in the oven."

He goes and pulls them out, himself. Never one to expect me to wait on him and he doesn't start now that we're wed.

I pour our coffee. "Is it very cold out, yet?"

"No," he shakes his head. "The snow's mostly gone already, but winter is nearly here. Soon we will have many a cozy night while stayin' in around a fire. Good weather for making babies."

"Patrick!" I swat him with the dish towel. He grabs it like he once did before and brings me close, planting a kiss on me.

"I thought you wanted children."

I close my eyes against his nearness, and then nod. "Oh, yes, my darling. I should like as many as we can fit in here."

"Well, we ought to get started then," he says, playfully. "But first I need to eat and those look delicious."

We sit down and he tells me about the horse that had to be shot, and that we need to head out to the Brinkley's this morning to check on Alice's condition. I am very eager to see my friend. He says we need to check on Mrs. Pavlock. My role as housekeeper and part-time nursemaid falls completely back on my shoulders, and I find I am more than ready for all the tasks out before me. It will be worth the hard hands, the calloused feet, the dusty hair and backbreaking hauling, if only to do all of it with my husband.

Suddenly he reaches for my hand, and I stop eating and look up at him. His eyes are bright. "This is how it will always be now, Janie. You and me, and God willin', children, together at this table and in our home. How did this happen?"

"Well, you answered my letter when you advertised for a housekeeper. And then we fell in love."

He chuckles. "You make it sound simple."

"All ended well, Paddy."

"It did," he agrees, then smiles at me. "Me own dear wife I don't know if it can get better than this."

I look at him and then dive into a thought I've had while making breakfast. "I was thinking... perhaps we ought to go fetch Widow Hawks - Esther - and have her come live with us."

Patrick sits back as he used to, relaxed and considering. "Well, there isn't much room here. Perhaps we should have a little side room off the kitchen, or a cottage in the yard."

He likes the idea, and I plunge in further, dreaming aloud. "It would help when the babies start arriving, to have an extra set of hands around. Then I can still cook and clean and help you with the office and the patients. We neither of us have family around to help as it were, and we'll need it."

He's nodding, agreeing, planning. "We'll set right off to get her, as soon as I finish all my rounds in the next few days."

"Kate won't be pleased with us," I warn, and he gives me a rueful grin.

"I don't think she's a mite pleased with us anyway, gettin' married and all. But she's cast off her own family. We're adopting Esther as grandmother for our babes. It is her loss."

"Perhaps one day she'll come around." I hope, but I don't think it will come to that.

"It's a grand idea, Janie." He smiles at me, but then his smile turns wistfully hopeful, and we retire upstairs before he sets out for another trip to visit patients.

I watch him leave, his bag in hand, to help ease discomfort and check on a child's cough, and then to take me to visit our friends and my dear Alice with her coming babe. He is mine, and we have created a life, a family, and a purpose here. It is enough.

# CHAPTER 48

I am tense as we make our way to the reservation. Though the natives are no longer roaming the plains and picking off travelers at a whim, the journey is still tight with danger. There are the wild animals, from wolves to bison, the uneasy summer weather, and of course the occasional group of self-named cowboys who are perhaps more like pirates.

We have joined a small wagon train that will continue further west, picking up and dropping off travelers as they move. It is safe to go in a group, and we are thankful for the numbers of men and women in the wagons around us. The grass undulates, reminding me once again of the ocean, though I do not long for it quite as desperately as I used to. The afternoon light is rich with golden color, even though the days are cool and nights colder. The people call to each other, hailing one another's children or shouting at a horse or cattle. Our own group is silent. Kate has joined the Doctor and me and she is stonily quiet, and keeps us from having our own light chatter.

I did not expect her to come with us. When we'd been back a week, I had asked her to accompany the Doctor and me to the reservation. I thought Widow Hawks might actually agree to return to Flats

Junction more readily if she could see that Kate still held some sort of love for her mother. And I wanted Kate to prove to me, and to Patrick, that she was not without redemption.

Her immediate response was to shut her door in my face. She was angry with me, of course, for marrying Pat, for settling back into Flats Junction as if I'd never left, for asking for her mother to come back. I waited until I was in the general to buy goods. She would not refuse to serve anyone, regardless of her feelings or mood swings, and when I had dallied long enough until we were alone, I begged her to reconsider.

"You're asking too much of me," she had snapped.

"No, I'm not," I'd retorted, knowing I was still pushing my luck. She would be swallowing her pride, and facing the fact that she was half-native, and thereby reliving all of the ridicule she'd endured as a child. I could not imagine what emotions she wrestled with as she and I bartered back and forth for a half hour.

In the end, I had left the general with her resounding negative in my ears, and had returned home to Pat. We would go alone to fetch Widow Hawks, because to us, she was family.

But the day we hitched up a borrowed wagon, Kate arrived with a tight bundle and an even tighter look about her eyes. She didn't speak to us and jumped into the back, her spine straight and her face looking away from us.

It has been three days on the journey to the reservation, and still she does not speak a single word to either Patrick or myself. I can only imagine the tempest in her heart. She is traveling with me - once a friend, and then a betrayer - and the man she'd thought would wed her. Her animosity toward us might never completely go away, of

this I am certain. And she is going against the independent nature she has spent so long cultivating in defiance of the way the town treated her. She is, in her own eyes, a non-native willful woman who has no need of family, especially the side that is Indian. What is so odd to me is that, considering what I've gathered from Widow Hawks, Kate would be welcomed whole heartedly into the Sioux community, whereas she has had to fight constantly in Flats Junction to remind people of her preferred status. Like me, Kate does not always choose the easy way.

I spend many hours musing over Kate's motives for joining us. I wonder if I will ever have a chance to ask her, or if she and I will ever have kind words between us again. Patrick doesn't seem to have half of my worries. He is merely glad she has decided to come. He seems to think she will have a change of heart when she sees her mother, but I do not have quite as much faith in Kate as that.

# CHAPTER 49

The reservation is dirty. It is the first word I think of as I look at the huts, the slapped together shacks that are ridiculously flimsy against the elements, never mind the winter weather that will arrive soon to the territories. In the haphazard cluster of dwellings, I see some traditional teepees, a few *wetus* with smoke curling from the cracks, and a lot of open campfires, rowdy children and gaunt dogs. There is a lot of mud, mixed with human debris. It is as if the tribes were trying to straddle both things; their community and the way of the white settlers, and in doing so were failing in both respects.

I am appalled that Widow Hawks, the neat, precise, graceful woman I remember, resides here. She is with her people for the first time in decade and this is what she now thinks to call home. I am once again thankful for my husband, who agreed with me that she must return to us.

Patrick is making inquiries as best he can. A few can capture the English words, and he knows so little of their tongue. Kate and I are useless, so we are sitting in the wagon, watching Pat gesture and pantomime. The man he is talking to finally shrugs, his face never once showing a flicker of emotion, and half turns to give a guttural call. Eventually a woman pokes her head out of the shack nearby. She approaches, and listens to Pat again. I think perhaps he has finally remembered Widow Hawk's name in *Sihasapa*. There is a nod.

He leads her to the wagon and helps her up. Behind her, the husband hands up two of the smallest children and goes back to the shack, his tall lean body bending against the breeze and the gaggle of young ones still around his knees.

The woman turns to us, her black eyes a beady gaze that passes over me and lands on Kate. She stares, completely unabashed, at Kate's broad cheekbones and glossy locks. I know she sees her own people in Kate's face, but she will not presume. Finally, she puts one of the children next to me and says, brokenly, "I take Chatan."

Chatan - I recall it is Widow Hawks' name. I nod, and then Patrick says, "Dowanhowee."

The woman pauses, looking between my husband and me. He nods, still holding the reigns and watching the horses, and the woman gives a little nod, acknowledging me. "Dowanhowee." Her voice makes the word sound earthy and rich.

I stare at Patrick and he gives me a little side smile. It seems he has remembered the name that Widow Hawks' family gave me so long ago. I am touched and delighted.

We follow the line of the rough road, around the meandering huts. I am shocked with how many people live here, and in the conditions they endure. I see several men sitting outside looking worse for wear with drink, and the women look worn and rough. It is as if they were placed here haphazardly, told to make a living from nothing, and perhaps that is what really happened. I find my lack of understanding frustrating and a bit frightening.

338

When we arrive at a very large teepee, the woman nods again toward a nearby *wetu*. Inside I hear strange chanting. She says gravely, "*Inipi.*"

I do not know what she means until Patrick has the presence of mind to say to me, "Sweat lodge, for healing." I try not to stare at the hut, realizing our new acquaintance has decided to give us the sights, as we are obviously rather ignorant white travelers. I wonder how Patrick knows this, but perhaps he often asked Widow Hawks what her people did for medicine, being a doctor and curious.

As we sit in the wagon and stare, Widow Hawks comes out of the teepee and looks at us. Patrick gives a short happy whoop and swings down to her.

"Esther!"

She gives him a warm smile, the light of it chasing away the questions. He gives her a hug, and in the meantime, I take it upon myself to climb down as well to give Widow Hawks a long embrace.

"You came back, then, Jane?" She asks me, though the answer is plain. "And married him? I am so glad."

"Now, it is your turn," I say, stepping back. "You must return, as I did."

She pauses, and I see doubt for the first time on her forehead. She is looking past us, to the wagon, where Kate still sits. As one, Patrick and I turn to look. Kate is not moving, not looking at our trio, her head turned away to look out across the reservation.

"Angpetu!"

The word is odd, and at first I do not realize it is a name except that Kate's head whips around at it. She stares at her mother, her face unreadable and her jaw set. I am struck with intense wonderment. Why make this journey, in silence, in anger, if only to reject her mother again in the end? Did she wish to see the reservation? What her people looked like en masse? Where her mother would perhaps die and be buried? I could not even start to ask all the questions.

Widow Hawks calls again, "Angpetu!" And then she moves away from us, toward Kate, who still stares at her mother. As Widow Hawks draws up with the wagon, Kate stiffly clambers down until they are face to face. I suddenly see all of the resemblance, from the straight nose and cheekbones to the carriage of their shoulders.

They do not embrace, and I suppose I do not expect it of them. Kate is still too angry at her mother, for the myriad reasons, and Widow Hawks too proud to ask what Kate will not willingly give. But suddenly I see Kate give a tight jerk of her head, affirmation of some sort, and with that, Widow Hawks turns and comes back to us, Kate following and the other Indian woman coming down too with her children, chattering away suddenly to Widow Hawks as if a spell has been broken.

I am confused, and do not understand what just happened, but before I can start to ask Patrick, he is smiling at me. "I think she will come back with us."

"I might have gathered that, darling, but I don't know what decided her."

He begins to explain, but is suddenly interrupted by several bodies pouring out of the teepee. I recognize Widow Hawks' sister-in-law Hantaywee, and a few of the adolescent girls. We are ushered inside

340

the tent flaps and I'm assailed with scents of tobacco, urine, fur, smoke and corn. Seated in a corner is the crumpled, but smiling form, of Eyota, Widow Hawks' mother, and there are four men lounging near the central fire. They all sit up when we enter, and stare at us, the way so many have done since our arrival on the reservation.

We are served food and Patrick is passed a pipe. Eyota smokes one of her own behind us all, and Widow Hawks is smiling, chattering in a mix of native language and English. I stare back at everything, from the mixed clothing to the oddly prepared food, even more unusual than what Widow Hawks used to make.

Kate sits next to me, and she refuses to eat or to join in any conversation. How does she stay so silent? It must be a trait of her people instilled in her. I do not think, even in my quieter days, that I could abstain so long from speaking to another person. She keeps her head down and her mouth tight, but I see Widow Hawks looking at her fondly, happily. It is as if Kate broke a barrier with arriving here, as if that was all Widow Hawks needed. I wonder if Kate too sees it that way, though perhaps she sees it as giving in to her mother, and that is why she is not quite so eager about all of this.

I smile and nod at everyone, and Patrick is talking to the men as best they can with their jumble of words. One of them continues to gaze at me, and I wonder why as it ought to be apparent I belong with Patrick. And then I realize he is not looking at me, but at Kate. She does not notice this, and I do not think she would take kindly to me making liberties to tell her that a man has taken interest in her, especially a Blackfoot.

The language washes over us, and every once in a while, Patrick gives my shoulder a squeeze. They eventually take him out, and he explains briefly,

"One of the family is ill. They want me to take a look and see if I can do anythin'. We'll be spendin' the night here, Jane. We will catch a wagon heading towards Flats Junction from the reservation so we aren't alone."

"We'll all sleep together?" I ask incredulously, looking around the teepee. It is the first full conversation I've had in English since we've arrived and I'm suddenly grateful he thinks to talk to me about all this.

"Yes, to keep warm, as it is. It will be alright; Esther is here and so is Kate."

"Will you be back quickly?"

"I don't know," he amends. "But they say it is not far to walk and if the illness is what they say, there will be little I can do."

"What is it?"

"Liver issue. Comes from too much of the drink. They'd do better with their beloved *pejute sapa* than liquor."

"The what?" I try not to let my sheer annoyance with all the language barriers show. It has been a trying day to say the least.

"Sorry - coffee. They love it. In fact, why don't ye pull ours out of the wagon to share around for tomorrow? Least we can do for hospitality."

With a brief peck on my forehead then, he is gone out into the late afternoon with the men.

I turn back to see Widow Hawks smiling at me. "What?"

She shakes her head. "It is so good to see you, Jane." There is much emotion in that comment, but she cannot say more to me with Kate sitting nearby.

Instead I try to talk of lighter things. "It seems my husband has the presence of mind to remember the bits of your language, though I do not even know how to pronounce my own Blackfoot name."

Widow Hawks blinks, as if trying to remember it, and then translates. "It is Dowanhowee - Singing Voice."

"Oh." It does not seem a fitting name for me. I have never been praised for my voice, though perhaps to the natives it is different enough to be considered a pretty sound. I try to sound it out, and several of the children clamber over to try and help me say it out. In the clutter of their voices, soft hands on my knees and leaning into my body, I see Widow Hawks smiling again at me, as if it is a vision she enjoys. I myself try not to wrinkle my nose at the pungent odors of fur and food that hangs tightly around the little writhing bodies. These are her family, after all, and I do not want to offend anyone.

"So, then, what do you call Kate?" I ask, trying, belatedly, to bring her into the circle of conversation. Her face swings around to look at me, but her expression remains neutral. She will not offer me her name.

"She is Angpetu, at least, to me, part of her always will be." Widow Hawks is looking directly at her daughter, as if memorizing her face, reminding herself of the girl and woman before her. "Radiant. Day. That is what her name means, and to me, she will be so until she returns to the ancestors."

I almost expect a rejoinder to that, but Kate stays silent, as if willing herself to be separate. It is all I can do to not shake her, to beg her once again to consider her mother. But it is enough that she is here. I cannot ask more of her, and by the softness around Widow Hawks' face, I know she feels the same.

# CHAPTER 50

We will arrive back in Flats Junction late in the afternoon after another five days of riding. Kate and Widow Hawks sit side by side in the back of the wagon. I often sneak glances at them. I have not seen them or heard them speak a single word between them. Is it the native way to say so little, to have an understanding with a simple nod of the head? Are they resolved to live near each other? Does Kate have any forgiveness in her for her mother's choices, and does Widow Hawks readily forgive Kate for her anger and rudeness?

Once I look back and I see their hands are clutched together, old and young fingers together but the same shade of brown. I am relieved and heartened by this.

I will live in Flats Junction all my life, so I am sure my questions will be answered in time. That is the way of life, I suppose; to seek answers slowly, in a long revealing meandering, instead of having it all wrapped up neatly and easily.

# CHAPTER 51

"Esther will stay with me until she has a place of her own." Kate announces this as we stop the horses near our home. It is shocking to hear her voice and it is slightly hoarse from misuse, but most strange is the declaration.

"Stay with you?" Patrick is the first to recover.

Kate gives him a defiant look. I wonder when they discussed this, or if Widow Hawks is only hearing of it now. She is on the other side of the wagon and I cannot see her face.

"Whatever you wish, Kate," I say, holding back the small smile I feel inside. Perhaps this is the way to reconciliation after all; stilted, angry, and yet not without merit. "We were thinking we'd do something for her here at the house, eventually."

She pauses, and then gives a curt nod and turns away. I give Patrick an incredulous glance and he gives me a cheeky grin in response and a slight shrug. I'm not sure if any of us is truly vindicated by the past few week's actions, but I feel as if we might all be on better footing now than ever before. That is comforting.

"Well, then, Janie." Patrick is at my shoulder, as we both watch the two silent, straight backs of Kate and Esther walk away from us, without another word between us or them. "That sure beats all. So before we return the wagon to Sadie and the extra horse to the Brinkley's, we ought to take a moment alone, do you think?"

I finally am able to give a laugh. "I think that would be lovely."

# EPILOGUE

"Robbie! Get your sister out of the peas! Her foot's caught." I pull my head back into the kitchen. Esther smiles at me from the kitchen table. She's hand feeding our second son and I'm well rounded with our fourth child. Patrick is in utter heaven as he putters through the bean poles, happily enjoying his children's chatter. He keeps near home when I am very pregnant like this, even though I am calm since delivering children healthily. He does not trust my blood, so he hovers. I do not mind. Having him close by is always wonderful.

Esther has blossomed in her age here. She sleeps in a little cottage we've made at the edge of the prairie on our land, so she only needs to step through the gardens to get into the kitchen. Her help is invaluable and the children call her Nanna. I'm hoping this pregnancy is not my last as I love having a brood. Being a mother and wife is overwhelming and beautiful.

Patrick comes in now, Daisy on his hip and Robbie following with a fistful of fresh pea pods. Both children have Pat's auburn locks, but little Johnny has my dark hair and eyes.

"Ready for supper, Paddy?" I ask, as he sets his basket of beans on the sideboard.

"Yes," he spins me around from the stove to a quick jig before kissing me and then tousling Johnny's hair. "Robbie, Daisy my lass, to the lab for our hands."

I hear their noises echo down the hallway to the laboratory, and the gush of water and splash. Esther meets my eyes and smiles at me. She knows how much I love this life, and how happy I am, and she is happy too. We have all made a tentative peace; us, Esther and Kate, and in this, our little world is as tidy as it will ever be.

Patrick comes back in, two shadows following, and we set to eat. As is our habit now, he says grace for us all, and we fall to the meal. Over the bowed heads, and jumpy arms and legs, and the jumble of toddler's voices, I look at my husband, with his youngest son on a knee, cutting a piece of meat for his daughter while answering eager questions from his oldest. Esther hovers over us all. We are all bursting with happy distraction, and I am so thankful I am able to share this with her, and give him the family he wanted so much. It is as if with this marriage, something I had never thought to do again, my life forever has more purpose than I could have ever imagined.

# The End

The End